A ROMANCE
NOVEL

TOO STRONG

Hayes Brothers Series Book Four

I. A. DICE

Also by I. A. Dice

HAYES BROTHERS SERIES
A sries of interconnected standalones
Too Much
Too Wrong
Too Sweet
Too Strong
Too Hard
Too Long

BROKEN DUET
Broken Rules
Broken Promises

DELIVERANCE DUET
The Sound of Salvation
The Taste of Redemption

Playlist

"Figure You Out" by VOILÁ
"Cruel" by VIOLÁ
"Slow Down" by Chase Atlantic
"Tip Toe" by PatrickReza
"HEAVEN AND BACK" by Chase Atlantic
"Pink" by Two Feet
"Grave Digger" by Matt Maeson
"On My Way" by MaRina
"Drift" by Benji Lewis
"Consume" by Chase Atlantic, Good Des Garcons
"Movements" by Pham, Yung Fusion
"TELL ME WHY" by The Kid LAROI
"Work Song" by Hozier
"Car's Outside" by James Arthur
"Think about it" by Dennis Lloyd
"Chills – Dark Version" by Mickey Valen
"I Can't Go on Without You" by KALEO
"Fahrenheit" by Azee
"Slip" by Elliot Moss
"Demons" by Jacob Lee

Dedication

To all of you who think tattoed hands make
the prettiest necklaces.

ONE

Conor

"You ready yet?" Cody shouts, battering the closed door with his fist. "Hurry up!"

Impatient as always. The party doesn't start for another hour, but he's all geared up, ready to roll. Always the first one jumping at any opportunity to fill Nico's garden with too many people and always the last cleaning up after.

The house is set, decorations in place, but no one's showing up for a while. Whenever we say six o'clock, nobody arrives until at least seven.

"Five minutes!" I shout back, pulling on my costume.

Jeans, t-shirt, my favorite watch from this year's F1 collection, and brand-new, snow-white Jordans. I check my reflection in the mirror, then glance at the time. Looks like I over-compensated because what do you know? I'm ready inside half a minute.

Cody lingers outside my door, casually leaning against the

opposite wall, eyes focused on the screen of his cell, fingers typing away. His costume is just like mine—low-effort—although, considering I bought my *'Error 404 Costume not found'* t-shirt online, I guess his required more effort.

He's wearing all white save for the red silk ribbon circling his ribs—courtesy of Mia for sure—and ending in a big bow over his chest. A large gift tag with *'To: All Women; From: God'* dangles from his shoulder, bouncing against his pec.

"No fair," I mutter, annoyed I didn't come up with that idea. "You're hardly a gift to women, bro. What's Colt wearing?" I dodge the fake cobwebs hanging from... well, everywhere as I follow Cody downstairs.

Having a woman living with us means an upgrade on the decorations. Last year, our older brother, Nico, wouldn't have allowed this nonsense.

Fuck, last year, we couldn't even dream about throwing a Halloween party.

Now look at him... He spent yesterday morning carving pumpkins and the afternoon shopping with his girl, Mia, buying more decorations than would fit in the house. He got up early today to help us put up cobwebs, lanterns, candles, and a million other different kinds of creepy shit she bought.

"No idea, but I bet his costume's as imaginative as ours," Cody says, entering the living room where Mia gestures with her hand, silently telling us to keep the volume down. Cody immediately lowers his tone, whispering, "Why aren't you dressed?"

"Five more minutes," she utters, weaving her delicate fingers through Nico's thick, black hair. "He needed a power nap."

An emerald engagement ring that belonged to our grandmother sparkles on her ring finger. She's been proudly wearing it for a week now, the message clear as day—engaged.

I never thought I'd see the day my brother popped down on one knee.

And I was right.

He didn't.

At least not in the traditional, widely accepted way. The way Mia describes it, he fucking *told* her to marry him.

Figures. Nico always gets what he wants.

Still, it'll never cease to amaze me how he morphed from a robotic, fire-breathing, workaholic, A-grade asshole to this guy, currently asleep on Mia's tummy. He's still all those things but has a softer side exclusively for his girl these days.

She sits in the corner of the couch, toying with his hair while Nico lays on his front, between her legs, arms flush with her sides, face nuzzled into her waistline. It's a common sight. Nico can't last ten minutes without touching her.

Good thing they're always fully clothed, or I'd have to bleach my eyeballs.

I cast a brief glance around the room, admiring the final result. Cody, Colt, and I did help decorate, but Mia kept going, putting her own touch on this place long after we called it a day.

The entire ground floor level evokes a sense of spookiness. Streamers of cobwebs drift from the ceiling like gauzy curtains. Paper bats and spiders flutter on thin strands, their wings rustling in the draft wafting through the open windows.

Gargoyles, skeletons, and limbless porcelain dolls with wide, painted eyes leer from every corner of the room, adding to the already eerie atmosphere cemented by the orange candlelight glow casting shadows across the walls.

The air is thick with pumpkin spice, and the finger food buffet waiting in the kitchen for Nico and Mia's first guests. They're throwing a separate party here, so I'll drift between ours outside and theirs inside tonight to see my older brothers.

Our party scene in the garden is equally spooky. Gnarled tree branches dressed in cobwebs twist and turn, plastic tombstones poke from the grass in a miniature graveyard, carved pumpkins grin alongside the house, and more cobwebs cling to the makeshift stage.

It won't be a typical Hayes College banger this time. After everything that happened with Mia earlier this year, we were very selective with the guest list. No Jake Grey's friends, and—much to Cody's relief—no Blair Fitzpatrick.

Although I won't be surprised if she weasels her way over here somehow. It'd be better if she didn't because Cody loses his shit whenever she's nearby.

He still has that sense of higher purpose wherever Mia's concerned, big-brother mode in full, over-the-top effect. It's a good thing we don't have an actual sister; she'd hate our guts.

"See? This is what you get for making him do manual labor, Bug," I tell Mia, jutting my chin at Nico. "He can't handle it."

"Any excuse to get between her legs." Nico rises on his elbows, maneuvering into a seat beside her, then pulls her legs onto his lap. "I let you throw a Halloween party, and *this* is what you're wearing?" His finger wavers between Cody and me. "Since you're trying to be funny, that gift tag should be on your dick."

"What are you dressing up as?" Cody asks, entertaining the idea by sliding the tag over his groin.

"If you say you're wearing matching costumes, I will not be held accountable for making fun of you all night," Colt says, entering the room.

"Magic eight-ball?" Mia chuckles, eyes sweeping his t-shirt. He's dressed in black, eight-ball emblazoned across his chest. "Let's see..." She taps her pouty mouth. "Oh, I know! Will you fall in love this year?"

Colt forces an amused puff of air down his nose, turning to reveal a blue triangle on his back with '*Google it*' written inside.

"This's no fun. You were supposed to take this seriously!"

"Other than you, and maybe Theo, no one's gonna dress up properly," Cody says, propping his hip against the back of the couch. "Girls will come as Harley Quinn, sexy cops, sexy nurses, or sexy... something, and guys will either low-effort this like us or go full Rooster."

"Rooster?" Mia pulls her brows together.

"Yeah, from the new *Top Gun*. I bet we'll see at least a few guys wearing pilot uniforms and fake mustaches."

"Those will be the guys getting laid tonight," Colt adds, adjusting his watch.

"Missed opportunity," Nico muses, taking Mia with him as he gets up. "We should get ready."

They head upstairs. Colt grabs three beers from the cooler in the garage on our way to the back garden, where we spend ten minutes checking everything's ready.

Six arrives soon after, dressed as a glow-in-the-dark skeleton. Pretty cool for a DJ.

Ten to seven, the doorbell rings, so I head back inside, not expecting Nico and Mia to be ready yet. Whenever they go upstairs together, they're gone for well over an hour.

It's a miracle neither I nor Cody nor Colt caught them in the act yet. Mia moved in with Nico in June, so I expected a memory bank full of unwanted visuals by now, but nope. Nico's uncharacteristically careful when choosing where and when they fuck.

Since we moved here three years ago, we walked in on him nailing countless random women. Not surprising since, save for his ex, he never took any of them into his bedroom. Always got his dick wet in the living room, the kitchen, the garage, even the stairs.

Since he got together with Mia, Colt, Cody, and I made it a rule to be extra loud whenever we get back home. We take our sweet time closing the door, and crossing the hallway, in case they need a quick minute to get dressed, but so far, no life-changing, psyche-scarring encounters. Fingers crossed.

I saw all my brothers in action at some point in my life, but I hope I'll never see Mia. She's my little sister by choice. It's fucking wrong to even think she's having sex.

I jog across the garage and up the stairs to let in whichever of my brothers arrived with ten minutes to spare. Definitely not Logan. That guy doesn't understand the meaning of punctuality.

It's not any of my brothers, though.

"Oh, hey," the girl outside says as I fling the door open. "You must be one of the triplets." She narrows her black eyes at me. "Conor, right?"

"Yeah, and you are...?" *Too young to be here.*

We didn't invite any freshmen. They're too wild—just finished high school and getting their first taste of college parties. And this girl is a freshman, for sure.

If that. Maybe she's still in high school.

She definitely shouldn't be here, but she's dressed for a party, so someone invited her. What's more, she's dressed as Wednesday Addams.

Bold, considering it's not a sexy version.

It suits her, though. Perfectly. Jet-black hair in two braids, fringe, and a black dress complete the look, contrasting her skin. She's not as pale as Wednesday, but it doesn't detract from the look.

"I'm Rose," she offers, rocking on the balls of her feet.

Cool... this doesn't fucking help me whatsoever.

I comb my hair back, growing uncomfortable. "I'm not trying to be rude, but I've no idea who you are or what—"

"Mia invited me," she explains, unfazed by my obvious exasperation, her genuine smile crinkling the corners of her big eyes. "I guess you'd call me her student. She gives me piano lessons three times a week."

Ah, right. Mia mentioned this girl, but I don't spend much time at home these days, and neither do Colt or Conor. We're mostly out partying or aimlessly driving around town, so we've not had a chance to meet Rose.

I step from one foot to the other, opening the door further to let her inside.

She turns on her boot, waving at the driveway, my eyes inexorably follow her line of sight. A death trap sits parked at the bottom of the concrete steps: a battered Mercury Cougar, a relic from another era with at least thirty years under its belt, if not more.

The car's battered like it rallied over the Himalayas, and no one bothered fixing the dents. The front bumper's only just clinging on by untrimmed zip ties, the side mirror is taped with packing tape, and I have no clue what color all that rust is hiding. Plus, it's belching out this huge black cloud of thick smoke that could stop your lungs working in a heartbeat.

"I'll pick you up after eleven," a girl in a stripy black and yellow top—or maybe a dress—shouts from the driver's seat. "Don't drink!" The bee antennae glued to her headband happily jiggle about.

Rose gives her a thumbs up, beaming from ear to ear. Before I take a better look at the girl behind the wheel, she puts the car in motion and rolls down the driveway, leaving a cloud of poisonous emissions in her wake.

"Eleven? The party will only just start getting good then," I say, stepping aside to let Rose step over the threshold.

"I bet, but I have little choice. She'll pick me up on her way from work."

"Hey, you're here!" Mia cheers, click-clacking down the stairs with Nico close behind.

"No. Fucking. *Way*," I boom, looking them over.

She's cute as always, wearing a sparkling crown and a black, red, and white tutu dress with a big Q and heart printed on her chest. The soft fabric swishes around her legs as she moves, but Mia's not why my jaw hangs open.

It's Nico. He's wearing black slacks and a shirt, a red K and heart displayed on his muscular pec. A long red cape flows over his broad shoulders, a matching crown atop his big head. He looks like a regal superhero. A deadly king ready to save his queen from imaginary danger.

"King and Queen of Hearts," Rose muses, closing the door behind her. "So fitting."

"My God you're whipped, bro. Wait till Colt sees you. This will be fun."

"Wait till *he's* whipped," Nico shoots back with a smirk.

I want to say *no way that will ever happen*, but I said that about Nico, so... yeah. I'm not making the same mistake again.

We'll all end up whipped at some point.

Mia pulls Rose into the kitchen, and Nico follows suit, a snarling Rottweiler, always at his girl's side.

Nothing here to see, so I join my other brothers in the garden, where people are finally flocking through the side gate.

As expected, most girls arrive wearing sexy, barely-anything-to-them costumes, while the guys put in minimal effort, although some are hilarious.

Justin Montgomery has purple cardboard wings growing out of his back, the words '*Booze Light Beer*' written in fluorescent green marker on his t-shirt. Another guy's chest is covered in gray paint samples, so I assume he's '*50 Shades of Grey*' and...

Low and behold, we have a winner.

The one red-haired guy in our circle of friends has five loaves of bread strung around his neck, a sticker with '*Ginger Bread Man*' written in black ink across his forehead.

No way anyone can top that.

Many toilet paper mummies, guys in black shirts with Superman t-shirts underneath, and scary rubber masks later, Brandon Price arrives. The king fallen from grace.

He's been on his best behavior since Nico threw him out of the house the night Mia was assaulted.

He's lost his pompous attitude somewhere along the way, working hard to earn our forgiveness. To prove he's not an incurable dipshit.

The jury's still out on that one.

Mia overheard me, Colt, and Cody debating whether to invite him a few days ago. The good-hearted little Bug she is, she said we should. We excluded him from the year-end and homecoming parties already. Other than a couple guys from the team, he's lost every friend he ever had.

Meanwhile, cred is due where it's due because he's been walking on water the past few months. I guess we'll see tonight how much he changed.

He enters the garden, the only guy to put effort into his costume: a green onesie covered in hundreds of tiny white plastic thorns. He must've cut up a whole box of plastic forks for the spikes.

"A cactus?!" Cody questions, shaking Brandon's hand. "What the hell, man? Why cactus?"

"Dig deeper," Brandon says, patting my back as I stop beside them. "What are those?" He touches a thorn.

"You want the technical term? Fuck knows. Spikes?"

"Kind of, yeah, but not what I'm looking for," he admits, shaking his head. "What do they do?"

"They hurt," Cody supplies, brows drawn together. "Is this a game? A rebus? I better win something if I guess."

"They're called prickles," Colt says. "He's a prickly cactus, so you could say he's a…" His eyes jitter between our clueless expressions, waiting for it to click. "He's a massive prick, you idiots."

I burst out laughing, but it takes Cody a few more seconds to catch on and join in. "Well, that sure is fitting. At least you know."

Brandon nods, looking up at the living-room windows, features pinched. He thinks it masks the pain in his eyes. It doesn't. "Will she sing tonight?"

"Yeah, but only a few songs. They're having their own party up there. Our brothers are coming over, and our parents too, so you better behave."

He's been pining over Mia since he saw Nico exit *Q* holding her in his arms. It's as if seeing with his own eyes she was no longer available made him realize he didn't just want to fuck her but keep her.

"Right, I need a beer." Brandon squeezes the back of his neck, heading for a table bending under the weight of kegs.

"Could I have one?" a familiar voice asks.

I turn to see Rose—aka Wednesday—a few feet away. "I thought that chick told you not to drink."

"That chick is my sister." A cheeky smile punctuates her

words. "What she doesn't see won't hurt her. So? Would you like me to beg?"

"No need, girl," Brandon says, leaping back to wrap his arm around Rose's shoulders, a slight curve to his lips. "Come on, I'll hook you up."

Oh, hell no.

I don't know where this sudden, intense, aggressive jolt zapping down my spine comes from, but the thought of allowing his hands anywhere near Rose has me on the brink of bursting into flames.

I'm not the Hayes who loses his shit for no reason (not pointing any fingers), so this is surprising.

Brandon might be trying to redeem himself, but he's still a fucking prick. There's no way I'm leaving Rose under his supervision. Mia would have my balls for that, I'm sure.

"Not your party, man," I say, breaking Rose from his hold. "Grab a beer and have fun, but don't try anything, or you'll be out the door in five seconds."

Brandon holds his hands up in defeat, no longer prone to arguing with us. He's gone from a show-worthy Doberman to a lapdog in the last six months.

"A beer, huh?" I ask, leading Rose across the lawn to the beeline at the drink table. "How old are you?"

"It's rude to ask a woman her age."

"When she's fifty." I elbow our way to the Bud Light keg, grabbing a solo cup from the stack. "You're at least eighteen, right?"

"Yes, since last week," Rose admits.

"Fine. You can have one."

She pinches her lips, biting back a smile. "Yes, Dad."

"Call me *Dad* again, and you won't even get a sip. And Wednesday doesn't smile, Rose. Lose the grin."

She snatches the cup from my hand, fills it until it's almost overflowing, then gulps half of the contents. "Oops. Too late."

"Oops, you're *grounded*," a voice snaps behind us. We both turn, standing face to face with the bee antennae girl.

Damn... busted.

"Wha-what are you doing here?" Rose wails, slapping the half-empty cup into my chest. "You're supposed to be at work!"

"I lied. I had to check I could trust you. Guess what? I *can't*. And you!" Her face grows red, bee antennae jiggling harder.

She's got a tight, black and yellow dress to match and even a stinger attached to her butt. She's shorter than Rose. Paler in complexion, eyes a striking silvery grayish color, hair like warm caramel up in a high, messy ponytail swinging side to side, tickling her bare shoulders.

"What the hell is so funny?" she demands, cheeks on fire as she pokes me with her finger.

I don't know what's so funny. I'm *not* laughing, but it doesn't stop the girl tearing the cup from my hand and tossing the contents in my face.

Feels like I've seen this before...

"You're enabling a minor!"

"Whoa, whoa, whoa," Cody leaps between us. "What the hell are you doing? Who are you?"

"I'm nobody." She shoves Cody aside, then grabs Rose by the wrist, pulling her toward the house.

I don't know why she shoved him. He wasn't in her way.

Both girls take five steps, and then Little Bee halts, spins round, and her eyes lock on mine, growing wide in horror like it only just clicked what she did.

"I'm so, *so* sorry."

Now I laugh, using the hem of my t-shirt to wipe the beer

off my face. "You ruined my costume, Little Bee."

"It's Vee," she snaps, rolling her eyes. "My name. It's Vee. Well, technically, it's Vivienne, but no one calls me that. Just Vee."

"I was referring to your costume."

She looks down like she fucking forgot what she's wearing. The red hue leaves her cheeks almost as quickly as it appears. With a new sense of determination glimmering in those striking, silver eyes, she snatches off her antennae. An exasperated exhale later, she shimmies out of the stinger, which, I now realize, was on a rubber band around her waist.

She comes closer, a walking contradiction. Every one of her moves is gracious, confident like she comes from old money, but she sure doesn't act it, throwing beer in my face.

Every look she sends my way sears right through me, forcing the rhythm of my heart into a higher gear. She's really pretty. The kind of girl I'd turn to take another look at.

The kind I'd openly stare at all night.

Her light brown hair works perfectly with the freckles peppering her nose and cheeks. Hundreds of them, maybe thousands. An entire freckly constellation.

Her black, laced, heeled boots stop an inch from my Jordans, and she peers up, angling her head to meet my gaze. She's not Mia-short but can't be taller than five-three. I'm naturally drawn to the perfect, well-defined cupid bow of her lips.

A faint scent of fresh linen and soap fans my face when she lifts her hand, weaving those delicate fingertips through my curls. My scalp and spine erupt in tingles that travel lower until the stimulating waves reach my dick.

I don't stop to think.

To be perfectly honest, I'm in an alternate dimension right now, blind, fucking *deaf* to everyone but this girl. I act on impulse, dip my head and take her mouth.

Don't ask why.

There's no rational or even irrational explanation for why my insides tie into knots when she touches me or why my chest turns to molten rock when our lips connect.

A bone-chilling pause settles over us. A mounting heaviness grows in the air before the temperature jumps a few degrees. A second ticks by. Maybe two at a stretch. The sheer surprise of this moment dawns on both of us, I'm sure, but I don't move away.

Her lips twitch under mine like she's about to kiss me back. She doesn't.

She pulls away.

And I don't get a chance to fucking blink before her open hand strikes my cheek so hard my head wrenches to the side.

Ouch.

I don't know what stings more: my cheek or my ego.

"You're unbelievable!" she snaps, arms akimbo, eyebrows scrunched together. "I throw a beer in your face, and you think I want a kiss? Read the room." She drops her hands, stepping closer again. "Don't move. I'm fixing your costume."

I'm too stunned to say one word. All jokes evaporate from my head, and I do as instructed while she pushes her headband into my curly mane, then wraps the elastic band around my hips, before hooking it in place, and adjusting the stinger over my dick.

"Before you say it's not as big as yours," she muses, admiring her handiwork, "at least you've got a proper costume now."

"So I'm a hornet?"

"I'd say you're a hoverfly but have it your way."

"Hoverflies can't sting," Colt supplies, standing somewhere on my right, the resident encyclopedia.

I was so preoccupied with Vee I hadn't noticed him join the show.

More people are crowded round since Rose and I got here, but no one's talking or elbowing their way to the kegs lining the table.

"No, but they follow you around if they like you," Vee admits, flashing a beautiful smile.

She throws beer at me, then gives me half her costume, slaps my face, and now she's... *flirting*.

At least, I think that's flirting.

I'm so fucking confused my head is throbbing.

"Now would be a good time to ask me out," she adds impatiently, glancing at her wristwatch: one of those novelty watches you win at the arcades. Hers has Donald Duck on the face.

"Dinner," I blurt out like we're playing *Taboo*. I'm on the clock here. No time to think. "Tomorrow."

"*Ruby's Diner*, nine-thirty," she confirms.

With that, she spins around, pulling Rose behind her.

What the hell just happened?

TWO

Vee

"Care to explain?" Rose mutters, struggling to keep up with me as we enter the obscene, enormous villa through the garage.

We squeeze past a line of cars, each worth at least triple my yearly salary from two jobs combined, and up *porcelain* stairs until we emerge in a marble-floored hallway.

Talk about ostentatious.

Seriously, what sane person needs a six-bedroom house when they don't even have kids?

Glancing around, making sure we're alone, my eyes glide across the oversized, sepia pictures of Newport at night hanging on the wall. It's an odd gallery of unconnected spots in town, no clear link: the lifeguard station at the beach, *The Olive Tree* restaurant, a private cab, *Tortugo*, the airfield where a few of my friends skydived last year...

The only plausible explanation is that those places mean something to Nico.

Rose nudges my shoulder, tapping her foot against the floor, one brow furrowed as she inserts more credibility to her signature impatient bitch face. It adds a few extra points to how good she looks dressed as Wednesday.

"Nothing to explain," I say, playing it down. "He's cute."

"You don't know him." She folds her arms over her chest.

So what? I don't know many people before meeting them. Isn't that the whole point of dates, to get to know someone?

Besides his handsome looks, that guy seemed fun. He didn't flip out when—on impulse—I threw beer in his face, and he has the softest lips I've ever kissed.

If you can call that tight-lip peck a kiss.

I've known less about some men I've shared proper kisses with in the past, so there's that. I'll learn more during our date. If he turns out rude, dull, or an asshole, no harm done.

'At least I'll know I seized the moment.'

My evening shift at the bar ends at nine tomorrow. Plenty of time to freshen up in the restroom and change from the uniform into my own clothes before meeting—

'Nice one, Vee. You don't even know his name.'

"I'll get to know him," I say, dropping the volume a few decibels as I spot the owner of this flashy house, the man who chose those sepia pictures, crossing the hallway. He yanks the door handle with so much force you'd think he's trying to rip the main door off its hinges when he opens it. "How bad can he be?" I continue, my voice near whisper level. "He didn't mind *Ruby's Diner*, so he can't be one of the uptight rich boys, right?"

Once bitten, twice shy.

A boy named Luke swept me off my feet back in high school. Never will I make the same mistake again. Never will I let a guy with more money than common sense trick me into thinking I could be more than his temporary fix for boredom.

Luke was the dream boyfriend—smart, sinfully hot with cute dimples on both cheeks, shiny hair, and a chiseled jaw. Well behaved, ambitious. What a *dream*. What a *catch*.

'*What a fucking pretentious, stereotypical douche.*'

How much he loved groping my ass, latching onto my neck as he squeezed me against the lockers, didn't mean shit once he parked his bright-red, convertible Porsche outside my house. The kisses, hand-holding, laughter... *irrelevant*. Like my personality that he adored, telling me every day I was cooler than his buddies.

The fact I let the asshole punch my V card? Who cares?

Not Luke.

Not once he saw where I came from.

Disbelief blazed from his eyes while he craned his neck left and right, gawking at his surroundings as he dropped me off one evening.

With each passing moment, his expression fell further. The smile almost permanently glued to his stupid, pretty face slipped off, replaced by a disgusted scowl. His nose wrinkled as if he caught the stench of decomposing fish guts, and... *see ya*.

We were over.

The next day, he walked past me like I didn't exist. From then onwards, my life's mission became avoiding rich boys.

Turns out, it's not that hard. As I've gotten older, so have my peers. Boys started paying attention to more than my ass, boobs, and long, caramel hair. They started inspecting *what* that ass was wearing, for example.

No designer labels? No second glance.

That's still valid, even though it's been over three years since I graduated. Of course not all rich men care about fashion.

Some wear the most obscure things, so they don't scrutinize my clothes, but... the sight of my thirty-seven-year-old, rusty car never fails to send loaded guys running in the opposite direction.

Working at a local newsstand and the bar across the street from *Ruby's Diner* doesn't exactly boost my social status, either. To be perfectly honest, my social status has always been in the gutter.

I don't let it affect me. I'm helping my parents and putting Rose through college.

That's good enough if you ask me.

I started working evening shifts at *The Well* to pay for Rose's piano lessons, but Mia refused the money. I could quit, but my car is falling apart. It desperately needs replacing, so I'm saving the peanuts I earn serving beer, so I can buy a more reliable one.

The engine failed in the spring, leaving me biking to work throughout summer while I saved enough cash to get it fixed. Too bad the mechanic then warned me that keeping my old Mercury in relatively good, safe shape would take another few grand just for parts.

'Better to save up for a few months and buy a car that won't need to be coaxed into starting every day.'

Rose scoffs, glancing heavenward like she's dealing with an oblivious, naïve child. "I guess you didn't pay any attention to the other two guys standing beside your date, did you?"

"Not really." My focus was solely on *him*, whatever his name is. The masculine yet soft energy, the deep brown eyes, curly, rebellious hair, and big hands. "Why?"

"Maybe if you did, you'd realize that, save for their hairstyles, the three of them are identical."

'Oh, no, no, no, no, no.'

My stomach bottoms out faster than an express elevator.

Identical triplets... that's more than enough information.

"Oh, *yeah*, sis. They're the Hayes brothers," Rose adds, her voice low like she's hoping to soften the blow. "You told *Conor Hayes* to ask you out."

"Shit," I whisper, my lungs decompressing instantly, shoulders falling limp.

He seemed so... I'm not sure what.

Not Hayes? Other than Nico, I don't know any of them personally, but Nico doesn't give off the best vibe. The few times he opened the door when I dropped Rose off for piano lessons, an unpleasant chill whispered across my skin, sending a burning icicle-like cool through my bones.

'*Not rich.*' *That's* how Conor comes across. Down to earth. Laid back, approachable, and unpretentious.

"Ugh, why didn't you warn me?" I ask, frustration elevating my voice to a disgracefully high note.

"How was I supposed to know you like him?" Rose folds her arms over her chest, an incredulous, slightly amused expression marring her pretty, young face. "You met five minutes ago, sis, and you already told him to ask you out!"

"I don't know if I like him. He seemed cool." I roll my eyes, heading back to the garage. With one hand on the handle, I pause, fish my car keys out of my pocket and fling them at Rose. "Wait in the car. I'll be out in five."

"What are you doing?"

"What do you think? I'm calling off the date."

The door thunks closed behind me. I rush down the porcelain stairs, weave past the sleek, expensive cars, and I'm outside. Despite the end of October, the evening air warms my skin. Nico's house is airconditioned. Cooler by five or six degrees than the lazy evening breeze kissing my hair. The temperature outside holds in the mid-seventies, the autumn comparably hot to the scorching summer we've had this year.

I stop by the stage, every fiber in my body responding to the beat of Fat Joe's "All The Way Up" playing from the DJ's setup. Girls grind against each other on a dancefloor marked out with retractable tape posts. They move in time with each other, sipping from red solo cups, each prettier than the next. But they pale compared to the stunning brunette who enters the garden through the side gate. My eyes are immediately drawn to her.

She's alone, enough bling adorning her neck to rival a jewelry store. Holding her head high, she stalks past me in a tiny, form-fitting dress hugging her flawless curves. The fabric slides a tiny bit higher with every confident step. Red-soled heels pierce the grass in perfect time with the beat.

Whoever this girl is, she holds the ultimate power in this exclusive ecosystem. There isn't one person in sight not following her sophisticated moves. She's not paying anyone any heed, though, her eyes fixed on something or someone on the other side of the garden.

The beat keeps pumping, the potent bass vibrating through my bones. Conor stands right where I left him—by the drinks table—immersed in serious-looking conversation with his identical brothers and a guy wearing a white t-shirt covered in large blue, red, green, and yellow dots.

He must be *Twister*.

Conor hasn't pulled my headband off yet. The antennae sway from side to side, and the stinger remains in place, passing for elongation of his dick.

'*What was I thinking?!*'

Now, at a safe distance, my cluttered mind temporarily under control, it's clear he's not how he comes across at first glance. His confident stance exudes an air of wealth and privilege. The t-shirt he wears stretches tightly over his broad chest, accentuating every muscle.

Despite his casual appearance, the devil's in the details. And those tell a different story. Gleaming white Jordans on his feet, gold watch on his wrist, and beaded bracelets stacked up his arm all scream luxury.

All my shoes combined aren't worth as much as one pair of his. At this point, with the engine desperate to heave its soul out every morning, even my car isn't worth as much as Conor's Jordans. The thought of him willingly accepting half my costume while he can afford a thousand drives me up the wall.

I don't know why. It's just a fucking headband and a DIY stinger stuffed with two rolls of crumpled toilet paper, but I'm glowing with barely controlled anger.

The polyester bee dress and headband set me back fifteen bucks. Not a fortune, but I bet Conor tips his barista more for his five-dollar, tall macchiato or whatever the hell kickstarts his morning.

My heart thumps faster, threatening to snap through my ribs the hotter my temper flares. A quick mental pep-talk and I'm off, marching across the pristine green lawn, my boots leaving a trail of flattened grass in their wake.

Conor casually rests his lower back against the table, broad shoulders relaxed, a half-smile playing on his lips. He's tall. At least six feet. His curly hair, styled in an intentionally messy way, makes him effortlessly hot. Golden flecks pepper his hazel eyes, softening the sharpness of his features, but his heated gaze is intimidating, intriguing, and arousing at once.

He looks like a man who knows exactly what he wants and isn't afraid to go after it. His confidence is magnetic, crushing, enough to extinguish the inferno of my anger for a moment.

A very short moment.

The second his eyes dip, roving my body, caressing every curve, I'm ambushed by a burst of self-consciousness.

"You're back," he says, his lips curling into a warm, genuine smile that incites the butterflies in my tummy to riot against my next move. "What do you need?"

My cheeks heat, an uncharacteristic blush pinking up my face. It's not what Conor said that throws me off track but *how* he said it... like he's ready to make every one of my requests come true.

I grit my teeth and visualize stomping my foot to get back on track with the anger. It works. My rage grows hotter, fiercer now that I know why I'm getting so worked up.

Because I wish he wasn't Mr. Richie Rich. I wish he was just an ordinary guy I could go to the cheapest diner with, who wouldn't make me feel embarrassed about my clothes. Somebody who could look at my thirty-seven-year-old car without that *'just stepped in dogshit'* expression.

People judge. *'And people with money judge hard.'*

But he is what he is. I've learned my lesson and won't make the same mistake again.

Dating wealthy men only ends in tears, if you're lucky.

"We are *not* having dinner tomorrow," I say, stepping closer to snatch back my headband off his head. "And you are *not* keeping my costume."

I wrench the stinger away, expecting the elastic to snap. I made it last night, and I'm not exactly a seamstress, so it's not the sturdiest construction. Instead of pulling off, the stinger jerks from my hand, hitting Conor's sensitive spot with enough force to make him kneel. His face flashes with pain, the color changing from red to white to green and back.

"Oh shit, sorry," I gasp, crouching before him, where he's clutching his jewels in both hands, stinger now at his waist.

"Why—?" he asks, the word pushed through clenched teeth, dark, sinful eyes unfocused almost hidden behind his curly mane.

"I didn't mean to hurt you! I thought the elastic would snap. I made this myself." I poke the stinger making it jitter left and right. "I'm useless at sewing. I didn't think it'd hold if I yanked hard enough."

"No." He winces, inhaling deeply as he gets to his feet, slowly straightening his spine. "Why aren't we having dinner?"

"Oh..." I stammer, standing back a step as he unhooks my stinger. "You're... you're... just not my type."

His eyebrows furrow, another question dancing on the tip of his tongue, judging by his lips falling apart.

I don't wait for him to find the right words. Grabbing the stinger, I mumble *bye*, bolt across the lawn, then inside, and slam the garage personnel door behind me.

Or try to slam it, but stupid Conor gets in the way, the door whacking him in the face.

'*God, this is a disaster.*'

His eyes water. Blood spews from his nose, staining the white t-shirt he wears.

It's not funny, it's terrifying, but I can't stop the nervous, shaky laughter bubbling out of my chest.

"See? You've got another costume ready." Add embarrassment to these first frustrated, guilty tears, and I'm officially a blubbering, snotty, trembling mess. "I'm sorry," I wail, tearing the stinger apart for its now precious toilet paper stuffing.

"My fault," he says, resting his back against a matte white Mercedes. Leaning forward, so I can wipe the blood off his chin and hands, he then lets me hold a big, crumpled ball of paper against his nose. "I should've expected you'd bang the door."

"I'm really, really sorry," I mumble, the words almost catching in my throat while I do a lousy job of containing the quiver in my voice. "I swear I'm not doing this on purpose."

He lifts a hand, wiping my tears away, his touch soft, the gesture careful, so affectionate my stomach sinks pleasantly.

"Calm down," he whispers, inhaling through his mouth. "Don't cry, Little Bee. I'm fine." He takes my hand, moving it gently away. "See? I'm not bleeding anymore."

Wiping my nose with the bloodied toilet paper, I sniffle, nodding fifteen times. "I'm sorry."

"Stop apologizing." His fingers dance along my cheek to the side of my neck, eyes following the gesture before they rise to meet mine. "Explain why you called off our date."

"I already told you." I draw deep breaths, willing my racing heart into a slower rhythm. "You're not my type."

Without warning, his strong hand wraps around the back of my neck. He draws me in, closes my lips with his, and slips his tongue inside so fast I have no hope of pushing him away before it happens.

His other hand circles my back, insistently holding, *molding* me to him, and... my mind blanks. I'm consumed by the moment. Every other thought fades away.

The heat radiating off his big body encompasses my senses, leaving me dazed. His taste halts the thoughts rushing through my mind. I drop the ball of toilet paper to the ground, weaving my fingers through his thick hair and. I. *Take.*

Endorphins flood my system the closer I press against him, teasing and kissing like I've lost my mind.

I have.

We just met, but it doesn't mean a thing. His touch is

electric as he pulls me close, the heat of his body searing my skin, the raw intensity of desire saying more than words ever could. The kiss evolves, turning feral, almost carnal. He holds me, firm but tender, and rediscovers my mouth like a starving man. The explosive chemistry between us makes the blood scream in my ears.

The kiss feels like an interlude to something bigger than life.

Conor's a drug. Opiates. One taste is all it takes to leave me craving more. I can't stop, the rational part of my mind unavailable while my body comes alive at our lips melding in breathless sync.

He's not my first kiss, but he might as well be. All others fade in comparison. His heartbeat thuds against my chest, a challenge mine picks up, matching the rhythm.

I've never felt this consumed by another person.

'I want more.'

More of his lips, more of his kisses. I want his warm hands against my bare skin, his muscles under my fingertips, his big body suspended above mine. Taking, claiming.

As if he reads my mind, his hand slides down my back, pulling me flush against him. The outline of his hard cock imprints itself on my skin, and my brain short-circuits.

The party happening around us fades into the background. The hot ball of pulsing ache burning between my legs begs me to curve into him further.

I knead my fingers through his hair, deepening the kiss.

I'm not sure how long we stand there, lost in each other. I wouldn't notice if someone walked in, but once we pull back, breathless, thirsty for more, dazed, and equally baffled by what just happened, we're still alone.

The realization we're surrounded by nothing but the sound

of our ragged, racing breathing fuels the fire. A rush of longing and lust floods my system. Conor's eyes rage with desire. Full of surprise that sets my nerve endings alight like a firework display.

'He's just as confused and turned on as I am.'

The urge to feel his lips back on mine is nearly palpable. I can tell from the hunger on his face that he feels it too.

"Not your type?" he questions, his voice husky as his thumb traces the shape of my lips. "I beg to differ."

"You're a great kisser…"

'But you're still an entitled, born-with-a-silver-spoon asshat like all rich guys.'

I swallow hard, still on him like duct tape, my hands unwilling to leave his shoulders. One deep breath and one step back help me regain a sliver of control. "But no date."

Undeterred, he leans in, kissing me again, this time with a soft, slow intensity, savoring every moment. He sucks my lip into his mouth, teeth coming together just shy of hard enough to hurt, then runs his tongue over to sooth the mild sting, sending shockwaves down my spine.

I should push him away to make him believe I don't want a date, but damn it, his lips are freaking magical.

"That will swell up real nice in a minute," he whispers, his breath warm against my cheek, his nose nuzzling mine before letting me take a hasty step back.

And as if nothing fucking happened, as if he hadn't just flipped my world on its axis, he pushes away from the car and heads out the door.

"I'll see you around, Little Bee," he calls over his shoulder.

I watch, dumbstruck, as he exits the garage, my heart pounding like a bass bin. What the—

I pinch myself hard, my nails biting into my skin. My heart

races, a fast-paced drumbeat in my chest when the realization hits... I'm *not* dreaming. This was real and... so confusing. I try and blink it away, inhaling a deep breath that does nothing to clear the chaotic whirlwind of my thoughts. It doesn't help me understand what just went down, either.

"He's unstable," I decide, clinging to the banisters of the porcelain stairs as I climb them on jelly-like knees. "Or drunk... or both." I pull my eyebrows together, still stunned by the unexpected kiss and how much my body and mind enjoyed being pressed hard against Conor's broad chest. "He's on drugs. Mushrooms, probably."

The volume inside the house has gone up during the last... however long I was gone. More people crowd the huge living room as I peek in, certain Rose isn't waiting in the car like I asked.

"Can't catch a break," I mutter, shaking the weakness off my limbs. Readjusting my ruined costume, and the mess that's now my hair, I emerge at the end of the corridor.

I don't know the Hayes. I know they exist, but I never had a reason to pay attention when they were mentioned until Rose started taking piano lessons with one of their fiancées. The one who makes me feel like I'm about to face the wrath of all Gods.

Nico Hayes.

I don't know why the sight of him engages my fight or flight response—and it's not like I'm going to fight him—but it does. Every time. Even now, when he spots me across the room from where he stands, arms protectively wrapped around Mia, his tall frame towering over her.

They're the most bizarre couple I've ever come across. A tiny ray of sunshine and the reaper.

Rose is there, chatting with Mia, her face illuminated by a smile before she playfully pushes Nico away.

TOO STRONG

'Brave. I wouldn't risk touching the guy.'

With a deep breath of courage, I trot over, doing my best to navigate the throng of people unnoticed.

"Hey," I say, stopping beside Rose. "I'm Vivienne, Rose's sister." Peeling my eyes off Nico, I meet Mia's green gaze. "I've not had a chance to thank you for helping Rose and—"

"Don't worry about it," she cuts in. "She's very talented."

That she is. She's always been musical. By the time she was three, she could sing along to every song on the radio, and before she turned six, she could play guitar.

"Well, thank you, and..." I turn to Rose, my cheeks heating under Nico's intense scrutiny. "We should get going."

She opens her mouth like she's about to plead, but she's cut off by a different voice, the hair-raising kind.

"Stay," Nico orders, his tone brooking no argument. "Rose wants to hear Mia sing. She's heading on stage in half an hour."

How am I supposed to say *no*?

I'm afraid to freaking breathe around this guy. My head is automatically nodding before I've had time to decide whether declining is safer than staying with the possibility of facing Conor again.

Mia beams, taking half a step out of Nico's embrace. "Come on, I'll get you something to drink."

"I'm—" My words pile into a verbal traffic jam as Nico tugs her back until she leans against his chest.

"Theo wants to test-drive your Ferrari. I'll be back before you start singing." He dips his head, kissing her softly.

"For the tenth time! It's not mine. Don't use me as an excuse to buy another car. I don't even drive."

"You'll learn. Be good, baby." He stamps another kiss on her forehead, bobs his head at Rose and me, then walks away, pulling a guy—I assume Theo—with him by his shoulder. Looks like it's settled: we're staying for the party... *Yay*.

THREE

Vee

Rose effortlessly glides through the crowd, not an ounce of doubt in her body as she strikes up conversations with anyone who crosses her path, whether she knows them or not.

She radiates confidence like a beacon while I'm a wallflower, hiding in the kitchen, nursing a glass of freshly squeezed orange juice—a far cry from the concentrated, artificial shit my father buys. This is the real deal. Freshly squeezed, jam-packed with vitamins and all-natural goodness.

I've never considered myself closed-off, but compared to my younger sister, in this setting, I'm an introvert. Tucked in the corner of the room, out of anyone's way, I wonder what the hell I'm doing at the fanciest Halloween party in Newport...

The kitchen is a feast for the senses: gleaming marble counters, state-of-the-art appliances, and an extravagant finger food buffet that defies the very definition of the term. Tiny smoked salmon tartlets, caviar blinis, truffle risotto balls, escargot in puff pastry, lobster tails on crostini... I wouldn't know the names if there weren't tiny cards detailing the name, ingredients, and allergens in flowing calligraphy beside every dish.

'What. A. Life.'

"What are you doing here alone?" Rose asks, bursting through the doorway with Mia by her side. "Come on, I'll introduce you to everyone."

If this was any other party, I'd be introducing myself rather than hiding, but I'm out of my element, intimidated by the luxury dripping from each and every tiny detail. Intimidated by the crowd whose rich, powerful, entitled aura couldn't be masked by even the most extravagant Halloween costume.

"What time are you going up on stage?" I ask Mia, my hip glued to the cupboards, my phone in hand.

I've never felt more out of place. This is so not how I imagined this evening. Rose was supposed to be here, and after checking she could be left alone, I was supposed to join my best friend, Abby, on the beach. A bunch of our old high school friends are having a Halloween bonfire by the pier.

But Rose can't be left alone.

The ungrateful brat.

As if it's not enough that I lie to our dad and her mom about the piano lessons. They don't know who Rose's teacher is. Dad didn't flip out straight away when her friends suggested Mia Harlow. That in itself wasn't an issue since we kept the Hayes surname away from his ears, but he did flip out when he learned the next day that Mia just so happens to be a future Mrs. Hayes.

Dad's not fond of them, hating the mayor for—I quote— *"being an obnoxious, rich elitist who doesn't give a damn about anyone other than the wealthy in this town."*

Rose whined for days, saying how talented Mia was and

how much she wanted to learn from her.

I caved. Not that I had any choice. Rose wouldn't quit whining until she got her way. It's her annoying superpower—wearing people down.

For the first time in my life, I lied to Dad. We told him we found an older gentleman who'll happily give her piano lessons, and *what a coincidence*... he lives just round the corner from where I got the job tending bar. It makes sense that I drive her there and back three times a week, doesn't it?

So, yeah... as if it's not enough I lie to Dad and Rebecca, now I've reduced myself to Rose's babysitter, watching over my three-years-younger sister while she lives her delusional dream, befriending Newport's elite.

She steps further into the kitchen, snatching the phone from me while I'm halfway through typing a text to Abby, exaggerating the complaints about my shitty evening.

"Nico's not back yet, so—" Mia utters, the words dissolving on the tip of her tongue at the sound of the door opening.

The man in question enters, his commanding presence flooding the room. I'm probably making this up in my head, but it feels like the air turns crisper than a winter storm with his arrival. He immediately turns into the kitchen, casting a quick, loaded look at Rose and me before tightly enclosing Mia's small frame in his huge arms.

He dips his chin, leaving a kiss in her hair with the intensity of a man who hasn't seen the love of his life for years.

Tension knots my body. The possessiveness in Nico's gestures knock the wind out of *me*, and I'm nothing but a passive observer: not involved, not on the receiving side of his dominant personality.

"You won't be driving that thing, baby," he says. "It's too

unpredictable. I'll get you something less powerful tomorrow."

Of course...

He bought her a car worth north of three hundred thousand dollars, and now he'll buy another one just. Like. *That.*

God, why am I suddenly so petty?

Mia says nothing about it, and less than five minutes later, we're outside, awaiting the show.

I head away from the crowd herding toward the stage and sit on an oversized outdoor couch in the deserted seating area.

I won't miss the show, I can see the stage just fine, but at the same time, I'm out of the way, where I don't risk being chatted up.

Or so I hoped...

Conor rounds the couch, taking a seat close enough that I get a hit of his heady cologne. "You stayed."

"I had little choice." I keep my eyes on Mia as she adjusts the height of her microphone stand. Cody's there, too. Or maybe it's Colt who drapes his hand across her collarbones, booming an introduction to the ecstatic crowd. "Your brother said *stay*, and apparently, I'm an obedient dog."

Conor lets out a short, amused huff. "Yeah, Nico's a tough one to say *no* to. Don't take him so seriously. He's mellowed out a lot since Mia."

I cock an eyebrow, watching the petite blonde on stage, seeming to float an inch off the ground with every move she makes. I didn't tell him which brother said *stay*, so I doubt Nico's mellowed much if Conor knew exactly who I meant.

"I'm sorry I let Rose have a beer," he adds, aimlessly passing a half-empty bottle of Corona from hand to hand. "I wouldn't let her have another."

"I wouldn't mind if she'd have two, but her mom's very

strict, and it's always me who gets an earful whenever Rose does something Becca doesn't approve of."

"I thought you're sisters."

"Stepsisters. Same father."

"That explains why you don't look alike."

True. No one thinks we're related. We're completely different, which is odd. I'm ninety percent Dad with light brown hair, silver eyes, and a heart-shaped face, while Rose took nothing from him. She's the spitting image of her mother save for her black hair and eyes. That must've been passed down from her grandparents or maybe even great-grandparents.

"Rose is a good kid, but she's careless. She gets in trouble a lot, so Dad relies on me to keep her safe."

"She's safe here," Conor says.

I take a good, hard look at the crowd of college guys ogling girls like candy. "Hardly. She's barely eighteen. Very gullible. She already thinks Mia's her best friend."

"And what's wrong with that?"

I can't stop a derisive snort flying past my lips. "Nothing wrong, but nothing realistic, either."

Girls like Mia don't befriend girls like Rose or me.

'Princesses don't hang out with the help.'

"She sure is amazing, though," I admit, unable to tear my eyes from Mia as she starts singing. Her voice is rich and full. Each note slips from her mouth like honey trickling over a razor blade, a raspy depth in the lower registers.

Conor nods in agreement. "She has a way of captivating an audience. I've heard her sing a million times, but I still get goosebumps whenever she's on stage," he admits proudly, jigging the bottle in his mouth to get at the last of his beer. "So, you're not mad at me?"

"I'm not. At least not about Rose."

"Good." He moves closer, his breath skittering across my neck. "Because I want to ask you something."

I turn to look at him, caught off guard by the sudden proximity. "I already told you we're not going out on a date," I whisper, heart racing as I try to anticipate his next move.

"That's not what I want to ask."

"What do you want to ask?"

He moves even closer, his lips near enough to mine that our breaths mix, reminding me of that kiss in the garage.

I'm frozen. Even my eyes are unable to move.

There's something in his gaze, a kind of blazing possessiveness that has my toes curling in my boots.

And then a thought that should've materialized the second he kissed me the first time pierces through me like a sharp arrow.

This isn't about a date.

He doesn't give two fucks about dinner. It's what might come after dinner that he wants.

'*Sex.*'

A jolt of excitement wrings me inside out. I shouldn't be excited. I should be offended. Hurt. Humiliated.

I'm far from it.

Sex is noncommittal. Purely physical. In bed, who fucking cares where I'm from or how much I don't fit with a man like Conor? No one. That's who.

'*Sex is easy. I know the drill.*'

A bit of fun, perhaps seduction if the guy's feeling particularly giving, maybe an orgasm if he's not self-centered, and we part ways.

Now *that*... that could work.

There's no denying the chemistry sparking and sizzling

between us. The closer he is, the more I'm turned on. The kiss alone ignited my mind and body, waking an itch I wouldn't mind him scratching. We could go to a motel, work through the desire, and part ways an hour or two from now.

'Everyone wins.'

My gaze idles from his eyes to his mouth and back. I moisten my lips with the tip of my tongue. A silent invitation.

The universal language I'm sure he speaks, too.

The ball lands in his court, and the sly smirk twisting his features says he understood. Shifting his weight, he closes the gap between us. He's close enough that his nose tickles the line of my jaw.

Hook, line, and sinker.

'God, I'm good at this.'

My body tingles with anticipation as the tip of his nose drags its way higher, dawdling as he brushes a line to my ear, his hot breath against my skin.

"Do you want a beer?" he whispers, his voice curling at the edges.

Shit.

This isn't seduction.

This is bold amusement.

The sentence falls like a hammer, breaking the spell. Disappointment settles heavily in my chest, the tension between us deflating as fast as a punctured balloon.

For a moment, I was caught in a dream-like state, thinking he'd kiss me before we'd go somewhere private. I *wanted* it. The thought of his lips on mine, his naked body pressing into me. The memory of that outline…

I shake that thought off, avoiding his scorching gaze as I scurry away, breaking the intimacy that's now well and truly gone. "No, I have work in the morning."

He clutches my chin between his fingers, turning my face his way. "What's wrong, Little Bee?" he drawls, his tone charged with a heavy load.

He watches me like he sees right through me. I'm pretty sure he does. I'm not great at hiding emotions.

"Why the pout?" His knuckles outline the contours of my face, eyes never leaving mine. "You didn't want me to kiss you, did you now? I'm not your type, remember?"

"I remember," I mutter. The pressure in my belly revives as his gaze drops to my mouth, his brown eyes sizzling.

So he does want sex? Ugh...

'What a weird game.'

"On second thought..." I remoisten my lips, giving him a taste of his own medicine. "I'll take that beer."

His grin widens. "This will be interesting," he adds, more to himself than me. "Alright, one beer coming right up."

It takes a moment before I get a hold of myself and realize that, however strong the pull between us, giving in means tears and disappointment at best.

He'll forget about me once he gets his fill, and I... I think I have whiplash from the pendulum motion of my thoughts.

Now that he's not close, reducing my brain to an infinity pool of desire, and I can think relatively straight... one night with him might not be a good idea if the way I crave another of his hot kisses is any indication.

Maybe he does come back with the beer. Maybe he doesn't. I don't get to see because Mia finishes her gig two minutes later, and despite Rose's pleas, we head home.

She's silent all the way back, staring out the window, eyebrows theatrically bunched in the middle, arms and legs crossed.

She's annoyed. *'So am I.'*

If not for her, I wouldn't have met Conor tonight. I wouldn't feel so jittery and feverish inside recalling the way he kissed me. I wouldn't wonder whether I'd made the right call shooting him down.

I park the car. The engine dies before I turn the key.

Great. Just what I need.

"At least we got home," Rose mutters, slamming the door.

My head hits the headrest as I watch her make her way round the clay pots Rebecca put out to grow vegetables at the start of summer. It was nice while the novelty pushed her to take care of the tomatoes, carrots, and salad, but her efforts faded quickly. Now, nothing but desiccated twigs poke from the soil.

I move my gaze further from the car to the place I call home, my stomach churning at how different this place is from where I've just spent a few hours.

No driveway here.

No porcelain steps lead inside a humongous villa.

My house is nothing like that. It's not even a house. It's a rickety trailer with faded blue paint peeling at the edges.

No marble floors, Persian carpets, or high-end appliances inside. Here, the walls are a dull, faded shade of yellow, adorned with family photos. The living space is small, crammed with mismatched furniture: a three-seater sofa, an armchair, and crammed in by the window, a table with just two chairs, so we have to take turns eating dinner.

The kitchen doesn't have an island, an oversized fridge, or a custom-made coffee machine. It's a kitchenette, complete with sink, stove, and mini fridge.

It's not much.

It's not really a house, but it *is* home.

TOO STRONG

Rebecca flings the door open, her curler-wrapped hair lit from behind and a once-black robe cinched around her waist. With both arms firmly planted on her hips, she waits for Rose to approach and blow in her face so she can check her daughter wasn't drinking.

Once satisfied, she steps aside, letting Rose pass, and glares at me, pointing her thumb through the door. A silent order to haul my ass inside.

"Why so grim?" she asks, squinting as she watches me climb out of the car. "What happened to your costume?"

I shrug, not in the mood to even think about the disaster my costume has caused, let alone relay the evening. It's too risky, anyway. When I get going, I don't think through my words, and it's a given the frustration bubbling inside me would make me accidentally spill whose house we were at tonight.

I may be twenty-one, but if my father finds out I entered the Hayes lair, I'll be grounded until I'm twenty-five, so it's safer not to open my mouth.

The air inside the trailer is thick with cigarette smoke and the chemical stink of cheap cleaning products. My dad sits parked in the armchair, eyes glued to the TV. A can of Coors is propped on his big belly, cigarette dangling between the fingers of his other hand. Despite his rough exterior, the wife beater he wears, and rugged looks, my dad's a real softie deep down.

He's always been there for us, working hard to provide for the family. He's not the fancy, eloquent type, but he's the farthest thing from a deadbeat you could imagine. Unlike my uncle, Dad's never been one to party hard or let anything get in the way of his responsibilities. He enjoys a few cans of beer on the weekend and smokes like a chimney, but we all have our vices.

Gummy bears are mine.

"Hey, Angel, how was the party?" he asks.

I occupy half his attention while his favorite actor waves his way into the studio, greeting the talk-show host with a firm handshake.

"It was fine. I'd tell you more, but I'm tired. By the looks of it, my car's dead again, so I'll be biking to work tomorrow."

"I'm not working tomorrow. I'll take you in, just wake me up when you're ready."

I smile small, retreating toward the bedroom. "Thanks, Dad, night night."

"Night, Angel."

As expected, Rose is already comatose on the lower bunk bed. The ASMR sounds of raindrops on windows emanate from her birthday present, a small portable speaker in the extravagant—for a speaker—shade of blood orange. She always drifts off straight away, while I toss and turn, searching for a comfortable position.

After washing up, I change into pjs, and climb the wooden ladder to the top bunk. The mattress sags beneath my weight, springs whining in complaint as they dig into my back.

I lay here under my cozy, weighted blanket, in the comforting hum of artificial rain patter and air conditioning, unable to keep Conor from hijacking my thoughts.

What is it about him that has me in such a tumult over one kiss?

My cheeks burn at the memory, then grow incandescent when shame hits me square in the jaw. I shouldn't have left without saying *goodbye*. He's been nothing but kind all evening, and I...

I was my usual, antagonistic, hot-headed self.

FOUR

Vee

The ancient jukebox in the corner honks out "Ocean Front Property" by George Strait as I cross the threshold of *The Well*.

The first fifteen minutes of my shift are spent getting used to the smell of stale beer, sweat, and the wet rag Polly, the owner, uses to wipe the counters and tables.

Shaky reproductions of the dim lights shine from damp furniture and a pool of spilled beer across the wooden floor that Johnny, Polly's husband, is mopping up.

"Hey, Gary." I round the bar, nodding to the regulars sitting at the counter—a mix of truck drivers home for the weekend and local small shop owners.

"Get me another, doll," Gary says, slapping a twenty on the bar. He sets his glass on top and pushes it toward me. "You okay? You look tired."

Polly's head pops like a whack-a-mole from the counter where she kneels by the glasswasher. "Don't tell me you're sick," she pleads, looking me over. "Tell me you partied all night."

"I'm not sick, don't worry. I couldn't sleep."

Because the thought of Conor Hayes kept me awake all night.

And the night before and every night since last weekend's Halloween party.

I've not seen him while dropping Rose off at Nico's for her piano lessons this week. A small part of me, the one I resent, was utterly disappointed.

He kissed me.

No, he consumed me. Every touch of his lips designed to melt me, turn me on, own me, please me, and then... *nothing*. I hoped he'd be home in the afternoons, playing hot and cold. Taunting. Teasing the way he did in the garden. I hoped he'd seek me out, try to make me change my mind about the date but nope.

No hot. Just cold.

I hate that it unnerves me this badly. Conor and I would never work, but at the same time, I can't obliterate him from my mind.

I'm sure he's in one of the elegant cocktail bars his older brother owns right now, enjoying a few beers with friends.

I doubt he ever set foot in a tiny place like *The Well*. No handmade, exclusive artisan liquor, jewel-encrusted decorations from high-end artists, or clientele in designer labels... just scratched-up bar stools and rickety, old tables.

A chalkboard menu with drink specials hangs on the right wall, and reasonably priced bottles line the shelves behind me. It's not fancy, but it's got character. A soul. Personal touch.

Old newspapers wallpaper the ceiling, sports or music channels flicker from two large flatscreens on opposite sides, and the walls are littered with things you'd find at a garage sale: broken clocks, mismatched art, lamps. A surfboard—wrapped in string lights to create a chandelier—hangs above the pool table.

I like the vibe. Casual, welcoming: the kind of place everyone knows your name. Somewhere you can let loose and be yourself without judgment because we're all on the same boat—working (or not) class, struggling to make ends meet.

Time moves as if standing still tonight. Minutes trickle by so, so slowly while I serve the patrons, my mind elsewhere.

In that damned garage last week.

Curved into Conor's chest.

With a huff, I grit my teeth, channeling all effort to think different thoughts. Less Conor-infested. More practical. I make a mental list of things to take care of after the weekend. I check if I'll have enough time before work on Tuesday, Wednesday, and Thursday to drop Rose at her piano lessons. That satisfactorily concluded, I double-check Becca's shifts, making sure she can take Rose to college.

Rose passed her driving license a few months ago, but can't afford a car without a job, so we're dividing and conquering the taxi schedule.

"Oh boy," Polly chirps, nudging me from my reverie. "Long time no see," she adds, beaming at the man breezing into the bar.

Following her line of sight, my stomach threatens mutiny as my eyes lock with Conor's. Money almost oozes out of his pores. The expensive details on his casual outfit scream he doesn't belong in a dive like this. Designer logo on his t-shirt, expensive watch adorning his wrist, perfectly white shoes.

He carries himself with a sense of confidence and entitlement, shoulders back, cool, aloof expression easily mistaken for him looking down on everyone in the room.

He isn't. That's just a first flawed impression.

It changes when a goofy smile curls his full lips as he rests his elbows on the sticky, damp counter.

His eyes taking a slow, heated sweep of my face is all the attention I get before his gaze runs along the contents of the tall fridge in the corner. "Corona, please," he orders, pulling a barstool closer.

"I'm sorry, we don't serve Corona, and we're actually closed to outsiders tonight. They have Corona in *Tortugo*. Try there."

"They sure do. Nicer bartenders too." He drags his eyes toward Polly. "Can I get a Corona, please?"

Polly, the traitor, nods once, snatches a bottle from the fridge, and pops the cap. "Lime?"

"No, thanks."

"What are you doing here?" I snap, ringing him up. "How did you find me? *Why* did you find me?"

"I'm having a beer. It's been a long day. And who said I was looking for you?" He tugs from the bottle, unfazed that the place fell silent. Everyone listens in like he's an international spy ready to divulge state secrets. "When do you finish work?"

"Once my shift ends."

He smirks, snaking the bottle left and right between his fingers. "Not long enough, huh? I thought a week would wear you down." He takes another swig, giving me a minute to process his question before repeating it. "What time do you get off, Vivienne?"

"Nine," Polly cuts in, boiling my blood. "But I wouldn't mind letting her off the hook sooner tonight."

How dare she pimp me out like that?

I turn to her, anger scorching a hole in my stomach. "I'm getting off early tomorrow for Abby's birthday, remember? I'm working my full shift tonight."

And, of course, as my hand whips toward Polly's chest, it accidentally swipes Conor's beer, and it spills... all over him. Where else would it spill if not over his thousand-dollar jeans?

"Beer in my face and on my pants," he muses, accepting paper towels from Polly. "You hurt my dick and my nose. What's next, Little Bee? You'll knock my teeth out? Break my leg?"

"I'm—"

"Sorry," he finishes, nodding a few times as he pats himself dry. "I know. You're not doing it on purpose." No annoyance taints his voice. He's amused, eyes sparkling as he waits for me to speak.

"I'm really not—"

"Really not *what*, Little Bee?" He muses with a smug grin. "Not really sorry? Not really doing this on purpose?"

Oh the nerve of him.

"Listen," I clip, the embarrassment long gone, replaced by an angry bee buzzing at the back of my skull. "Just leave." I pull out the money for his beer from the till, handing it back. "Go, okay?"

He pushes my hand away. "Not until you give me one *valid* reason you won't have dinner with me. And don't say I'm not your type. You don't kiss a guy like—"

"Shut up!" I wail, my cheeks aglow with embarrassment, stomach tight at the reminder of his perfect lips devouring mine.

I don't fucking need a reminder.

'I've replayed that kiss for a week straight.'

It's etched into my very being by now.

"You're *you*, okay? I'm just me. It's a waste of time."

His eyebrows bunch, but it's not him who speaks.

"You're you, he's him, and I'm all out of beer, doll," Gary says, rolling his eyes between us. "Grab me another, will you?"

TOO STRONG

"I'm *me*?" Conor asks. "What's that supposed to mean?"

I pour another beer for Gary, worrying my lip as I reluctantly meet Conor's gaze. "What car do you drive?"

"Tonight? A Mustang, why?"

Tonight? How many cars does he have? How many cars does one person need? Isn't it just one?

"Have you seen my car?"

He nods, accepting another Corona from Polly. She's got things to do, but she's not moving, gaze anchored on Conor as she drinks every word falling from his mouth.

"Yeah, Mercury. Classic."

"A classic piece of junk. Is that a Rolex on your wrist?"

He glances down, checking which expensive watch he's wearing today. It's not the same one he wore last week, so I bet he's got a whole collection.

"No, it's not."

"But you have one," I continue, handing Gary his beer.

Conor straightens in his seat, a hard edge to his brown eyes. "You won't go out with me because I own a Rolex?"

I stare back, nervously twirling a strand of hair around my finger, racking my brain for the right words.

"More or less," I admit, my voice shaky. "I won't go out with you because, in social terms, you're here..." I stretch my arm, making a line in the air as far above my head as possible, accidentally knocking a few hardly-ever-used wine glasses tinkling from the rack bolted into the ceiling. "...and I'm here." I make another line, significantly lower. Low enough he can't see it because it's almost at my knees, hidden behind the counter.

Judging by the look crossing his face, he's starting to understand where I'm coming from, but I keep talking, determined to nail the point until no doubts remain.

"Let me paint a picture for you. I'll fast forward a few dates at the diner and go straight to meeting your friends and brothers. Imagine I arrive at Nico's house, parking my rusty car beside your shiny Mustang."

He's visibly annoyed now, one fist clenched on the counter, jaw set tight as he claws the label off the bottle.

"I'll be late because I just finished my shift here and got dressed in the toilet at the back." I motion to the door behind me. "I'll wear a Walmart dress, buckle-laced boots, and the handmade jewelry Rose makes, trying to fit among your friends. They'll ask what college I go to, I'll say I work two jobs. They'll ask where I live, I'll say trailer park."

"And you think anyone will care?" he asks, his tone dripping sarcasm. "You think I care?"

A derisive snort saws past my lips. "Everyone will. Don't pretend they won't. Don't pretend *you* won't. I know you only asked me on one date, but I'm not wasting my time. I know this will never work."

"You know nothing about me, Vee." He grinds his teeth, jumping from his stool. "But you sure paint a vivid picture. Looks like I overestimated you. See, I thought you're cute, carefree, and confident, but you're actually judgmental and fucking shallow if you think I, my family, or friends give a damn where you live, work, or what car you drive."

He nods his goodbyes at Polly and Gary, then turns on the sole of his sneaker, marching out of the bar, jeans still wet.

My cheeks burn bright. My skin bursts into prickles and I've never felt more embarrassed. I didn't mean it to come out the way it did. I wasn't judging *him*. Only myself.

We're from two different worlds. Two ends of a spectrum. While it was supposed to be just one date, what's the point in getting to know him better when the end is easily predictable? Building my hopes up if he'll toss me aside in a few days? I get attached too fast to not defend myself. It's enough I can't shake him off after one kiss. A date will be the last nail in my coffin.

"You'll regret it," Polly sing-songs, wiping the counter with the old, wet rag. "I know the Hayes are loaded, but I bet you've not spent time with any of them. They're decent people, Vee."

I fold my arms, tapping my foot against the floor. Polly's like a cool, crazy aunt. The kind that helps you pick out your date outfit and gives you advice on impressing the guy. The kind that helps you sneak out to parties by lying to your parents.

Now she's anything but cool. The other aunt. The one who smells like moth balls and the seventeen cats she lives with.

"How would you know?" I ask.

She's fifty-three. I doubt she spends her weekends partying with the elite.

"Cassidy, soon-to-be Mrs. Hayes, is good friends with my youngest, Mary-Jane. Logan comes over whenever anything needs fixing, and never charged me a dime."

"Logan?" I mutter under my breath, labeling the Hayes by more manageable categories than just their names. "Is he the one who owns *Stone and Oak*?"

Polly nods, snatching five glasses from the counter. The bar is starting to empty, only a few people left nursing their drinks. Gary will remain parked by the counter until closing. His bushy mustache twitches in amusement as he eavesdrops on our conversation. Johnny's nowhere around, probably cleaning the toilets at the back or rearranging the sign above the front door into something cringy that he considers funny. Last week it was '*I drink therefore I am*', and the week before, '*We sell water. Frozen and floating in liquor'.*

"Yes. And you met Shawn the other night when he cuffed the two guys who started that brawl."

"The Chief of police?! He's a Hayes?"

"The oldest brother," Gary confirms. "Stand-up guy, he is. His kid's in kindergarten with my granddaughter."

"Well, that's just two out of seven. Besides, I'm not saying they're bad people. I'm saying I don't belong in their crowd. Have you seen Nico's fiancée? She's like something out of a Disney movie. Cinderella or whatever."

"She's gorgeous, but she's lovely, isn't she?" Polly continues, cocking an eyebrow. "You're wrong if you think they'd judge you. Cassidy didn't come from money, sweetheart. And Theo's wife worked as a cart girl at the Country Club." She leans her hip against the fridge, arms crossed, eyebrow still raised. "I can tell you like Conor. Your face lit up the moment he walked in. It's just one date, Vivienne. He's into you."

The kiss last week speaks in favor of her statement. I do like him. Otherwise, I wouldn't have told him to ask me out, but...

At twenty-one, I no longer believe in fairytales. And Conor Hayes asking me out is just that, a fairytale. It won't work.

But it isn't Conor's fault.

It's mine.

My insecurities won't allow me something as simple as a meal at a cheap diner.

Jesus, so much drama over one dinner.

'So much drama because you like him.'

"You're overthinking," Gary says, swilling back half his beer. "And that means you're not sure you made the right call."

Oh, I made the right call considering how invested I already am and that I'd end up as nothing more than a notch on Conor's bedpost, but assuming he and his brothers are entitled, condescending assholes might've been too much.

I grab my bag from under the counter, flinging it over my shoulder. "I'll work the time back next week," I tell Polly, coming out from behind the bar. "I promise."

"Don't worry about it. Have fun!" she yells after me, amusement tingeing her voice.

I bust out the door, scanning the street. Conor's still there, leaning against the side of his Mustang parked further down the road. The cherry of his cigarette flares, a cloud of smoke droning around him as he takes a drag.

"I'm sorry," I say, coming closer, sweat oiling my palms. "I realize that's all I've been saying since we met, and it means nothing by now, but I am sorry."

"What are you sorry for? Everything you said? Or that you judged me even though you don't know me?"

"Neither. I mean, both. I'm sorry I've made it sound like you're the problem. It's not you, okay? It's me."

"Ah, the famous *it's not you, it's me* bullshit..." He flicks his cigarette butt into the sewer before raking his fingers through his hair.

"Ugh," I huff, clenching my hands into fists. "That came out wrong..."

"Then tell me how it was supposed to come out because everything you said tonight is fucking ridiculous."

"It's not ridiculous, Conor. We're from different worlds."

He pushes away from the car, close enough now to dip his head and look me in the eyes, his hot breath warming my cheek. "Money doesn't define me. You've labeled me a *rich prick*, but that's not me." His voice is barely above a whisper now, the electric current between us back in full force, almost cracking like lightning in the cool evening breeze. "You'd know if you'd let me take you out."

My mind races.

I'm trying hard to resist him, but my willpower splinters when he lifts his hand, ghosting his knuckles along my cheek.

"One date, Vee. That's all I'm asking for now."

'If it were that simple.'

"No. I can't, I..." I say, my voice trembling, heart pummeling my chest. "Please, just stop seeking me out, okay?"

"Why?" His narrowed eyes search mine like he's trying to pull my thoughts straight from my head. "You've not given me a single rational explanation."

'Because this has already gone too far.'

And he only kissed me once.

Because he consumed my every thought this past week. Because it would take a split second of inattention to absolutely lose myself in him.

'He has no idea how quickly I'd get attached.'

I don't want to be another one of his conquests.

'Another notch on his bedpost.'

I don't want to be a temporary fix for his boredom.

"I..." I bite my lip. "I just can't."

He watches me for a long moment, expression unreadable. Then, with just a single nod, he hops behind the wheel and drives away, leaving me alone. Torn. Filled with regret.

FIVE

She talks to herself.

Quietly. Sometimes quietly enough I can't make out the words. Other times I wish I hadn't heard.

When she did it at the Halloween party, I was ready to snap. What the fuck does she mean *people with money judge hard*? I clamped my teeth shut just in time when I realized those words weren't meant for my ears.

Anyone's ears.

Vee didn't seem aware her unfiltered thoughts slipped out.

It's fascinating.

Hurtful because she seems to think all I want is her to end up just another notch on my bedpost, but fucking fascinating nonetheless.

She unconsciously gives me a first-row seat into her thoughts, and while I might wish I didn't hear some of them, I want to know how she operates.

And I sure fucking loved hearing that she was thinking about our kiss all week, so there's that.

It's not a constant string of words. Vee doesn't blurt out everything, just some random lines. I've gathered so far that she only does it when she's deep in her head. It's like her thoughts race a million miles an hour, and if some aren't spoken, she can't focus.

It's odd. Quirky. I love it.

Most of it.

But what she muttered and what she intentionally said aloud brought me to the same conclusion.

She thinks I'm too rich for her.

Something like this has *never* happened. Not that I've never been shot down by girls; that's no novelty.

I've been shot down because they preferred one of my brothers. Because I'm careless. Because I'm too young to ask a beautiful thirty-year-old mom to a three-year-old daughter out for a drink, but never because I have money.

Too little money, sure. A Russian Princess, or whatever her title was, told me to beat it last year while we partied in Vegas, but *too much* money?

Who would've thought it could be an issue?

Despite the shit Vee said, despite her judgmental attitude and between-the-lines accusations, color me fucking impressed. For the first time, I met a girl turned off by designer clothes, expensive watches, and brand-new cars

I hold my hands up; Colt, Cody, and I have had it easy thus far. Mom and Dad paid our expenses until our twenty-first birthday a couple months ago. Nico bought us cars at seventeen, took us in so Mom didn't watch us party, and pumped our accounts with cash every month since we started high school.

I. A. DICE

We *did* have it easy. And we're off to a great start, thanks to Nico gifting us portfolios worth almost two million dollars. Still, it doesn't make us entitled assholes. We don't look down on anyone with less money.

We've been helping with Mom's Charities since I remember. And Colt is Nico's right-hand man these days, working his ass off managing our brother's many businesses.

Cody spent the summer doing hands-on manual labor for Logan, and I've rebuilt Nico's business websites from the ground up.

I lean against the side of my car outside Nico's house, glaring at the pebbled driveway. It's not the same Mustang he bought me four years ago. Along with the portfolios, we got new wheels: another beacon of our privileged life.

Taking a drag of my cigarette, I blow a long, forceful plume of smoke past my lips, anger and disappointment mixing in my veins.

I've been back here for half an hour, smoking one after another, though I'm mostly a social smoker. Parties, beer, good company all warrant a smoke. Not tonight. Tonight, I'm checking how many cigarettes in a row it takes before my head starts to throb, or my stomach ejects its contents.

Three aren't doing it. Maybe five's the number.

Maybe I should smoke faster.

Or maybe I should stop staring at the house, trees, and my own shoes like they somehow offended me and get inside.

My brothers know what happened last week. The kiss, my sudden unexplainable *need* and *want* for Vee, the charged air between us.

We don't brag about who we hook up with, but the magnetic pull between Vee and me feels like a ton of bricks weighing down my chest. I couldn't stop obsessing over the kiss for hours. I had to tell someone. Let it out. Vent, because every second on the couch with her while Mia took the stage was an exercise in self-control.

I've never tried so fucking hard not to drag a girl onto my lap, fold her into me, and kiss her.

I can't get her out of my head. I don't fucking want to. She unlocked something primal, wild, and unattainable I never knew existed deep within me.

I'm losing my mind here. Who gets so hooked after *one* kiss? God, but what a fucking kiss...

I still feel her lips against mine. Soft, full, eager. It's been days. *Seven* long days, but the memory lingers, taunting me nonstop. Her warm body pressing into mine, her fingers tugging my hair, her breath catching when I deepened the kiss...

That sweet, soft, surprised little moan I swallowed. The way she melted into me, fitting like a puzzle piece.

My sudden obsession wouldn't be this surprising if my goal was to drag Vivienne into my bedroom and fuck her senseless, but the thought didn't cross my mind until she was gone.

Despite way-too-many beers, my cock was rock hard before I even stepped in the shower later that night and it wasn't long till I painted the tiles with my cum, reliving the kiss until my orgasm rattled through me.

A frustrated groan scrapes up my chest once the cigarette ends. I'm basically smoking the filter. I toss it onto the driveway, almost snapping the bridge of my nose between my fingers, a heavy sigh saws past my clenched teeth.

Fuck.

I'm overreacting.

So she doesn't want to go out with me... who cares? She's

not the first and won't be the last. Granted, most girls at college would rip their right arm off for a date with me, Colt, or Cody while Vee acts like I'm Hugh Hefner trying to buy a night.

Still, it's no reason to drive myself batshit crazy.

Other than that cute, quirky first impression and mind-blowing kiss, she's not exactly a catch with that judgmental worldview.

I cross the driveway, wondering why Nico never had it paved. The crunch of gravel grinding under my sneakers sets my teeth on edge. To be fair, everything has since I left Vivienne standing alone on the street.

The garage stands open, Nico's four cars and Cody's Mustang parked in a neat line. Colt must be putting out fires, tending to emergencies at Nico's cocktail bars or *The Olive Tree*.

Lights flicker from Cody's second-floor bedroom window, making it my destination as I enter the house. He's either watching a violent action movie or gaming online. Neither is as important as me venting, though.

I jog upstairs, two steps at a time, then knock loud enough to wake the dead.

One.

Two.

Three seconds.

Long enough for Cody to shove his dick back in his pants if I guessed wrong, and it's not an action movie he's watching.

Though there's plenty of action in porn...

"Come in!" he yells.

Pointless, considering I'm already pushing the door open, casting a quick glance around in case I'm imposing.

The TV is on, the qualifying session of the Japan Grand Prix about to end. Shit. I forgot it's race weekend. I promised we'd watch it together.

At least Ghost, the python now considered a family pet, is here, though not giving two fucks about the race, curled into a large coil at the foot of the bed.

"What's up?" Cody asks, eyes glued to the flat screen.

"Wanna grab a beer? Or five?"

Now he looks over, eyebrow raised. "Didn't go well, I take it? What did she say?"

"That I'm too rich for her."

"Too rich? You're not rich, bro. Nico's rich."

"I own a Rolex, a brand-new car, designer clothes, and..." I get comfortable in the wing chair by the door. "She's odd."

"I thought that's what you liked most."

I nod, temporarily lost in my head. "She's just... I don't know. I don't understand this girl. You know I don't take them out—"

"So why are you pining?"

"I'm not pining," I growl.

I so am.

Don't know why, but I am.

I want that girl so fucking bad my skin itches.

"When she suggested a date, the idea grabbed me so hard I can't shake it. I want that fucking date. Just one for now. See how it goes, but she's acting like I asked her to marry me."

Cody mutes the TV, drags his feet off the bed, propping both elbows on his knees, and offers his full attention.

Fine.

Beer can wait. Maybe he'll notice something I'm missing.

I relay mine and Vee's entire conversation, holding nothing back, not even how she looked me over when I walked into *The Well*. How her voice quivered when she spilled beer over my jeans.

They're still damp. I smell like a goddamn brewery.

Halfway through my monologue, Colt arrives with a case of Coronas, eyebrows drawing together as he tunes into my words. "Who looked ready to burst out crying?" he asks, throwing himself onto Cody's bed. "We talking about that Bee girl?"

"Not really talking," Cody muses, opening the case and popping the caps off three bottles. "Conor's airing his laundry."

"Ah, right. Nothing better than your unfiltered thoughts at full volume. Start from the top."

"But this time," Cody says, "...keep some details to yourself. We don't need to know she smells so fucking fresh or how pretty her eyes are to understand your point, bro."

With a heavy sigh, I rewind, catching Colt up so he'll throw his five cents in at the end. I don't know why I bother. Asking him for advice about women is like asking Logan.

Pretty fucking useless.

How Logan keeps Cassidy happy, glowing, and in love with him is anyone's guess.

"So?" I urge when I'm done.

They just sit there, silently processing. The room is quiet save for Ghost slithering away toward the door like he's had enough of me talking and is now thinking *fuck this, I don't wanna live here anymore.*

"Any ideas?" I ask, the words entirely too desperate, hinting how much I need their help to figure this out.

"It sounds like there's more to it than you two being from different worlds," Cody says, swigging his beer.

"Yeah? Like what?"

"How the fuck should I know? I spoke one sentence to her."

"She might have had a bad experience with someone like you," Colt suggests, leaning his shoulder against the headboard, a frown creasing his forehead.

"What the hell do you mean *someone like me?*" I snap, my temper on the rise. "You think I'm a rich prick?"

"So fragile," Cody chuckles, shaking his head. "Relax, if you're a rich prick, so are we. I think what Colt means—"

"What I mean is maybe some trust-fund asshole hurt her, and now she sees all guys through the same pair of glasses. Or..." he trails off, leaving the idea hanging in the air.

God, I swear, one day, I'll smack his stupid face. Colt loves building tension, turning the screws with these long pauses. It's mildly annoying most days, but tonight he's pushing my buttons with expert precision.

"Or? Or what?" I reach for another beer, the condensation dripping freezing lines down my fingers.

Conor shrugs. "Or she's not used to being pursued. Maybe you intimidate her."

"So I'm basically screwed, right?"

"Giving up so easily?" Colt tuts. "You like this girl. That's what's making you chase her even though she keeps telling you *no.*"

"Find out what bothers her," Cody adds, combing a few loose strands back into his bun. "Maybe she's not ready for anything serious. Or she's afraid you only want something casual. You tried digging deeper?"

"Yeah. As much as she let me." I groan, my head smacking the wing chair. "I wanted to kiss her so badly I was practically fucking drooling."

"Then try again. She already shot you down two times, a third won't do your ego any more damage," Colt says. "You said she mentioned her friend's birthday tomorrow, right? They'll probably be going out somewhere in town."

"Or she lied to get rid of me."

"Or that." He smirks, pulling his phone out. Detective Colt on a mission. "We'll see."

Everyone compares him to Nico because they're both sharp, intelligent, and shrouded in danger, but in some ways, Colt resembles Logan. Careless despite his excellent work ethic and outgoing enough he's on a first-name basis with half of Newport. He's probably texting his friends, asking if anyone knows Vee or her friend—Abby—and where they'll be tomorrow night.

Fingers crossed he gets some intel.

SIX

Conor

"Got your girl," Colt says, barging into my bedroom late on Saturday. "She's heading to *The Ramshack*. We're going out."

"*The Ramshack*? Where's that?"

"You know that rundown building two streets over from the arcades? The one with boarded-up windows, green paint, and a plastic mermaid hanging over the door?"

"That's a bar?"

"Apparently so. Live music every weekend. Some local band is playing tonight. Get moving. We're leaving in half an hour."

I sit up, slinging the PS controller aside. "I don't need a wingman, bro. I'm going solo."

"She already said *no* twice, and I've not seen it once. If she shoots you down again, I want to fucking watch. You're not taking this away from me. Get. Dressed." With one last pointed look, he retreats, closing the door behind him.

Of course the idea of witnessing Vivienne delivering another low blow to my stomach is too entertaining to pass on.

Having little choice in the matter, it takes me less than twenty minutes to grab a shower and meet them in the kitchen, buzzing like a fly on a hot day.

This can't be normal.

I've seen Vivienne twice, kissed her once, and I'm already acting like a stray dog that found a new owner.

"Heading out?" Nico asks, peeling his eyes from the screen of his laptop. "You need a ride?"

"Yeah, that'd be good. I was going to drive, but since you're offering, I won't mind a few beers," Cody admits, taking three bottles from the fridge. "Mia's out?"

"Yeah," he grinds out, clearly on edge, though it's not half as prominent as six months ago. He came a long way in taming his unbearable personality traits for Mia. "Dinner with Aisha."

"So you're not drinking," Cody states, popping the caps off.

It's not a question. Never is while Mia's out with her sister, father, or even us. Nico drives her wherever necessary and back, keeping off alcohol if his girl is the passenger.

"Where are you going?" he asks, pushing his laptop aside. "Club or another frat party?"

"*The Ramshack*," Colt supplies, grabbing the keys to Nico's G Wagon from a bowl in the hallway. "It's round the corner from the arcades."

"New bar?"

"Old one. Just not our scene," Cody says, making a beeline for the garage. "Shotgun!"

Yeah, no shit. He calls shotgun every time, like Colt or I would argue. Not a chance. Cody gets motion sick in the back, and neither of us enjoys stopping every five minutes, so it's a given he rides up front.

"Why the change?" Nico asks once we're all buckled up and he's reversing out of the garage. "You prefer your usual spots."

Cody looks over his shoulder, eyeing me with the question, checking how much—if anything—he can divulge. Satisfied by my lack of head shaking, he looks straight ahead. "Conor's hunting. Remember Rose's sister?"

"Vivienne?" Nico's inquisitive stare shifts to the rearview mirror. "You like her?"

"Understatement," Colt cuts in. "She shot him down *twice*, and he's still chasing."

Having brothers is fun.

They have a way of digging under my skin, knowing exactly where their pokes and prods will hurt most and piss me off to my back fucking teeth.

So much fun...

"She told him he's too rich for her," Cody adds, his tone brimming with amusement.

I don't need to see his face to know it's split in a Joker grin.

"She thinks I'm a spoilt asshole," I grunt, my foot bouncing against the car floor.

"Way off the mark." Nico turns left at the traffic lights, speedometer racing over the speed limit. Another thing he never does if Mia's in the car. "The rich part, I mean. You are a touch spoilt. Look at yourself. You're going after a girl who thinks you've got too much money, and *that's* what you're wearing?"

I scrutinize my tee and jeans. Granted, they're both designer, but no huge labels are plastered anywhere, so I fail to spot a problem.

It always makes me laugh whenever I see anyone strut the streets with huge *Dolce&Gabbana* prints covering their tees. *Look at me! I can afford this!*

TOO STRONG

Yeah... no. You can't. You saved up and bought the most obscene tee with the biggest logo to rub in your friend's face. All for show.

People who have money don't buy ostentatious clothes. Take Nico. He's got more cash than he could spend during three lifetimes, but he doesn't own any *look at me!* clothes. He doesn't feel the need to prove anything to anyone.

"What's wrong with my clothes?"

"Not your clothes, Conor," Nico clarifies like he's talking to my five-years-younger version. "Watch, bling, belt. You'll walk into that bar and stand out like a sore thumb. Lose the watch."

"So I'm supposed to change who I am?"

"You're looking at this the wrong way. I'm not saying never wear a watch again but show her you don't need it and you're no different without it. Know your audience, bro. If she didn't like spiders, would you bring one? You wouldn't, so don't wear things that immediately remind her you're... *rich*." He chuckles at the last word.

I don't like when he does that. After years of not hearing him laugh, hearing it now reminds me of psychopaths for some unknown reason.

I don't see how losing my watch will work, but *fine*. I hand it over to Nico for safekeeping. "She won't magically forget who I am just because I'm not wearing a watch," I say, massaging my wrist. "Fuck, I feel naked without it."

"Of course she won't forget, but you won't be flashing it in her face all evening. If you want her to get to know you better, keep her focused on *you*, not your bling. Got it?"

"Makes sense," Cody says, unbuckling his seat belt once Nico parks by the curb.

There's a line outside the bar. Immediately everyone turns,

staring at the two-hundred-thousand-dollar car my brother drives.

Good job not sticking out like a sore thumb.

Thankfully, a quick crowd scan tells me Vee's either inside or not here yet.

"Thanks for the ride," Colt says, his elbows landing on the driver's side door the second Nico rolls the window down. "You gonna stay up late?"

"Call me and check. I might pick you up."

"Alright." He taps the roof twice, sending him on his way.

Normally, we'd aim straight for the door, pat the bouncer's shoulder, and enter without spending a single second waiting in line, but it won't fly here. A, the bouncer watches us like he's thinking up an excuse *not* to let us enter at all, and B, we're supposed to lay low.

I light a cigarette, deeming the occasion social enough.

"This sucks," Cody mumbles, leaning against the building at the back of the queue. "Can't we slip him a hundred and get in already? How long will this take?"

"About ten minutes," a girl in front of us says, spinning on her heel. Big, blue eyes roam the three of us, not a hint of timidity marring her expression. "I'm Ana. You guys clearly don't belong here."

"What makes you say that?" Colt grumbles, equally unhappy about the wait as Cody.

Ana's redhead friend turns around, every bit of her exposed skin shimmering with glitter lotion. "The car, your clothes... your surname," she lists, tongue flicking round her lips. "You're the Hayes brothers, correct?"

Cody theatrically grips the back of his tee, circling round to look over his shoulder, unnaturally craning his neck. "Do I have a label on my back?"

Ana giggles, running her hand down his arm as the line moves. So do we, three whole steps.

"You don't, but your surname might as well be tattooed on Nico's forehead," Ana admits. "Everyone who pays attention knows who he is." She licks her lips again. "So? What brings you here of all places? Cocktail bars don't do it for you anymore, or are you looking for fresh pussy to tap tonight?"

I almost choke on the smoke, hacking my goddamn lungs out, but Colt's stoic expression hardly changes as he looks her over, ever so casual. "That an offer?"

She grins, taking a step closer, every move designed to stiffen his dick. "Maybe. Buy me a drink. We'll see what happens."

He grabs her by the arm, nothing tender about that touch or the look he sends me as he motions his chin at the door.

I guess sixty-seven seconds is enough time wasted in line. Cody urges the other girl along with a motion of his hand. By the time we reach the door, Colt's already dealt with the bouncer.

From the smirk stretching across the guy's face as he retracts the tape to let us pass, it's clear he got more cash than he'd typically ask for.

The first thing that hits me is how heavy the air feels compared to outside. The room is dimly lit, walls decorated with photos of bands that must've played here over the years. The space is packed beyond capacity, the crowd thicker than molasses, air saturated with artificial smoke, the stench of spilled beer, dampness, and sweat.

"C'mon." Cody nudges me under the ribs, pointing at a round bar at the center. "Let's grab a beer," he adds, arm casually draped across Ana's friend's—whatever her name might be—shoulders.

Never takes him long to scout a girl ready for a bit of fun.

We snake our way through the swarming crowd, passing the stage where the local rock band plays. They're good. Rock guitar riffs raise the hairs on the back of my neck, music raw, pulsing in the air with a gritty energy that infects everyone in the room.

This isn't what I'm used to. We go clubbing often, but our usual spots, with their sleek decor and flashing lights, seem almost sterile compared to this grungy chaos. The dancefloors there are either white, glass areas that blink in time to the DJ's music or clearly segregated wooden parquets.

Here, the dancefloor spreads every which way in a wave of bodies dancing to the rhythm dictated by the band. Even the metal staircase is alive with people swaying and jumping. There's no sitting area. No tables or plush couches for VIPs to lounge on.

Instead, a few retro booths line the walls, like in an old-school diner. The owner clearly didn't care about impressing anyone with luxury or exclusivity; they tried to create a space where people could come together and lose themselves in the music.

The lack of a dress code is another striking difference. In our favorite clubs, one wrong outfit choice is enough to get turned away at the door. But here, people wear whatever they want, from shorts and hoodies to bikini tops paired with tiny skirts.

Despite losing the watch, I'm still overdressed. My shoes are too clean, my t-shirt too crisply pressed, my jeans not showing enough signs of excessive wear.

The weight of people's gazes follows me to the bar. It's unnerving. The scrutiny, side-eyes, and behind-the-hand whispers. Weird. New. Unexpected.

"Three Coronas, and two appletinis," Colt tells the bartender, raising his voice above the music.

She taps her index finger at the drink menu taped to the counter. It's pretty short. Mostly beer and cheap wine, with three cocktails that hardly live up to the definition. Vodka with Red Bull, Greyhound, which is just a fancy name for vodka and grapefruit juice, and Cape Coddler, which—again—is just vodka with cranberry juice.

I'm starting to see a theme.

"Just get beer," Ana tells him. "Any."

A moment later, five bottles of Corona are pushed across the counter. No condensation on the bottles, meaning we'll be drinking it at room temperature. *Awesome.*

The barmaid frowns at the hundred-dollar bill Colt's holding out. "I don't think I've got enough change," she says, opening the till. "You got a twenty?"

"No, but you can open me a tab."

She cocks an amused eyebrow. "A tab? First time in *The Ramshack*, I take it? We don't do tabs, handsome." She grabs the bill with a cheeky smile. "I'll tell you what, I'll hold onto that." She slips the hundred down her cleavage. "I'll note what you're ordering, then give you the change at the end of the night."

"I plan on having more than two drinks," Colt says, pulling another three bills out. "Keep this. It should cover the bill by the time we're done."

"Sweetie, I know you're used to paying ten dollars a bottle, but it's five here, so a hundred bucks covers four rounds. You think you'll be ordering sixteen?"

"Probably no more than ten. Get me a booth, don't make me wait in line when I come back, and you'll keep the change."

A glowing smile is the only answer she gives before hailing a bouncer. She says something in his ear, gesturing at Colt, and the guy nods, no facial expression whatsoever.

"Follow me," he says, leading Colt and Ana—his girl for the night—toward the few booths left of the stage.

"So? What's the game plan, bro?" Cody asks, sitting *his* girl for the night—the redhead—on his lap once the bouncer has shooed the previous occupiers of the booth away, clearing a few empty glasses in the process. "You see her anywhere?" He slides his hand down to the girl's hip, then lower, slowly, making her squirm.

Good. He's into her, and that means he'll be otherwise occupied. Better than him getting in my way, trying to help, and doing the exact opposite. I tug from my bottle, scanning the crowd, not counting on much. Vee's short, so spotting her among the party-goers might be mission impossible.

But luck's on my side.

She just arrived, hair back into a high ponytail. Hips dressed in a denim skirt sway from left as she aims for the bar, arm-in-arm with another girl.

Must be Abby, judging by her pink birthday sash.

"Bingo," Cody whisper-cheers, nudging me to get moving. "Don't blow this. We'll be here if you need us."

"What would I need you for?"

"Good point."

I down another mouthful of beer, shifting closer to the edge of the seat, but suddenly everything goes to shit. A group of guys catches up with the girls, and one winds his hand around Vee's waist, yanking her away from Abby.

Every muscle in my body seizes painfully. Violent, zestful energy sweeps me from head to toe, growing incendiary at the puzzled, frightened look crossing her face.

It doesn't last long.

A second later, her beautiful smile lights up, replacing

my violent twinge with jealousy ringing in my mind like a school bell.

The guy whose grubby hands grope Vee's waist has the demeanor of a labradoodle. His unrelenting smile so dazzling it's blinding and if he had a tail it'd be wagging all over the place.

"Fuck," I hum, the word nullified by the surrounding noise.

If that's her type, then she was right... I'm not it.

But I can't let this girl go without a fight to save my fucking life.

SEVEN

Vee

Two hands grab the counter either side of my waist.

A pinch of surprise comes first, but the pleasant smell of Conor's cologne douses any unease I might have felt. I recognize it immediately. Spicy but fresh, a hint of citrus and something mildly sweet. Unmistakable. No other man I know uses cologne, let alone one this pungent.

"You really are a hoverfly," I say, keeping my voice steady though I can't deny my heart flutters and stomach cramps. This is the last place I'd expect to see Conor. "How did you find me here?"

"That guy who…" He trails off, fingers gouging the hardwood counter hard enough to snap a piece away, "…*touched* you earlier… is that what you're looking for?" He dips his head lower, the taut muscles of his jaw sweeping my cheek. The jealousy resounding in every word he speaks heats my skin. "A puppy who'll wag his tail whenever you look at him?"

TOO STRONG

Maintaining my composure around him is almost impossible on a normal day, and tonight I've got three drinks in my bloodstream, making the task that much harder. I'm flattered, turned on, and apprehensive all at once.

"What are you doing here?" I ask, shifting my thoughts away from the heat radiating from his chest hovering over my back.

I shouldn't have let Abby pour the drinks. Had I known I'd bump into Conor, I'd have told her to take it easy with the gin, but I didn't, so my courage is justified. Artificial but justified.

"I think this is stalking," I add, internally cursing my best friend for making gin and tonic half-an-half.

The band's not helping either, playing "Work Song" by Hozier, the melody and words caressing my mind the same way Conor's caressing my body.

He takes half a step forward, trapping me further as if encouraged by how I curl myself into him, his breath hot against my ear. "You like the chase."

A fit of shivers tingles along my spine. Damn it. He's not wrong... the hot and cold, the run and chase. This undeniable attraction between us is growing at an alarming pace.

In moments like this, when it's just us, his intentions are clear. *'He wants me.'* Whether the date is a speedbump he thinks has to be conquered head-on before we fuck, or sex isn't his end-game, I can't tell.

It hardly matters right now. I'm drunk enough to let Conor have his way with me if he makes a move.

I turn around, still graceful enough that I don't force him to step back. I doubt he would. He's not offering me more space, his gaze piercing into mine.

"I'm not sure if I should be flattered or scared," I admit, but instead of flirty, it comes out stern.

Damn the gin.

"Never scared, Little Bee." He lifts his hand to touch my face, his thumb stroking my cheekbone. "Not with me."

My skin ignites, and blood runs a fever, pulsing in the right place as if he found a nerve on my cheek directly connected to my clit. I swallow hard, dazed by the loaded look flooding his eyes, caught in the stacking tension.

A group of drunken guys elbow their way over and knock me out of the moment. One of them rams Conor's back so hard he crushes me into the bar, the hard edge digging into my shoulder blades.

Conor curls one arm around me, hand firmly pressed against the small of my back. Plastering me to his chest in one swift, tender move, he simultaneously shoves aside the guy who just rested his elbows on the counter.

His head whips our way, eyes narrowed as he sizes Conor up and down. "You got a problem, man?" he asks, the words slurred.

"Not yet." Conor shifts me to his side, using his body as a shield. "But you're begging to have your jaw dislocated."

The guy's eyes flash as he looks me over, a self-assured smirk spreading across his face. "What are you drinking, babe?"

Conor takes a fistful of my dress, molding me into him, his grip like a vice. The music thumps in my ears, a backdrop to the brewing confrontation.

"Getting there," Conor says, a hint of danger layering his voice. "Before you open your mouth again, take a second to decide if pissing me off is worth spending the rest of the night in the emergency room." He looms closer to him, towering over the guy by a good five inches. "See, I don't throw my fists often, but when I do, I don't hold back."

The guy snorts, toughing out his wavering confidence. He

glances over his shoulders, probably searching for backup. Instead of his friends, a group of girls stands there, giggling and swaying to the music. Before he turns to Conor, the bartender comes over, one eyebrow raised in silent question.

"Five bottles of Corona, and..." Conor's expectant gaze lands on me. "What are you having?"

"Separate bill," I tell the bartender. "A bottle of champagne and two glasses, please." I shove my hand in my purse, ignoring the way Conor's jaw tenses. "Don't even think about paying."

He swallows hard, like it's physically painful to watch me whip a fifty from my purse.

"How do you expect to keep the bottle secure while you're dancing?" he asks, grabbing the tray with beers. "Anyone can slip something inside the moment you look the other way."

"This isn't that kind of place. We come here a lot, and nothing ever happened."

"It doesn't mean it won't, Little Bee." His eyes narrow as he curls his fingers under my chin, tilting my head toward the light. "How much have you had to drink tonight?"

"What?"

"You're either tipsy or horny. Which one is it?"

'Both.' "Neither."

"It can't be both and neither, Vee."

A blush creeps onto my cheeks flushing to my neck and stiff-peaked nipples strain against the tight fit of my blouse. "I said it out loud?"

That's not a novelty. I talk to myself all the time, but I'd rather keep my no-filter mind away from Conor's ears.

"You did." His hand moves higher, tracing the outline of my lips. "You're drunk and not mine yet, so no orgasms tonight."

I bite back a smile. "Yet?"

"Yet," he emphasizes. "It's been two weeks since I kissed you, and not an hour goes by that I don't think about it."

My breath catches in my throat, eyes widening. Something in his voice makes my head reel. Never in a million years would I expect a man to be so... honest.

"Two weeks, Little Bee," he repeats, his thumb glossing my bottom lip. "Two fucking *weeks*, and we're still at zero dates." He pulls his eyes from my mouth, pupils blown. "I want that date, but you're tipsy tonight. Any answer will be tainted by alcohol, so I'm *not* asking you out, but know this..." He leans in just a little, enough that his warm breath fans my skin. "I'll be watching you all night. That bottle of champagne and your flute better land on my table whenever you go dancing. I want you safe, Vee."

I'm at a loss for words. He sounds so sincere. So caring. And at the same time, he stares like he's barely holding back from ripping my clothes off and fucking me right here, right now.

What's worse, my resolve is stumbling. I'm submitting to the pull, rational thinking be damned.

I shouldn't have had those three drinks... Conor's right. I'm tipsy. Everything I feel and think is a byproduct of that. I can't trust my body's reactions or the little devil sitting on my shoulder whispering, *what if you let him take you out?*

Yeah, what if?

I grit my teeth, shaking the weakness off my limbs as I look up. "I am safe."

"You are if I've got my eyes on you," he confirms. "Now go join your friends, baby. It's taking more restraint than I've got not to kiss you, and I'm not doing that while you're tipsy."

Disappointment swells behind my ribs, but there's more. A sense of calm. He cares about consent. Or me. Or maybe both to an extent. He cares enough that he wants me one hundred percent in control of my mind before he makes another move.

It's unexpected.

Most guys would seize the opportunity. After all, I'm not wasted, just tipsy. Happy, mellow.

"Okay," I say on an exhale. "Thank you."

His features soften, despite his jaw clamping tighter. "I still want that date, Vee." He runs a gentle hand over my cheek, briefly glancing at my lips. "Think about it."

With that, he turns, and within three steps, he's swallowed by the thick crowd.

EIGHT

Vee

"Right, how about we take this back to my place?" Brian, my date this evening, asks after we're done with desserts, then bursts out laughing at the dumbstruck expression undoubtedly painting my face.

Yes, I'm on a date and *not* with broody Mr. Hayes, who watched me like a hawk from his booth last week.

Last *week*.

You read that correctly.

I'm with Brian. Tall, blond, handsome. Odd. A little inappropriate. Not my type. He's friends with a guy Abby almost dry-humped at the dancefloor last week. He's a... distraction. Someone who fails miserably to take my mind off Mr. Hayes.

I expected to see Conor the day after he tracked me down at *The Ramshack*. He said he still wanted a date, and once I sobered up, the *want* that coursed through me while he held me at the bar was still there, convincing me to give him a shot.

But he backed off.

I don't understand why. I stayed safe. Didn't dance with anyone. Kept a watchful eye on the bottle of champagne and my flute. I was good, yet I somehow pushed him away.

I blink at Brian a few times, a mixture of surprise and annoyance flooding my system.

Is sex all he wanted from this evening?

"Relax, sweet cheeks. You think I'd straight-up ask you to come home with me for a quick fuck?" he adds, grating my nerves with his patronizing tone.

"Maybe. Don't pretend you've never done it," I retort, the words dripping with sarcasm.

"Not with girls I like." He winks, high-fiving himself. He's done that a lot tonight. "But, hey, if you're down for some action, I'm game."

Abby warned me about him. She said he's a pothead with zero ambitions, but he seemed cool while we talked at *The Ramshack*. I guess he wasn't high then. He sure is now, his eyes bleary, unfocused, cackle perforating my eardrums every thirty seconds.

Or maybe I had too many drinks last week to notice whether he was high.

My blatant flirting with Conor speaks in favor of that.

I clench my jaw, pushing the fuzzy memories aside, but Conor's soft lips brushing my ear as he whispered still sends tingles down my spine six days later.

"Thanks, but—" The rest of the sentence hits an abyss as a movement out on the street snatches my attention.

Or rather the shiny Mustang does as it comes to a screeching halt by the curb right outside the window. Conor exits the car, eyes locked on my face, a deep eleven lining his forehead.

Relief rattles through me, powerful enough to knock off

the weight that's been dragging my shoulders down since he disappeared in the crowd.

When I dropped Rose off this week, he wasn't home, fueling my obsessive thoughts by purposely avoiding me.

What the hell have I done wrong?

Why isn't he seeking me out?

Did he find someone else?

Has he lost interest?

Question followed question for six long days, and now... he's strutting toward our table, familiar determination written all over his handsome face.

"My roommates are having a party," Brian says, oblivious to my sinking stomach and chaotic mind. "We'll have a few beers, yeah? Your friend, the blonde one, is there. I think Roach has the hots for her."

"Roach? Which one's he?" I ask to keep him talking, my heart battling with my mind.

One flutters, filling my chest with warmness, while the other kicks up through the gears. God, I need my meds altered because those contradicting thoughts come on too strong.

It's like having two people whisper completely different things in my ears, and I have no way of silencing either.

One voice wants me to fling my arms around Conor's neck and kiss him like there'll be no tomorrow. The other is vexed I don't have enough time to set a convincing scene: I'm on a date with a great guy, having *so* much fun.

Why a part of me thinks about setting the scene is a mystery considering I've spent the past week lusting after Conor.

Yep, dose adjustment is in order. This is not working well.

I watch Brian's mouth open and close, but for the life of me, I can't hear a word he's saying. My ears are dialed into the

TOO STRONG

sound of the overdoor bell chiming as Conor enters the diner, his broad shoulders squared back, head high, stride long.

He looks like he owns this place.

He looks like he owns *me*.

My pulse picks up pace, my heart pounding in my chest to the beat of his Jordans hitting the floor. The sound reverberates across the room, drawing everyone's attention. No doubt in their minds where this tall, broad-shouldered man is heading.

Toward me and my date.

Brian.

"That's right, focus on Brian," I school myself quietly, tuning into his ongoing monologue.

He's talking... What is he saying? *Black hair.* He's not talking about me, then. Some other girl? *Big-ass joint.* A frown marks my forehead. What on earth does black hair have to do with a big joint. Is he smoking hair? Did he find one in his joint?

God, this makes no fucking sense.

Rightly so. I'm only catching every tenth word. Maybe not even that, the rest a distant drone, a hum in the background, drowned out by blood singing in my ears.

I rub my hands on my jeans like I'm ironing the fabric, but the truth is, I'm wiping off the sweat. A jolt of nervous energy sends anticipation, dread, and excitement whirring through my body.

Three more seconds and Mr. Hayes stops by our table, the scent of his cologne pungent in the warm, stuffy air.

And just then, Brian's monologue ramps back up, hitting my ears in full volume.

"Man, you should've seen it!" he screeches. "He was so high he woke up while we were still partying, took a leak on the flat screen thinking he was in the shitter, then vomited all over Jessica."

Lovely...

So much for setting a scene.

I wish I could simply sag, fold inward, sink to the floor, and hide under the table. Instead, I'm frozen in place. Heat prickles my neck and colors my cheeks.

Brian looks up, either sensing someone standing over him or maybe noticing my gaze shifting to Conor. "Can we help you?"

"You can't," Conor says. "But just so we're on the same page, I'm stealing your date."

"What?" Brian sputters, the sheepish, incredulous look of a guy who cums too fast crossing his face. "No fucking way, man. She's here with me."

"She came here with you, but she's leaving with me," Conor insists, his voice low. "Come on, Little Bee. You've tested my patience enough for one night." He jerks his head in Brian's direction, eyes locked onto mine but darting to my lips like he can't help himself. "I'm not a violent guy, but you sure make the idea appealing."

I think my cheeks are on fire. "You really are a hoverfly. How did you find me?"

"Rose," he says simply.

The little traitor. I told her not to mention my date with Brian to anyone, especially not the Hayes.

Conor curls his finger under my chin, tilting my head back. "Are you done, or are there more vomit-themed stories you're dying to hear?"

The glint in his eyes, the curve of his mouth, the resolve etched in his face... stick a fork in me. I'm done.

I give up, and the little devil on my shoulder does, too.

I'm too intrigued to fight him.

The pull is too strong.

TOO STRONG

"Fine." I throw my hands up in defeat. "You win. One date, Conor. Make it count," I say, turning to Brian. "I won't lie to you. This wasn't fun. Maybe it would be if you weren't high..."

Brian nods like his clockwork's running down. "Yeah, that's fair, sweet cheeks. In my defense, I'm always high." He leans forward, elbows against the tabletop, fingers interlocked to support his chin. "Tell me more about you, beauty."

My eyes widen as I try to understand what's going on. I can't believe this sudden personality switch-up. Maybe it's the slow-release effect of whatever he's smoking, or maybe I was too distracted by the rush of disappointment that it wasn't Conor taking me out to notice Brian is exactly what Abby said.

Stupid.

The disappointment, I mean. It's stupid because I called off the date, but isn't this how women are built? We change our minds a lot, and I have the added difficulty of my sluggish brain.

I've always been a slow thinker, prone to all-consuming irrationality, courtesy of ADHD, that worsens with Conor's proximity.

Maybe if I weren't overthinking whether shooting him down too many times to count was a good idea, I would've noticed my date with Brian was headed for disaster the moment we entered the diner.

"What's her name?" Conor asks, grabbing my jacket from the back of the chair.

"I know her name," Brian clips, "But I like calling her cutie."

"You called her *beauty*. Come on, man, dinner is on me if you tell me her name."

Brian frowns, his brain cells working overtime, gaze unfocused, and I'm even more embarrassed.

"Thought so," Conor says, taking my hand to help me up.

"Since you've already eaten, how about we visit the arcades?"

I growl a defeated sigh, shoving my arms into the jacket he's holding. "Sounds like a plan."

***

This is surreal. I'm in the passenger seat of Conor's Mustang, looking out the window once I've successfully peeled my eyes away from how he grips the steering wheel.

My insides tingle. The air buzzes and crackles, the tension unnerving but exciting all the same.

Something as unimportant as how he rests the inner side of his wrist on the rim, his relaxed fingers hanging over, has hundreds of butterflies flapping their wings in my belly, sending tiny sparks of energy shooting through my fingertips.

I peek again. He's so intriguing. Hot and cold. Sweet and stern. Tall, broad-chested, eyes dark and deep but playful despite the powerful aura buzzing around him. I think it runs in the family. All the Hayes I've seen at the Halloween party exude this crushing confidence.

He turns left, spinning the wheel one-handed, his long, slim fingers arrow straight while the middle of his palm does the work. Careless, so freaking *sexy*.

'Get a grip. He's just driving!'

"Where did you find that guy?" Conor asks, draping his arm over my seat as he turns around, looking out the back window while parking between two cars.

The air moves. The smell of his expensive, decadent cologne clouds my other senses. I doubt he needs to look over his shoulder. The car has cameras and motion sensors, but I don't point it out. The warmth of his arm behind my head makes my body react in a slow sizzle. Unconsciously, I shift closer to the middle of the car. Closer to him.

Like a moth to a flame.

'I'm gonna get burned.'

He's everything I'm not interested in: rich, entitled, privileged... and yet if I focus long enough to see past that, he's everything that makes me tick.

"Long story," I say, pulling down an inconspicuous breath.

It's not a long story, but I won't tell Conor I grabbed the first opportunity to go out with someone. Anyone, really. Anything to stop thinking about the guy beside me.

Brian and I had only exchanged five sentences last week. Might be why I didn't notice he's not remotely close to my type. Or maybe I noticed but purposely ignored the red flags.

"Okay, don't tell me." Conor kills the engine, a small smile twitching his lips. "C'mon. I've got an order to fulfill."

"An order?" I step out of the car, coat in hand because Conor turned the heating up to eleven. Now, chills gallop across my skin as the cool evening breeze nibbles my bare shoulders. "What order?"

"You'll see." He rounds the hood, takes my hand, and weaves our fingers together like it's the most natural thing in the world.

It's not.

My spine turns rigid, a metal pole so taut it could be played with a bow. My palms grow cold, but flames lick my flesh, a glimmer of panic spiking through my system. This feels too nice. *'I could get used to him holding my hand...'*

His scent swirls in the air, potent, drugging, sending my heart flapping along my ribs. Confusing doesn't begin to cover the turmoil running rampant inside my head.

"It's not even been a minute, and you already want to ditch me?" Conor asks, his voice playful as he leads me down the busy street.

"No, of course not." It's the last thing on my mind. "Where did you get that idea?"

His eyes are alive, sparkling with intensity as he stares through me. "You're shaking, Little Bee."

Oh... I take a deep breath, calming my racing pulse. I've never felt this self-conscious. The newness of his fingers pumping gently around mine makes me ridiculously aware how close he is. How well my hand fits in his. Like they were made to fit together. How smooth and warm his skin is.

How fucking *nice* this feels.

I've dated a few guys since high school. Although *dated* might be an exaggeration. No meaningful conversations, cuddles, or hand-holding. I was too busy working and helping my family to indulge in a real-deal relationship, but... a girl has needs, so we made out and fucked.

We were mostly intimate in an erotic way. Even when I sat in their laps at parties, their hands roamed the sensual parts of my body: thighs, ass, boobs. Every touch a prelude to sex.

No dinners, movies, or late-night beach strolls. We met at parties or school and got together spontaneously. No grand *we're a couple*, or *you're my girlfriend* declarations. It was kind of a given. Exclusive while it was fun. An odd dynamic that always worked fine.

'Now... holding hands? That's a first.'

"Get used to it," Conor says and my eyes snap to his. "I'll hold your hand a lot."

My mouth parts, but words don't escape as the realization hits me... I've been mumbling again.

TOO STRONG

God, I have no self-control around this man.

"You're very sure of yourself." I swallow the bitter aftertaste of embarrassment. "What makes you think you'll have the chance to hold my hand a lot? What if I don't enjoy tonight? What if this is our first and *last* date?" I glance his way, slightly tilting my head to see his face and I catch him smiling.

"If you decide you don't want to see me again at the end of the evening, I'll wave a white flag and leave you alone. Deal?"

A sinking feeling settles in my gut.

Why, I don't know. Too many conflicting emotions hit me to decide what I want right now, so I bob my head, frowning more when Conor smiles wider, glancing at our interlocked hands.

"What?" I ask, following his line of sight to find my fingers squeezing the life out of his so hard my nails turned white with the effort. "Sorry," I mumble, loosening my grip but not letting go.

"Do something for me." He tugs me closer, spins me around, and pulls me in, my back flush against his chest, his arms boxing mine, one hand covering my tummy. It's possessive how he holds me, his fingers splayed wide.

Possessive, hot, *protective*.

Firm but tender.

"Close your eyes," he urges.

"Why?"

"Trust me for one minute, will you? Close your eyes."

I huff my exasperation but do as he says, blocking out the bright, colorful lights flashing and twinkling over the street and reflecting off the shop windows.

His heart beats softly against my back, my mind catching the steady rise and fall of each breath in his chest.

"Now what?" I whisper, surrendering myself to the feel of

him behind me, my blood running a fever.

"Focus on the smells."

I want to ask *what*, but I don't. He's going somewhere with this. He's isolating my mind, encouraging it to switch off some senses and amplify others.

Smells take a direct route to the limbic system, extending to the olfactory bulb in the brain. It's well-known that smells evoke powerful memories. I think that's what Conor's trying to achieve. He's wiring my brain to associate the smells around us with this moment, so I'll think about tonight whenever I get a whiff of something similar.

"Cotton candy, caramel-coated nuts, waffles," he lists, brushing his nose up my cheek.

I inhale, concentrating on the sweet aroma mixing with the saltiness of the sea, creating a distinct, uniquely coastal scent.

"And then there's you." His lips graze my ear, introducing a brand-new avalanche of desire. "You smell like fresh linen. Soap, spring rain... Warm, soothing. I can't get enough of it." His grip engulfs me, firm and full of longing.

I'm caught between fear and desire. Half of me considers pulling away. The other half sways dangerously close to surrender. I'm scared how quickly he's tearing apart my defense walls but excited he knows how.

"Now listen," he whispers, his warm breath kissing the shell of my ear as his fingers trickle down my arm.

My stomach tightens on cue. One simple touch makes me question every assumption I've made about him thus far.

I wait, shepherding the sudden pang of desire coursing through me, expecting him to whisper, but he's silent. "What?"

"Jesus, woman," he chuckles. The amusement cocooning his tone arouses more butterflies. "Listen to the sounds around us."

"Oh, okay..."

The air is pierced by the buzz of people enjoying their evening. Excited chatter spills onto the sidewalk. The arcades nearby come alive with cheerful shouts and the sound of coins clattering into slots.

"Remember this." His warm lips skitter along my skin, arms tightening their hold, curling me further into him... and I fit so well. Perfectly. "I already know, Little Bee."

"What do you know?" I ask, my eyes closed as the smells and sounds infect my senses, the moment imprinting itself on my hard drive. I wiggle out of his embrace, spinning to face him. "*What* do you know, Conor?"

He takes half a step back, eyes heavy with some emotion I can't place. Maybe if I had more time, but it's gone in a fraction of a second, blinked away. His whole posture changes back to his usual carefree casualness.

"That it won't be our last date."

It makes sense.

Perfect sense considering what I said, but at the same time, I have a nagging feeling that's not what's on his mind.

NINE

Conor

"You can't be serious," Vee says, narrowing her silver eyes like she's adding stern credibility to her words. It would throw me off track if not for her rosy, kissable lips twisting into a smile when we stop by the row of claw machines.

Same lips she closes round a straw, sipping a cherry Slurpee.

Same lips I can't fucking wait to taste again.

"You know the odds are stacked against us, right?" she continues, trailing her fingers along the lever. "It's rigged. I read that it takes anything between thirty to fifty tries to win."

I hand her my cup and the half-empty bag of caramel nuts I bought on our way here, then nudge her hip so she steps aside, out of the way. "You'll have to be patient. I told you I have an order to fulfill."

She leans against the glass, eyeing the toys inside, focused, amused, and a little curious. "You've got an order for a plushie?" she asks, biting her lip.

TOO STRONG

It's a signal girls use to tease, but Vee's not teasing. She's doing it unconsciously, I can tell. Not that it works any different, enticing me to replace her teeth with mine.

"Last time I was here," I say, derailing all thoughts of my teeth and Vee's lips before I reach the point of no return and claim her right here. "I won that." I tap the glass, pointing out a green, big-eyed t-rex, then insert a few coins in the slot. "I gave it to my nephew, Noah. He took it everywhere for weeks." I pause, watching the claw dive, grab the toy, then let go as soon as it pulls up. "They went for a walk down the pier last night, and Logan didn't notice it fall out of the buggy. He ran back, but it was gone, and Noah's been crying ever since so I need another one."

"Oh..." she utters, her features softening like her voice as she watches the claw plummet again. "That's nice of you."

"Don't sound so surprised. I *am* nice." The claw grips the t-rex and this time, it doesn't let go. The prize tumbles out of the machine straight into my waiting hands. "One in thirty?" I tease, pulling my phone out to snatch a picture before sending it to the Hayes group chat.

Me: Got a replacement. I'll be over soon to drop it off.

"You got lucky," Vee muses. "Someone must've played earlier and gave up too soon."

"You wanna bet?"

She sucks the straw again, looking me over from under thick, black eyelashes. She's fucking stunning. Caramel hair in a ponytail, a few loose locks flirting with her neck, eyes so gray you'd think they're contacts, and that freckle-peppered nose she keeps scrunching in the cutest way. The shape of her mouth, the arch of her dark brows...

I'm a goner.

So fucking whipped. So fucking into her it knocks the breath out of my chest. I wonder if this is what my older brothers felt when they first met their girls.

Probably not. Theo kept Thalia as a friend for months before growing a pair to make a move. Logan was a no-strings-attached deal with Cassidy before he realized he's in love, and Mia wasn't even Nico's type, so this weird attachment I feel toward Vee can't be normal or common.

"Sure, why not?" she says, putting her game face on. "If you win the next one in less than thirty... no, forget it, less than *forty* tries, then—" She meets my eyes, lifting her chin slightly. "Yeah, what then?"

"I get one wish."

My lips, her lips, and no distance between.

I thought I could do it. I thought I could last the entire evening without stealing a kiss, but whenever I look at her, my mind summons the memory of our kiss in the garage. The way she felt pressed against me, the sweet little sounds she made, how she tasted, and how every touch of her hands on my head, round my neck, and in my hair drove me half fucking stupid with need.

The more I think about that kiss, the more I want her. The more I understand she's made for me, the more I crave her body, mind... the whole package.

"Okay, but more than forty and the wish is mine," she says, eyeing the plushies.

"Deal. You're going down, Little Bee." I'll smash my hand through the glass and cheat if I have to. Anything to kiss her again.

A short vibration in my pocket has me pulling my phone

out to check a new message in the group chat. It's not as lively as it used to be. We still talk and banter, but not as much as we used to. The feed is mostly pictures of my nephews these days. Be it those already growing and crawling or those still cooking in their mommies' tummies.

I'm not gonna lie; I can't make out the babies on ultrasound pictures unless Colt points out the head, arms, and legs.

Logan: Lifesaver. Thanks.

Theo: Who's the girl, bro?

I scroll up to the picture, nothing visible but Vee's hand holding the Slurpee in the background.

Damn, he's good.

I guess I can't blame him for being nosy. It's not like I ever took a girl out anywhere. I usually meet them at frat parties, and the only place I take them is the bed, bathroom, or car.

Cody: Mrs. Hayes in the making.

Cheeky fucker. My thumb wavers over *f*, but I change my mind about replying and slip my phone into my back pocket.

I have more important things to do than entertain my brothers.

"Which one do you want?" I ask Vee, getting a kick out of seeing the corners of her mouth twitch in amusement.

She's got the prettiest, most genuine smile I've ever seen and, when paired with a raised eyebrow... perfection.

There's not one thing about her I don't like.

"Have you got a niece?" she asks.

"Not yet."

I. A. DICE

Not that Logan isn't trying his hardest. Cass is a long way off her due date with baby number two, but Logan's already begging for number three any chance he gets. I doubt he'll stop begging until he gets a daughter.

Good thing Cassidy's patience could rival our mother's.

"Three nephews so far. Two more on the way," I say.

Give it a couple more years, and I'll need a list with names to hand for Christmas shopping. Shawn's got two boys, Josh and Aiden. Logan's got Noah and Eli on the way, and Thalia's due this month, a boy, too—River.

Five kids.

Add Nico and Mia's kids to the mix when the time comes, plus however many Logan talks Cass into, and we'll have enough to start a Hayes football team.

And that's even before Colt, Cody, and I get started.

Vivienne eyes the plush toys, rapping her knuckles against the glass. "Okay, grab another t-rex so Logan can stash it somewhere in case this one goes walkabout too."

"Good thinking, but once we have a spare, we're not leaving until we get you that..." I point at a gray bear with big black eyes. "He'll keep you warm at night." *Until I take over.* I feed a few coins into the machine, gripping the lever. "Count."

One, two... ten. With each unsuccessful attempt, I grow a little less confident and a lot more frustrated, my wish at the forefront of my mind, begging to be fulfilled.

The sound of the coins clinking, the whir of the gears, and the plushies tumbling fade away. I'm not the only one growing anxious. Vivienne's watching with bated breath as the claw plunges again and again.

By the twentieth try, I'm out of coins. "Wait here. I need change."

I grab two more Slurpees and cotton candy while I'm at

the counter, then go back to Vee, whose body barricades the machine like she's defending national secrets.

"Twenty more tries," she reminds me, tearing off some candy, pushing it into her open mouth and... fuck.

Just like that, all I think about is how sweet she'd taste if I kissed her now.

"Wouldn't it be easier to find the same toy online?"

I shrug, dropping more coins into the slot. "Sure, but what's the fun in that? The shop won't grant me a wish if they don't deliver on time."

She stuffs her mouth with more cotton candy, and I'm barely keeping my hands to myself, watching her lick her lips, oblivious to how sexy she looks. How titillating her every move is.

The claw loses the t-rex halfway to the hole on the fortieth try, catapulting my temper sky high. There goes my wish, floating out of view like a runaway balloon.

"You win, Little Bee." I grab my Slurpee, gulp three large sips too fast, and cringe, experiencing a bad case of brain freeze. "What's the wish?"

She's silent for a long time, staring me down like she's peeling the layers of my psyche. Whenever I snuck a look at her while I tried to win the t-rex, her eyes were on me, not the prize. She watched my face grow taut, my annoyance mounting with each failure, and she's watching now while frustration corrupts my voice.

I'm a sore loser. Always have been. Now, the stakes are so high it's a goddamn miracle I don't throw a tantrum (im)patiently awaiting the verdict.

"Kiss me," she whispers, eyes not leaving mine.

My body lets go of the tension it's been holding. Relief rattles through me, and two weeks' of frustration slide off my heart and mind like melting snow off a roof. I don't give her a second to think it through.

Not a second to change her mind.

I take a step forward and almost fucking tackle her, catching her lips with mine as I pin her against the machine, my tongue finding hers before she even wraps her arms around my neck.

Two weeks since I last kissed her. Two weeks of thinking about this girl non-stop.

I lean into her, letting her feel the weight of my body and the hard-on that sprung to life in seconds.

She's everything. The kiss is fucking everything. Hard, demanding, thorough. My fingers tangle through her hair, and she responds like she's been electrified, trembling in my arms. My chest tightens.

My cock twitches and balls pull taut.

She marks her disapproval with a soft, low moan when I come up for air. Her eyes dart to my lips with a hint of wildness, like a psychological switch has been flipped. Finally, her hunger matches mine… raises the stakes.

She grips my collar and yanks me back, her heart drumming against my chest.

The fire of her body, the softness of her lips… that fucking cotton candy and cherry Slurpee taste on her tongue… addictive. Drugging. I want more. I want it all, but not yet, and definitely not here.

Not until she admits she's mine.

I pull back enough to watch my thumb trace her bottom lip. "That was my wish, Little Bee."

"I know," she hums, her chest heaving, arousal painting her flushed face. "I think you deserve it for your determination."

I clasp her chin between my fingers, tilt her head back, and take her mouth in another kiss.

Kiss*es*. Short, biting, full of passion that heats my blood, giving me second-degree burns. I bite her bottom lip and soothe the ache, licking along the seam of her mouth.

It doesn't matter that we met two weeks ago. That this is our first date. That we didn't get off to a great start. None of it matters. Only the intensity of this moment. The emotions coursing through me. How she flips my world upside down and simultaneously anchors me in place.

I already know...

And I've never been so certain of anything.

It's absolutely insane, but no matter how much I try and fool my brain, the nagging certainty won't fade.

Vee's mine. She just doesn't know it yet.

"Let's check if your theory's correct," I say, pulling away when someone clears their throat nearby.

It's a father with two toddlers at his side, a condescending look tainting his face. "This is a public place," he clips.

"And this is a public display of affection," I fire right back, moving Vee in front of me, her back to my chest.

"There are kids here," the guy adds, clearly looking to pick a verbal fight. "This is inappropriate."

"Kissing is inappropriate?"

"That wasn't kissing—"

"No? I feel sorry for your wife, man. If you're waiting for an apology, don't hold your breath. And if you don't want your kids seeing people kiss, don't bring them out at ten in the evening."

He huffs something incomprehensible, stares me down a moment longer, and caves, taking his kids outside.

I wrap my arm around Vivienne, placing one hand on the lever. Before dropping another coin into the slot, I dip my head, stamping a kiss in the crook of her neck, inducing goosebumps and... *holy mother of—*

My dick's not catching a break tonight. It won't settle until I rub one out later. And I'll have to because the sight of Vee's nipples straining against the fabric of her t-shirt is fucking art.

She's not wearing a bra.

How have I not noticed? How firm and perfect are her breasts that I *didn't* notice she's not wearing a bra?

She tilts her head back against my shoulder so I can see the machine.

"You're stalling," she says. "Play."

I inhale a deep breath, inching the lever forward. "Are you in a rush?"

She lets a heavy sigh past her lips. "It's getting late. I promised my dad I'll be back at eleven."

I release the claw in the wrong place, watching it barely grasp the t-rex's tail, coming up with nothing.

"Your dad?" I spin her around, my heartrate accelerating. "How old are you?"

"Relax, I'm twenty-one, but while I live under his roof, I abide by his rules." She parrots what I think is supposed to be her dad's stern tone.

"His words, right?"

She nods once, moving to lean against the machine, out of my reach. "He's very protective. I don't have a curfew or anything, but if I say I'll be back at eleven, I keep my word. Besides, I have work in the morning."

I glance at my wristwatch, checking how long we have left. It's already a quarter past ten. Fuck. "Is your car outside *Ruby's*, or can I drive you home?"

Her cheeks flare pink instantly, twisting my insides tighter and tighter. She's embarrassed, those silver eyes darting sideways, a glimpse into her raw, unguarded parts.

I fucking hate she feels like this around me. I hate that she thinks I'd judge her for living in a trailer.

"I don't need a ride," she says, no longer at ease but wound up tight again. "But if you could drop me off at the diner by half-ten, that would be good."

Which means we've got five minutes before we need to head out. "Okay, but don't tell your dad you'll be back this early next time." I pull her back to me, cuddling her into my chest, then pop more coins into the slot.

I should've paid attention when Cody taught Mia how to cheat the claw machine.

***

"This was fun," Vee says, her face fixed in faint surprise as I park the car outside the diner.

The slight undertone of confusion in her voice is both cute and infuriating. She must've thought her judgmental opinions would be proven right and can't quite believe I'm not every fucking plague she expected.

"I want to see you again, Little Bee," I say, watching her lips curl softly. She hands over the two t-rexes; the second one won on the forty-fifth try. "Sooner rather than later."

The need to kiss her writhes inside me, almost uncontainable. It will have to wait, though.

I will have to wait.

She enjoyed tonight. The tension I summoned, asking if I could take her home, drained after a moment of my arms around her. She relaxed and let her guard down. So much so that she started muttering random sentences as if the barriers holding them in place tumble when I'm around.

I don't think she's noticed she speaks out loud, and I won't point it out, enjoying her words too much to risk her not letting me inside her head, even if unknowingly.

She whispered *he smells so good* when the second t-rex tumbled from the machine, and *this is nice* when I took her hand in mine. A very faint *wow* when I stamped a short, biting kiss to the crook of her neck as I opened the passenger side door.

If the way she kissed me back before, melting in my arms—where she belongs—wasn't clue enough, those tiny peeks into her mind sealed the deal: she's into me. Maybe just as much as I'm into her.

I don't think knowing it should make me feel like I'm floating six feet above the ground, but we've had the strangest start, and I'm not taking those little things for granted.

Still, I'm not clueless. I pay enough attention to know that no matter how good Vee feels with me, she's a long way off trusting me. She's ashamed of her life, something I honestly cannot wrap my head around, and at the same time, something I want her to work through fast.

I keep reminding myself this is still fresh despite how overwhelming my sudden obsession with this girl is. We met three weeks ago. Went on *one* date.

She doesn't know me well enough to form a proper opinion, and that's why I'm not kissing her again until she's sure I'm not who she has me pegged for.

"I'd like that, too," she admits, grabbing the handle.

"When are you free?"

"I finish work every evening at nine, and I don't work Sundays."

We could have dinner tomorrow, but that might be pushing

my luck. She needs time to process what she learned tonight. Time to miss me. That sense of longing I'm trying to evoke is why I stayed away from her the whole goddamn week.

Patience is a virtue.

And it's working so far.

"Sunday it is. Can I pick you up?"

Her cheeks immediately pink up—another punch right in the fucking gut.

"Maybe some other time." She leans out of her seat and I feel her lips on my cheek. "Goodnight."

Oh, Jesus... *fuck*.

A brutal stab of lust pierces me, convulsing my nerve endings. It's so potent it obliterates my resolution to not kiss her. I grip her neck, seal her lips, and cup her face with my other hand, barely holding off dragging her across the middle console onto my lap.

I don't.

But I do bite her bottom lip, watching it swell up nicely, the image enough to help relieve some tension when I get home.

TEN

Dad waits outside, leaning against the trailer, his rough hand gripping the white fence marking the boundary of a makeshift porch. The wood's rotting, white paint peeling, a sad, *sad* state of affairs.

Clouds of smoke swirl around Dad, dissolving in the cool evening air as soon as he takes a drag of his cigarette. His normally carefree expression is marred by a slight frown as he watches the hood of my car.

I'm frowning, too.

I've been frowning non-stop since steam came hissing from under the hood, pleading with my car not to give up. At first, it was a slow, gentle hiss that seemed like nothing to worry about. But now, my Mercury is a boiling kettle, spouting out so much steam I can't see where I'm going.

The car judders beneath me as I press on the brake. I can't tell how far off the fence I am, but I bet if I try to roll any

TOO STRONG

closer, I'll hit it for sure since I can't see through the thick steam clouds. It's like driving through a dense fog.

I glance at my dad, the prominent wrinkles around his eyes telling me all I need to know.

This is bad. Really bad.

Dad strides across the narrow pathway, his heavy work boots thudding against the ground with each step. He rolls the sleeves of his flannel shirt to his elbows, approaches the car, and steps back when a massive cloud of scalding steam hot enough to cause second-degree burns erupts from beneath the hood as soon as he cranks it up. A cigarette dangles from the corner of his lips, the ash clinging to the edge, threatening to drop. Sweat beads along his hairline as he examines the engine, eyes narrowed in concentration.

With a defeated sigh, I open the car door and grab my bag from the passenger seat before stepping out and slamming the door shut harder than intended.

The sound echoes across the trailer park, startling the neighbor's Rottweiler. They keep him in a large pen at the side of their trailer like he's livestock. The metal creaks under his weight when he jumps against it, barking loudly, his mouth foaming.

I feel his gaze follow me as I approach Dad, his cigarette hanging onto his bottom lip by sheer will.

"Hey, Angel," he says, his voice gentle and soothing. "How was the date?"

I told him about Brian. To be perfectly honest, over the years, I've told him about everything that was happening in my uneventful life. Right until Rose begged me for two days to sneak her out of the house into Mia's Halloween party.

Thanks to her, for the first time ever, I have a secret I can't share with Dad. He's laid back, loving, and caring. Mostly stays out of our way, but he'd lose his mind if he knew we entered the enemy's lair.

I never gave the mayors or city council members much thought until Robert Hayes was voted in a few years ago. My dad fumed for weeks, complaining the town would get swallowed up by rich corporations while small shop owners would be run out of business. He said Robert Hayes only cared about keeping the elite happy and their wallets stuffed.

The years went by, and the talk in town was the exact opposite of my father's predictions. Our new mayor took care of everyone, putting particular focus on small shop owners.

His wife organized a few events, raising money for renovating the pier and key tourist attractions and installing new lights across the town to reduce the cost of electricity consumed by the city so that, in the long run, the money could be better spent on other things.

During his first election period, he did more for the ordinary folk here than his three predecessors combined.

It wasn't a surprise when he was re-elected, and now, with less than a year to go, he still pumps money into the infrastructure, repainting the shopfronts on the main street and prettying up the town.

But even with everything good he's done, my dad still detests him to his core. They're roughly the same age, and as I refuse to believe my dad's a bitter old man, I've guessed his undying reluctance has more to do with something that must've happened between them back at school than Robert's mayor post.

"Vee?" Dad urges, the last drag of his cigarette hanging from his lips before he tosses it on the ground and crushes it under his muddy boot. His eyes search my face as he waits for me to say something.

TOO STRONG

"Oh, yes, sorry..." I mutter, tearing my eyes from the dissipating steam. "It's dead, isn't it?"

Dad bends over the engine again, his fingers moving nimbly as he inspects the damage, wafting his hand left and right to get a better view. "I think your water pump's gone." He straightens up, wiping his hands on his jeans.

An exasperated groan swells in my chest. "Great. I bet it'll cost a fortune to fix."

"Not necessarily," he replies, sending me a reassuring smile. "I'll drop you off at work in the morning and get Uncle Hal to take a look at the car."

Uncle Hal isn't actually my uncle. He's Dad's best friend from high school and my godfather. Even though he's not a mechanic by trade, he knows his way around cars well enough.

Up until two years ago, he worked on my Mercury whenever something bigger than what Dad could fix needed to be done. Since he had a stroke, he's been in a wheelchair, no longer able to fix cars.

Dad slams the hood shut and snags another roll-up from a tin tray, his expression curious. "Now tell me about that date, Vee. I don't like that you're evading. Was he a douche?"

I let out a soft chuckle. Yeah, Brian was definitely a douche, but Conor... Conor was everything but. Completely different from what I imagined. Despite the designer clothes, expensive watches, and a fancy car, he's down to earth. Funny.

He kept stuffing his face with caramel-coated nuts and gulped his Slurpee too fast more than once, like an impatient kid. He hadn't done a single thing tonight I didn't find hot, clever, or endearing, and that kiss...

Oh my God, that kiss. I swear my mind went off like a Roman candle when his lips met mine.

Conor's nothing like the men I've come across thus far. He acts like he doesn't have a care in the world. He laughed so much tonight I bet his face will hurt tomorrow, but when he kissed me, he did it with such raw, feral intensity it felt like he wanted to eat me.

I think he did. His hard cock jutted against my hip, size impressive even through his jeans. That's not surprising. He looks like he's packing, and he sure kisses like he knows how to use his size to elicit intense pleasure.

The kiss alone was so sensual, so full of want, that my panties dampened on cue.

I swallow hard, avoiding Dad's curious looks as I turn to get inside. "He's okay," I say, keeping the answer light, brief, and lying only a little when I add, "We had dinner at *Ruby's*, then took a walk down the pier."

"You don't sound convinced."

I feel his eyes drilling into my back like he's trying to read a lie from my body language. I shrug, pull the door open, and step inside the stuffy trailer where the scent of pork chops hangs so thickly in the air I can almost taste it.

"I don't know him all that well, but I had fun, and we're going out again on Sunday."

Dad nods, glancing at the wall clock. It's already ten past eleven, meaning I've got less than six hours to sleep before my alarm blares at five.

"I guess you already ate, but there are leftovers in the fridge if you're hungry."

"I'm not," I lie again.

Damnit, it's starting to become a habit.

Dinner with Brian was a few hours ago, and I had a small salad, too nervous to stomach anything else. I'd love some food but stuffing myself with a greasy meal minutes before bed will mean tossing and turning for hours.

"We have to leave at half-five," I say, covering my mouth to yawn. "I'll knock on your door a few minutes earlier."

"I'll be up," Dad promises, but instead of heading for bed, he flumps into the armchair, switching on the TV to watch a recap of whatever match he missed while working today.

"Night, night," I mutter, dragging my feet across the floor.

It's been a long week. Long enough that I regretted agreeing to work overtime at the newsagents. Now that my car needs work again, I'm glad I did. The extra cash will come in handy.

I wash up and change into my pjs, careful not to make any noise as I climb to my bunk bed. Rose is asleep, her phone on the pillow, an inch from her face. She only does that when she and Liam get back together.

Looks like she's giving her douche-of-a-boyfriend another chance after she caught the asshat flirting with another girl.

I bury myself under the comforter, pulling a fluffy blanket close to my chin, my eyes already closed. Just as I hit that blissful moment when I'm seconds from falling asleep, the vibration of my cell has me nearly jumping out of my skin.

Unlocking the phone, I squint against the bright screen.

Abby: Why am I not your friend anymore?

I frown, reading her text a few times and understanding less with every pass.

Me: You sure you got the right number?

Abby: Yes! How is it I have to find out from Tammy that you've been snatched away from your date with Brian by CONOR HAYES?! I want to know everything. How? Why? When? Where?

Last week, *The Ramshack* was so packed she never saw me talking to him. I didn't tell her about it or about *him*, knowing damn well she'd find a way to have him join our party.

It's no surprise she knows who Conor is. She pays attention, indulges in the gossip flying around Newport that I always tune out. I'm sure the Hayes brothers are a big part of that whispered information.

And of course Tammy, the waitress at *Ruby's*, blabbed as soon as she had the chance. Abby and Tammy are friends, both working at the diner.

Me: I'll tell you everything, but not now. It's late, my car broke down again, and I'm working at six. Talk tomorrow.

Abby: You think I'll last until you finish work to get all the details?! I won't get any sleep now! You'll tell me on your way to work. I'll pick you up at half-five.

I send back a kiss emoji, forcing my eyes shut. Instead of sleep encompassing my exhausted body, my mind replays the evening. Every word Conor spoke, every touch of his hand, every look, and those two kisses lull me into a dreamless sleep.

***

The next morning Abby pulls up in her car, a beat-up old thing, a twin brother from another mother to my Mercury. Except my car doesn't reek of stale cigarettes. She smokes like a chimney, lighting one up when she tugs at the hand brake.

I wave at her from the door, silently asking her to wait, then tiptoe down the hall to let Dad know he won't be needed.

Hearing him mutter, "I'm up, I'm coming," I crack the door wide enough to speak through.

"It's okay, Daddy. Abby's taking me. See you tonight."

"I thought I heard her car," he says, his voice groggy. I'm sure the whole park heard. She's got a hole in her exhaust the size of my fist. "Call me when you're done, Angel. I'll pick you up."

"Yeah, okay. Thanks."

A minute later, I hop in the passenger seat, throwing my bag in the back, ready for the interrogation of a lifetime.

Abby's a great friend. The nosiest person I know. Her excitement shudders through the car, making the air crackle with energy as she shifts in her seat, leaning closer to me with a wild grin.

"So? What are you waiting for! It's been seven seconds already, and I still know nothing. Spill!" she squeals, making her seat groan with her excited bounce. "How did it go? How did you even meet Conor, and why don't I know you did? When? Where?" She crunches into gear, swallowing a deep breath when she runs out of steam. "What did he say? What did you say? Where did you go? Did you kiss? Fuck? Was it good?"

That's Abby. Blabs faster than she thinks, projectile-vomiting words without filters. I laugh, her excitement contagious and helping me relax. I've not had time to think about how bizarre meeting Conor was and how I feel, so letting it out helps organize my thoughts.

I tell her about the Halloween party, leaving no stone unturned. The more I say, the more her cheeks flush hot pink, and her lips twist into a dreamy smile after I mention he kissed me.

She's silent throughout the story, navigating the roads as she unleashes an excited gasp here and a *no way!* there.

"That's about it," I admit once I circle back to last night.

"About *it*?!" she booms, turning to face me. "That's *everything*! God, I'm so fucking jealous, Vee! Hot, rich, great kisser, and I bet his dick is huge. There are rumors about the Hayes brothers, and they're very..." She spreads her hands, demonstrating the size, her eyes widening for impact, "...*very* generous."

"We've not gotten that far," I mutter, the size of Conor's cock against my hip last night not something I want filling my head at six in the morning. It's enough that my panties were soaked all evening. I don't need that at work.

"But you will, right? Don't go all Mother Teresa on me here. I need the dirty, girl. Ride his dick! What have you got to lose?"

I roll my eyes but can't help a pleasant thrill washing over me as her words activate a string of vivid fantasies.

"We just met..." I trail off, my excitement doused when the main issue rears its head, reminding me of its existence. "He's loaded, Abby. I mean, he's sweet. Pretty intense, too. We fit so well, but I'm not his equal, you know? He says he doesn't care where I live, where I work, or what I drive, and maybe he doesn't, but what happens when I meet his friends? When he sees me beside all those gorgeous, done-up, rich girls who don't have to work two jobs? Who do you think he's going to pick?"

Abby sighs, shaking her head. "You always do that," she mutters, clearly annoyed. "You're overthinking and finding problems where there are none. You're way too insecure. Comparing yourself to others is dumb, girl."

She veers onto the curb outside the newsagents too fast, the front of the car screeching against the sidewalk. A loud crack tells me she might've wrecked the bumper.

TOO STRONG

Not for the first time.

Killing the engine, she turns to me, a hard edge to her narrowed, brown eyes. "If Conor said he doesn't care where you live or what you drive, take his word for it. Any guy put off by it wouldn't be so relentless. That's A, and B, as for his friends, who fucking cares what they think? You're not dating *them*. You're dating Conor."

"We're not dating. We've been out once. Don't go bridesmaid-dress shopping just yet."

She mimics my tone, letting out a thread of gibberish before actual words come out. "Whatever. Don't pretend you don't want him. I wouldn't be hearing a detailed rendition of every one of his fucking kisses and touches if you didn't."

"I didn't say I don't want him, but I don't know what to do," I whine, thwacking the back of my head against the headrest, my eyes closed. "It just feels like he's from a different world. Like the differences are too big to overlook."

Abby reaches over and squeezes my hand tight. "Look, I get it. It's surreal, right? But sometimes, you just have to take a leap of faith. You never know where it might lead. And if it doesn't work out, so what? At least you gave it a fair shot. Give it a few more dates, then decide if he's worth it."

I nod, her words sinking. She's got this effortless way of dredging my frenzied thoughts, plucking those that matter, and helping me navigate life while my mind's a ball of wool tangled by a kitten's games.

"You're right. I'm just... scared, I guess."

But when I think back to last night, there was no fear. Everything Conor said, how he acted, held my hand, and looked at me... I have no experience with dates, but the few Abby's been on didn't look like mine.

Mine was so much better.

So much more.

She leans back in her seat, giving me a reassuring smile. "I know, babe. You get infatuated fast, so keep that in check for a while but don't let your unfounded insecurities hold you back. You're amazing. You deserve someone who sees that."

I take a deep breath, feeling a newfound sense of determination taking root inside me. "Thanks. I needed to hear that."

"Anytime, girl. Now get your ass to work, then call me when you're done. I'll stop by tonight and help you pick an outfit for Sunday."

ELEVEN

Conor

I'm early.

Twenty minutes too early, to be exact.

I park by the curb outside *Ruby's Diner* and scan the street for Vee's Mercury.

She's not here yet.

There's still time, but my stomach flips, my mind conjuring scenarios where she doesn't show up at all. Tapping my fingers against the elbow rest, I distract myself by watching a family enter the diner. A little girl with pigtails giggles as she pushes past her parents' legs to get in first.

Three more steps and they're inside, no longer a good distraction.

Minutes tick by slowly, so, *so* slowly. Bang on four o'clock, my leg's jiggling, my mind so restless I feel fucking stupid. I turn in my seat, looking out the back window, into both side mirrors, and straight ahead. No sign of Vee.

TOO STRONG

She's not coming.

Fuck.

Grabbing my phone from the passenger seat, I shoot Mia a text. I've spent all morning subtly digging for information, looking for a woman's point of view. An opinion.

Fine, not that subtly. I straight-up asked what the fuck I'm supposed to do with a girl who thinks I'm an entitled, spoilt, rich ass. A girl I've not stopped obsessing about for three weeks.

A girl I already consider mine.

Me: She stood me up.

Mia: It's one minute past four. Give her time. Maybe she's stuck in traffic somewhere, or she lost track of time getting ready.

Yeah, okay, that makes sense.

Girls take a while to get ready. I doubt she took a quick shower and threw on her favorite t-shirt and jeans like I did. She's a girl. Her hair is long, silky, soft, and smells—

Veering off-topic here. Her hair is long, so it takes longer to dry and style than my curly mane. Plus, both times I've seen Vee, she wore makeup. That takes time, too.

My internal monologue comes to a screeching halt when I see her, and suddenly the nerves that twisted my stomach a moment ago take a turn for the worse.

She's riding a fucking bike, her cheeks rosy, hair tossed by the wind as she pedals down the street, eyes locked on my car.

My chest hitches painfully.

I've done my research. The nearest trailer park is barely inside the town's limits, a twenty-minute car drive from here. On a bike, that's twice as long. And that's if the closest one is the one where she lives. What if it's the one next town over?

My teeth gnash between my lips as I shoot from the driver's seat, closing the door as she halts beside me, scuffing the asphalt the same way I did years ago when I owned a bike.

"Sorry I'm late." She pants a little, gulping down crisp air. "My uncle came by, and—"

"Why are you on a bike, Vee?"

She frowns, air-bitten cheeks reddening as she looks at the old, rusty bike. "My car broke down."

I open my mouth to say she should've fucking called me and I would've picked her up, but my hands ball into fists before I speak.

She doesn't have my number.

And I don't have hers.

"So... are we still on for dinner?" she asks, uncertainty painting her face.

I hold the handles of her bike, steadying it while she climbs off and adjusts her jacket. Pointless, considering I grab both lapels in one hand and gently tug her a step closer.

"Of course we're on for dinner." I kiss her. Slowly tracing the contours of her lips with teasing pecks before I slip my tongue inside, building momentum until she sighs. The sound low, needy, and all her. "That's how you say *hi* to me from now on. A kiss before you say one word."

She blinks.

And again.

And once more, like she's not sure what to say. "I... You seem to think one date equals dating. We're not *dating*, Conor. We're going out on a *date*. That's different."

"Baby, call this whatever the hell makes you feel good, but promise me one thing. While we're..." I air quote for impact,

"...'not dating but going on dates' I'm the only man you do that with. The only man you kiss. And you better not let any other fucking man touch you, either. Understood?"

Winning. I'm winning big time. Vee bites back a smile, narrowing her eyes like she's ready to scold me, but instead, she rises on her toes and pecks my cheek.

"Only if it works both ways."

"I have no intention nor interest in any other girl, Vivienne. I mean it. Now..." I say, chaining her bike to the stand nearby, "Save my number and give me yours."

"Why?"

"So you can call me next time your car breaks down. I would've picked you up."

She pulls her cell from her jacket pocket. "You can have my number, but you're not picking me up."

Yeah... I'm losing again. She's so fucking stubborn.

"Why the hell not? Vee, I don't care where you live or what you drive, but I do care that you biked forty minutes to see me. I don't want that happening again."

"It's exercise. Exercise is good for you."

"Save. My. Number," I grind out.

She rolls her eyes, cocking an eyebrow, silently urging me to dictate the digits. I can already tell there's no way she'll call if she needs a ride next time, so I have just a few hours to form a foolproof plan and take her home tonight.

If I know where she lives, I can pick her up whenever.

She saves me under *Conor Hayes*, the most emotionless way to save a guy in your contacts, then calls me, so I have her number, too.

"Okay, what's the plan?" she asks, tucking her phone back in her pocket. "*Ruby's?*"

"No."

The smile she's been trying to hold off disappears. Two small wrinkles crease her forehead. It's all very tentative how she minutely examines the light, boyfriend-style jeans and skintight black cami she wears like she's peeping around a corner of someplace she's not supposed to be.

'*I knew this was a mistake,*' she mutters.

That hurts. Fucking *guts* me.

With shaky fingers, she combs any tangles from her ponytail and tugs her top, ironing out nonexistent wrinkles.

Every move she makes holds a weight of insecurity.

I hate seeing her like this. I hate that she feels she's not good enough. It's evident in her words and her stance: her shoulders slumped, eyes downcast.

I planned to take her to Nico's restaurant. Treat us both to a nice, three-course meal and a bottle of my favorite wine, then hit the Country Club for a couple of drinks and a late-night round on the mini-golf Nico had added earlier this year. It's been a hit with the older generation bringing their grandkids over.

But now, looking at how unsure she is, I know taking her to a high-end restaurant is the worst idea. We've not spent enough time together yet to switch to my turf.

She won't be herself. Won't relax. She's too self-conscious about how she looks and what she wears, which is ridiculous because she's absolutely fucking breathtaking.

"It's early," I say, making new plans under pressure. "We'll grab something from the stalls on the pier for now and come back for dinner later."

Doing good on my promise from last night, I grab her hand, lacing our fingers even though it's less than five steps before I open the passenger side door and let Vee inside.

TOO STRONG

"The pier isn't that far," she says, buckling up as I hop behind the wheel. "We could've walked."

"We'll spend most of the evening walking, Little Bee. You've had enough exercise for one day." I put the car in gear, making a U-turn in the middle of the road. "What's wrong with your car?"

She releases a heavy sigh. "The water pump and radiator gave up. I can't decide whether to fix it or scrap it. It's probably not worth fixing, but I don't want to bike to work all winter."

My hands crush the steering wheel trim, an overwhelming *need* washing over me.

How fucked up is it that I want to take her to the dealer and buy her a new, reliable car?

She'd look great driving a convertible, and Nico's dealer would hook me up with a good deal on a Mustang.

I also know Vee would freak the fuck out if I'd mention it. We're not officially together, at least not in her eyes. But to me... she's mine. The thought is so embedded in my mind I'm already possessive to the point of unhealthy.

I never considered myself that kind.

Nico, Logan... even Colt, they're the possessive types. The *don't fucking touch her, or I'll rip off your hands and shove them up your ass* types. Nico surely takes the crown, though Logan's not far off, and I bet Colt will be just as bad when the right girl comes along.

But me? I've always considered myself pretty permissive. Never once had the urge to stake my claim.

Everything is different with Vee.

Different and unfamiliar.

Especially that primal, fucking feral need to keep her to myself simmering beneath my skin. It's intense, threatening to choke me whenever I think of anyone touching Vee.

Too bad she's so cautious. Untrusting. Something deep in her mind saying we're too different, that she's not good enough for me.

I've never been more determined to prove someone wrong.

Buying her a car will have to wait. In the meantime, I can help fix hers.

"Let me take a look at it. I know my way around cars."

"Thanks, but I think scrapping it is the smarter option," she says with a shake of her head. "I don't want to waste any more money on it. Something else will break down soon enough."

"I don't want you biking to work, Vee. It's not safe."

She gives me a small, amused smile. "I've been biking all summer. Newport isn't exactly a high-crime area."

"It's not the safest, either."

I want to caveman-style this, tell her she's not riding the bike, period. That I'll be taking her to and from work and *end of fucking story*, but, again, it's not the best route.

All I'll do is scare her off, so instead of embracing the new, unhinged part of my personality, I nip the topic, filing the issue away in my mind to come up with a plan later.

I park the car near the beach and take Vee's hand once we're both out.

"What do you want to eat? Burgers? Hotdogs?"

"I'm not hungry yet," she admits, bending to take her sneakers off when we hit the sand. She buries her toes with a quiet, content sigh. "How about ice cream?"

"And a big coffee," I agree, pecking her head. "What flavor?"

"Surprise me, but no more than two scoops." She points over to some benches nearby. "I'll wait there."

"Are you allergic to anything?"

TOO STRONG

"No, but I guess you are. People who aren't allergic don't think to ask. What is it?"

"Raspberries and asparagus."

Here's hoping she won't sneak either in my food if I piss her off.

I'm back in five minutes, balancing two coffees in one hand and two chocolate vanilla ice creams in the other. "Safest choice," I say, handing her one of each. "We're going back to the arcades later. I promised you a teddy, but we ran out of time."

Vee sits on the sand rather than the bench, legs crossed, fingers drawing various shapes. She nods, taking a long, slow lick of her ice cream, the gesture sending my blood flow downward.

I'm not sure if she does this on purpose or this is how she always eats ice cream, but my dick stands to attention, begging to be touched. Begging to get inside her.

I've tried ignoring the desire. The lust prickling my skin, the need to feel her come undone beneath me, on top of me, and around me, but I can only ignore it so long. I'm nearing the limit.

"Do you come here often?" she asks, watching the lazy waves gently ripple the shore.

The beach is relatively quiet, a few people scattered around, most with kids or dogs. The air still feels warm, but a gentle breeze picks up, delivering a salty maritime scent.

"You'd be surprised. We've spent a lot of time here since we met Mia. She's not very outgoing, and at first, she wouldn't go clubbing with us, so we brought her here."

"I didn't know you were so close."

"She was ours before she was Nico's."

'Of course he likes her. She's gorgeous.'

I smile, hearing a hint of jealousy taint those whispered

words. "She is gorgeous, but I don't like her. Not how you imagine. She's like our little sister. Keeps us in check. We kept her safe until Nico took over." I tell her how we met and about how Cody took the older-brother role too far earlier this year.

"Sounds nice. I always wanted an older brother who'd look out for me, but it's just Rose and me."

"She's a good kid, you know?"

"She's not. She sold me out when I specifically told her not to mention my date with Brian to anyone."

Yep, Rose sold her out big time. I didn't ask for updates or information, but Rose took on the wingman role and texted me of her own volition.

Rose: Vee's on a date with some idiot. Ruby's diner. Pull your head out of your ass.

Cheeky little thing.

I finish my ice cream, grabbing my coffee next. "It'd be nice if I apologized for ruining your date, but we both know you didn't mind. And just so you know, you ever try to go out with anyone else, I'll find you and ruin that date, too."

She straightens her spine, looking me over with a heap of reserved curiosity shining in those stunning silver eyes. "You're moving this along too fast, Conor. I told you—"

"It's a date, and we're not dating," I cut in. "I'll try to match your pace, but don't expect me to lie or pretend I don't want everything right *now*, okay? I want you, Vee. Mine. It's as simple as that."

She looks straight ahead, then heavenward, then sideways, and it's enough of a hint that she's chasing her thoughts, holding lengthy conversations inside her head. *'Nothing simple about this,'* she finally whispers to herself.

I grab her by the waist, maneuvering her arms and legs until she straddles me comfortably, hands bracing my chest, knees digging into the soft sand.

"It's only as complicated as you make it."

She grabs the zipper on my jacket, sliding up and down. "You haven't once asked why I talk to myself. I know you've noticed. You answer me sometimes."

"Is there a reason?"

She nods, peering up at me. "I always do that, but not as often as I have the past few weeks. I've got ADHD. When my meds are right, I'm mostly fine. As in, not talking to myself—"

"I like that you do."

She pinches her lips together, holding back a smile. "Do you know what Shibuya Crossing is?"

"Yeah. The pedestrian crossing in Tokyo."

"Busiest one in the world. Three thousand people cross at a time there sometimes." She grabs my hand, toying with my fingers. "Now imagine it's not people but cars going anything between five and a hundred miles an hour. No traffic lights. Just intuition guiding drivers to the other side."

"Is that how your head works?"

She nods, dropping my hand. I immediately curve it around her lower back. "Too many thoughts cross at once. When the meds work well, the traffic's slow, almost smooth." She grabs the zip again, smoothly sliding it up. "But when meds stop working, I jump from one dose to another, and everything jams up." She yanks the zip hard up and down, fast enough to make it catch, stop, then start again. "Thoughts multiply, get stuck in traffic, blare their horns, and some have to rush around others to cross. Some make it, some get tangled. Speaking a few aloud helps decongest my mind."

She looks up again, silver eyes meeting mine. "Is that... okay, or is it too much? I'll understand if you want to run now."

Run? No way. The visual explanation of how her mind works might be the most fascinating thing I've ever heard.

I move my hand higher up her back, grip her neck, and pull her in for a kiss. A soothing kiss. Designed to calm, and hopefully take the edge off her agitated mind.

She sighs into me, not an ounce of fight in her body. Nothing but pure need as she ghosts her hands across my jaw, opening her lips for me again and again. She's fucking perfect.

"You're not getting rid of me," I say, moving lower to kiss the porcelain column of her throat, desire creeping up on us. "Grab that thought." Another kiss that becomes a nibble, a soft bite of her fresh-smelling skin, and then I suck the flesh, hard enough to leave a mark. "Imagine it's an ambulance. Every other thought makes way for it to cross, baby, so let it cross."

TWELVE

Conor

We didn't step out of the first base zone. If *kisses only* is what's considered first base... I've never seen the diagram.

We made out between talking, drinking coffee, and eating dinner. Vivienne stopped muttering random lines for the rest of the evening, her mind calm regardless of how possessive and downright suggestive our kisses grew as the night progressed.

As the whole *week* progressed.

It flew by so fast I didn't notice Friday arrive again. This time, I've not been purposely keeping a distance. I've not spent my afternoons fighting an internal battle to not wait for her at the front door whenever she dropped Rose off like I did for two weeks.

No, this week, I was with Vivienne. This week, we're making progress. One month since our first kiss, and we're *two* dates in.

Three, if you count tonight.

Seven, if you count every evening I spent at *The Well*, arriving half an hour before Vee's shift.

Her dad and some Uncle Hal fixed her car, so she's not biking. If that's not good enough, she's starting to trust me more each day, finally believing I don't care where she's from. Every day, she lets me get away with more.

More kisses. More hugs. More hand-holding.

We ate takeout in my car all week, alternating between burgers, pizza, and Chinese. Once I fed her, I spent three or four hours parked at the counter, sipping non-alcoholic beer and filling the moments, while Vee wasn't serving customers, with questions. By now, there's little I don't know about her past and favorites.

Purple, gummy bears, oranges. *The Notebook*.

She's superstitious—refused to enter *The Well* one day because the owner stood a ladder at the entrance while changing the slogan. He had to get down and move it before she stepped inside.

Quirky.

My kind of quirky.

I skip classes every Friday the thirteenth.

Prioritizing her thoughts with *ambulances* took root. It helps Vee navigate her busy mind whenever she's overwhelmed. It also helps me push some important ideas across.

We're making progress, but she's still happiest on neutral ground. *The Well*, the beach, the arcades, and *Ruby's Diner* are places she's one hundred percent comfortable with me.

As soon as we step out of her comfort zone, I lose her. Not entirely, but she morphs into a mouse in a roomful of cats. Wary. Uncertain.

It's clear as day when I kill the engine outside *The Olive Tree*. After days of surviving on greasy takeout and the bland food at *Ruby's*, I thought it's time we eat something decent, but the look crossing Vee's face tells me I overstepped.

'I'm not dressed for this,' she mutters, pinching the fabric of her gray, scoop-neck, flared dress. I know that's what it's called because I've spent countless hours shadowing Mia from one boutique to another over the past two years.

Sometime during the many shopping sprees, I became an expert on necklines and fabrics.

Unlike my brothers who invented the best excuses their brains could concoct and fled, I didn't mind holding Mia's bag or fetching different sizes.

It's not something I'd tell my friends, but it will come in handy one day when I'll trail after Vee, helping her pick clothes.

"You look gorgeous, baby." I help her out of the car because I'm sure she'll stay put if I don't.

We don't take five steps before she whispers, *'I look cheap.'*

Anger rages through me, flash-flooding my system. I tug her hand hard enough she has no choice but to brace against my chest.

"You don't look cheap, Vivienne. I never want to hear you say something as ridiculous as that. You're beautiful, and this dress..." I run my fingers along the curve of her hip, waist, and higher until they curl under her chin, "...this dress drives me fucking feral with how the neckline shows off just the tops of your breasts." I grip her jaw, making sure she's focused solely on me. "Ambulance thought, Little Bee. Pay attention. The whole ride here, I kept my eyes firmly on the road because every time I looked at you, I wanted to stop, bunch that dress at your waist, and make you come on my fingers."

She swallows hard, eyes wide like she can't believe I said that. There's a hum in her, low, lustful, so fucking *needy*. I love it. I can't get enough, and I'm learning how to turn on that needy desire that appears more often lately. In her and in me.

I've not touched her yet. Not licked, fucked, or even fingered her. God only knows where my patience comes from. I sure don't have much when I hit my shower every evening and fuck my hand until I come, imagining Vivienne naked in my bed, panting, gasping, begging.

"Well..." She bites her lip, moving closer to press those perfect boobs into my chest like an invitation. "I wouldn't say no."

Jesus fuck.

My cock's a pole in my jeans. I'm sure she feels it rubbing against her hip, twitching, almost barreling through my zipper as I snake my arm around Vee's back, bringing her against my chest.

Mine.

She needs to know and accept that she's mine before I claim her body because, once I do, there's no going back. Once she gives herself to me completely, I won't let her leave.

"Is this a date, or are we dating?" I ask.

She inches away, the lustful gleam fading from her blown pupils. "That's one way of changing the topic."

"I'm not changing the topic. Answer the question."

Glancing over her shoulder at the restaurant, she stiffens again, and that little mouse demeanor returns. "It's a date."

"Then you're getting food, not orgasms."

"Oh..."

"What's wrong?" I run a gentle hand down her cheek, loving how disappointed she looks. "You thought I'll fuck you and be done? It doesn't work like this. You want an orgasm? Tell me you're mine."

She folds her arms, all pretty defiance. "You think I'll believe you never had casual sex?"

"I did, but with you, I don't and I won't. I won't touch, lick, or fuck your pussy until this..." I gesture between us, "...is *dating*, not just dates."

She rolls her eyes, trying to dismiss me, but I don't miss how she rubs her thighs together, searching for friction, the little tease.

"I saw that, baby."

"No, you didn't."

She does it again. Harder, on fucking purpose. I bet she can tell by my jaw clamping tight that her move strikes the right chord, and my resolve falters.

I'm a patient person. Jerking off like I'm sixteen again takes the edge off, but she's testing my limits.

In desperate need of a distraction, I lead her inside. Instead of her wet pussy and the pornographic images filling my head, I focus on the waiter, my glass, the giant fish tank behind the bar, the other people... anything. Anything other than Vivienne and how much I want her to admit we're dating.

She doesn't speak either, flipping the menu back and forth, her expression growing more confused by the second.

"Where are the prices?" she finally asks, almost inaudibly.

Shit. I forgot there are no prices listed anywhere. Either you can afford to eat here, or you can't. *The Olive Tree* isn't the kind of restaurant that'll charge seven-hundred dollars for a steak, but the lack of transparency helps evoke a sense of exclusivity.

"Nico decided not to put them on the menu."

"So how do people know what they'll pay?"

"They can ask the waiter or check the bill at the end."

She scrunches her face, setting the menu aside. "Why did you bring me here? I know you have money, Conor. No need to show it off."

TOO STRONG

"Don't start with that judgmental attitude," I warn, a vein throbbing on my neck. "I brought you here because the food is nice. Because we've been on your turf since the start, and it's time you get used to my turf, too."

She chews her bottom lip like an uncertain little girl, her eyes no longer spitting fire. "I'm sorry, I didn't mean it that way. I know you're not showing off. I just—"

"I know, baby. Too much traffic in your head. Can I order for you? I'm pretty sure I know what you'll enjoy."

She nods once, her eyes trained on something behind my back. "Your brother's here with his wife," she whispers, looking like a deer caught in the fucking headlights.

I turn, spotting Theo and Thalia crossing the room, eyes on us. "Looks like we're about to have company," I tell the waiter. "We'll need a few more minutes before we're ready to order."

"And a bigger table," Theo chirps, gripping my shoulders with both hands. "Hey, bro. Mind if we join you?"

"Not at all," Vee says, her tone sheepish, but her words catch me off guard.

"Perfect." Thalia smiles, stepping out of the waiter's way when he joins another table and two chairs to ours. "I'm glad we bumped into you. I hate eating alone."

Theo rounds the table, introducing himself to Vee. "Hey, I'm her husband and apparently invisible."

"Theo," Vee says, giving a small smile. "The game designer, right? I'm Vivienne."

"Yup, that's me. This is Thalia. Don't mind her moody ass. She's three days away from her due date and not handling it well."

"Try taping a watermelon to your belly, smartass. We'll see how good you'll be doing after nine months. And you're not invisible, but since I'm off work, I'm with you almost twenty-four-seven. You're a bit much to take lately."

"*I'm* a bit much to take?" Theo scoffs, grabbing the tumbler to fill Thalia's glass with water. "You should see *you*, little one. I love you, but I'm not getting you pregnant again for a long time." The playful tone and smile across his lips ruin the stern look. "I'm thinking at least three months."

He's been bitching about Thalia's cravings, requests, and general tiredness to anyone who listened for nine months straight, but he secretly loves the midnight shop runs and foot massages.

I nudge his shoulder. "A girl, this time, alright? There are already too many Hayes boys. I want a niece."

"Logan's on it," he says, spreading a napkin over his knees. "I don't think I'd make a good dad to a little girl."

"She'd walk all over you," Thalia agrees.

It takes twenty minutes before Vee truly relaxes. Once she does, I can't peel my eyes off her smiles as she chats with Thalia and banters with Theo, effortlessly fitting in with my family. We eat dinner, then dessert, and for the first time, Theo and me aren't wrestling once the waiter sets the bill on the table. He purposely overlooks when it happens letting me take care of it..

"We should go out together sometime," Thalia tells Vivienne when we leave. "Oh, I know! I'll get Cass and Mia, and we'll all go to *Q*."

"You're nine months pregnant," Theo reminds, standing behind her, his hand caressing her big belly. "So is Cass, remember? Besides, you know Nico will hire the Black Ops team if you try taking Mia out. Invite the girls over for a night in."

"I didn't mean tonight, Theo. Next month. And Mia goes out with the triplets all the time, so—"

"So we're invited, too?" I chuckle, pecking her cheek. "A

night in might be the better option for now. Even if Nico doesn't mind Mia going out, Cass is still far off her due date, so Logan will latch himself on and ruin your night."

"Ugh! What is *wrong* with you all?" she huffs. "Okay, fine. Once I push this baby out, I'll call you, Vee. We'll set a date." She hugs her, kisses my cheek, then lets Theo take her to their car.

"She's nice," Vee says quietly, twisting her fingers around mine. "And Theo's funny."

"That he is. You met Theo and survived, so now you'll meet two more."

***

Twenty minutes later, I park at the back of the bar, lean across the middle console, and catch Vee's chin between my fingers.

She's been mindlessly fidgeting the whole ride here, mumbling something incomprehensible.

"You'll like them. I promise."

She creeps closer, a silent invitation to seal her lips with mine. I do, slipping my tongue inside her sweet mouth. Every time we kiss, I'm falling so much fucking deeper.

And I want her so much more.

"C'mon," I say when my pants get too tight.

She fuses our fingers together, not letting go even when I open the door to *Tortugo*—my favorite cocktail bar in Newport.

The familiar earthy scent of soil hits my senses one step inside. Clay pots with plants line the floor, spreading over the rusty metal shelves screwed into the exposed red-brick walls. Latin music sets the pace while the buzz of conversation drifts across the tables, making the space feel grounded but lively. I've loved this place since I first crossed the threshold three years ago.

Cody's by the bar, chatting with Justin. Colt sits at a table by the window with Finn and a few chicks from the cheerleading team, their former captain, Blair Fitzpatrick, notably absent.

There was a time the cheerleaders wouldn't show their faces at any gathering without their leader. After what happened earlier this year, they stayed in the shadows.

We've been hanging out with the football team guys more since Brandon made it his life's mission to brown-nose his way back into our and—more importantly—Mia's good graces.

Half the cheerleaders date football jocks, but with Cody's fire-breathing attitude whenever he sees Blair, they stayed out of our way, and I believe after a month or so, they were sick of missing parties and social gatherings so they kicked Blair out of the cheerleading squad almost unanimously. The two girls who voted against are missing tonight, just like their bestie.

To be perfectly honest, I don't give a fuck if Blair hangs out with us. It's not like I have to talk to her. Besides, she knows better than to start a conversation.

Mia made her peace with the bullying she endured for years, and that's the only thing I care about. But Blair won't show up if Cody's around, even with mine and Colt's blessing.

While the two of us don't like the girl, Cody spews fucking fire the moment he sees her. He was always closest to Mia, his big-brother attitude over the top at best. I get why he hates the girl who hurt Mia. I'm no fan, either, but Cody needs a fucking chill pill because he's starting to stoop to Blair's level.

How is gatekeeping her from every college gathering different from the shit she's done to Mia? It's bullying, whichever way you look at it.

But... tonight, I'm glad Blair's not here, considering how condescending she can be. She'd make Vivienne even more uncomfortable than she already is.

Vee follows me to the bar, two steps behind, and Cody immediately drops his conversation with Justin, turning to face us, his eyes darting to our entwined hands.

"Hey, *Little Bee*," he emphasizes with a smirk. "Good date?"

"It was nice," Vee admits, melting into my side, her fingers pulsating around mine.

"Name your poison." Cody nods to the drink list above the bar. "Beer? Wine? Maybe a caipr—" He frowns, looking over his shoulder. "Colt!" he yells, grabbing his attention. "What's that blue cocktail called you always make for Thalia?"

"A beer's fine," Vee says. "Any, I'm not fussy."

Cody waves Colt off, signaling we no longer need the name, and turns to the bartender. "Get us Coronas." He takes another quick peep back, counting heads. "Eleven. Two Diet Cokes and…" He sizes me up with a smirk. "Nachos."

"Double portion." I pull out my wallet.

Cody slaps my hand away. "Put that back in your pants, or I'll do it for you. My turn tonight. I've got a tab open."

Vivienne fidgets beside me when Cody hands her the beer. It's unnerving how she went from calm and beaming during dinner to this unsure-of-herself girl within minutes.

It'll pass. She's just careful. Needs time to take in her surroundings, settle her mind, and get to know everyone before lowering her guard.

I tug her hand, turning her to face me when Cody and Justin stroll toward Colt's table.

"Tell me something. Am I even remotely close to the guy you thought I was at first?"

Her white teeth sink into her bottom lip. "Not when we're alone."

I. A. DICE

The unspoken *but* lingers in the air, driving me nuts.

"Was I different at *The Olive Tree*?" I wait until she shakes her head before I continue, "I don't have a split personality. What you see is what you get. Same goes for my brothers and friends. Even Brandon's not an uncurable dipshit, so I need you to give them a real shot."

She looks at the crowd by the window, eyes skimming up and down like she's sizing someone up. One look that way makes it clear who.

"That's Anastasia," I say. "She's pretty cool, though she likes getting on Colt's nerves a bit too much. Don't be surprised if he drags her out of here once she crosses a line."

"So she's his girlfriend? She's beautiful."

I tilt her head so she'll look at me. "You're beautiful, Little Bee. And no, she's not Colt's girl. It's just sex, but he's territorial over the girls he has in his bed while they hold his interest, so she's off-limits to everyone while they're fucking."

Two little wrinkles appear between Vee's thick eyebrows, and her cheeks pink up. "Are you?"

"Am I what?"

"Territorial about girls who temporarily hold your interest."

"I'm territorial about *you* because this..." I point between us, then sneak my hand around her back, forcing her closer, "...is in no way temporary." I dip my head, fastening her lips with a kiss.

It's nothing like the kiss in the car. She doesn't give in. Doesn't part her lips for me or let me taste the silk of her mouth. Her muscles bunch under my fingers, so hard they have no give.

I pull back, my blood growing hotter, annoyance coursing through my veins. "Tell me what's going through your head, Vee. You want to leave?"

"No. Of course not." She shakes her head, making the few loose strands of hair dance around her pretty face. "I'm just not used to this..."

"Not used to what? Meeting new people?"

"Kissing. Well, not like this. Ugh," she huffs, her features pinched. "You messed everything up, Conor. I thought we were building this up to... you know, *sex*, but you said it won't happen until we're dating, and everything suddenly changed."

"What do you mean? Nothing changed, Vee. I told you at the start I want you for myself."

"I know I just... I didn't think you meant it, and now I know you do, it's... it's just that..."

"Deep breath, Vee," I cut in, seeing her slip into traffic jam mode. "Slowly, okay?"

She forces all air from her lungs, then inhales deeply, blinking like it helps clear her mind. "I've never been on dates before," she admits quietly. "And now that you took sex off the table, your kisses mean different things. Things I'm not used to."

"And what are you used to?"

She worries her bottom lip but releases it when my gaze drops there. "Well, most of my previous kisses were... foreplay."

One sentence and a multitude of unwanted images invade my head. All those men, however fucking many there were before me, touching her delicate body. Kissing those perfect lips, pawing her soft skin with their grubby, unworthy fingers.

We both have a past. I'm aware she's not untouched, and I'm not a fucking caveman. Virginity isn't important. In fact, I'm glad she's experienced. That way, I don't have to worry the same way Nico does sometimes—that he's all Mia knows, and maybe one day she'll want to know more.

It's bullshit, really. He worries for nothing. They're so good together despite how different they are that I know they won't fall apart, but it doesn't stop Nico crawling out of his skin to give her everything she might want.

So yeah, I'm glad Vee's not innocent, but imagining her with other men gets me riled up all the same. The possessiveness stirs a brand-new flavor of hell inside my mind. And that's something *I'm* not used to—feeling this territorial about a person.

"You got used to holding hands. Now get used to me kissing you whenever I feel like it because I will. A lot." Proving a point, I seal her lips again, and this time, she lets me taste her the way I want.

Not for as long as I want, though. When she starts pulling away, I suck her bottom lip, bite hard enough to make it swell, then lick along the spot, soothing the ache.

"This will swell up real nice in a minute," she says, throwing the words I've said almost every time I kissed her right back at me. "Why do you like this so much?"

"One look at you, and everyone knows you've been making out. Means they know you're not available."

THIRTEEN

Conor had one beer, then switched to Coke when Cody gave me another bottle. Every minute, I'm easing into the new setting and people a bit more, invalidating my doubts.

Conor's brothers aren't the same as him, but despite their varying personalities, neither makes me feel uncomfortable. Neither makes me feel worse or like I don't belong.

In fact, Cody's been talking my ear off, making fun of Conor and how many times he barged into his room earlier today, showing off yet another t-shirt he wanted to wear for our date.

Colt's less talkative. Stiffer than his brothers, surrounded by a broody aura, but his eyes are kind. Despite his quiet, simmering demeanor, I get a feeling he actually likes me.

I'm neither the best judge of character nor great at reading people, but how he watches Conor's hand rest comfortably across my collarbones says a lot. He seems genuinely pleased.

Sitting on a high barstool beside Cody, my shoulders relax,

and I cross my legs, leaning back on Conor's chest while he talks with Brandon.

Goosebumps cover my arms whenever the pad of Conor's thumb traces up and down my shoulder, soothing gently like he's trying to keep me at ease.

It's working.

"Conor said you work at *The Well*," Colt says, stitching together the longest sentence I've heard him say since we walked in here half an hour ago. "I've never seen you. Been there long?"

I arch an eyebrow. "You go there?"

He nods, taking a large swig of his beer. Once the bottle's empty, he sets it on a tray in the middle of the table, ready for the waitress to grab when she passes. It's thoughtful. A small detail that shows he's not a self-centered asshole.

A jab of shame has me feeling smaller and ruder than ever. I've made assumptions. Judged them before getting to know them, and I hate that I did. I usually give people a chance. Even Brian got one despite Abby's warnings.

"Not long," I add. "Since Rose started piano lessons with Mia."

"She doesn't need lessons," Cody cuts in. "I've heard her play this week. She's good. Not Mia good, but close."

"She played an old keyboard for years. If you think she plays piano well, you should hear her play guitar."

"Guitar? She didn't tell me that."

Conor leans over me, snatching me another Corona once a waitress exchanges the tray of empties for a full one.

"I shouldn't," I say, turning to face him. "I'm driving."

"No, you're not. I am."

I hook my finger in the collar of his t-shirt, tugging until he leans in closer. "That's sweet, but you can't take me home. I've got a car outside the newsagents."

I don't. Uncle Hal's working on it today, but Conor can't take me home. I don't know if my dad knows what the triplets look like or what they drive. Probably not.

Then again... better safe than sorry.

His lips form a lazy smirk. "Liar, liar. You told me Abby dropped you off, remember? I'm taking you home, Vee. It's non-negotiable."

My lips fall apart in protest that's cut short by Conor's lips, tongue, and a sweet, tender kiss. I'm momentarily speechless. Tingles scuttle up my spine, cracking the foundations of my resolve.

He's kissing me at the table.

We're surrounded by his friends and brothers. I'm sure most figured out I don't belong with them from my clothes and the handmade friendship bracelets adorning my wrists, yet here he is, kissing me for everyone to see, like he doesn't care what they think.

I'm starting to believe he really doesn't...

He sees something in me. Something I don't notice, and he keeps proving that my trailer home, Walmart dress, and old car mean nothing.

"You can't do that," I mutter, flinching back, gloriously dazed, my chest full and fluffy.

"Do what?"

"Kiss me to get your way."

A smile splits his face. "I can, and I will. Now tell me I'm taking you home tonight. What time do you need to be back?"

"Curfew?" Anastasia asks over the table. "Sucks, doesn't it? My mom's a nutcase. I'm twenty-one but need to be home by midnight, or she hides my car keys." She steps closer to Colt, her moves more conspicuous than she thinks as she nestles her butt between his legs and maneuvers his hand across her waist. "What time do you need to be home?"

"Midnight," I admit, twirling my beer around. "It's not a curfew, but Dad's old fashioned. While I'm under his roof, I try not to overstep."

"My dad was the same!" another girl cries, her speech slurred as she drinks the rest of her pink cocktail. "I was so glad when I finally moved out!"

Cody chuckles beside me. "And lived by yourself for how long, Kelly-Ann? A month?"

"Twenty-three days," Anastasia corrects.

Kelly-Ann purses her lips, then flashes everyone a cute, drunken smile. "God hasn't put me on this earth to do laundry or cook my own food." She shrugs. "That's something my husband will provide. Until I find one, I'm more comfortable with my parents."

"Kelly-Ann here wants to be a trophy wife," Conor says, loud enough that she can hear, but she doesn't look one bit offended.

"Nothing wrong with knowing what you want, Conor. Some men want trophy wives."

"Ditto." Brandon clinks his beer bottle to her empty glass. "But you know trophy wives aren't supposed to be as ambitious or smart as you, right?"

"Kelly-Ann just started pre-med," Conor tells me. "She wants to be a neurosurgeon."

"I *will* be a neurosurgeon," she corrects in a stern tone. "You just wait and see."

"No one doubts you, sweetheart." Brandon waves a waitress over, ordering Kelly-Ann another drink.

I'm left a bit dumbstruck and a lot speechless. Once again,

I. A. DICE

I realize I've been living a lie, making assumptions about the rich based on one guy who left me with a bruised heart back in high school and a few uptight people at the newsagents.

Now, I'm brought to question everything I thought I knew. My worldview fragments so fast I can't keep up.

Sure, I'd gotten a dirty look from two girls who left a while ago, but everyone else has been pleasant despite their designer clothes and glaring diamond jewelry.

"I should go powder my nose," Anastasia sing-songs, leaning back to kiss the underside of Colt's tense, square jaw.

"Crossing lines, A," he snarls. "Remember what happened last time you did that?"

She smiles sweetly, pulling an innocent face as she massages her right butt cheek. "The memory's a little fuzzy."

"That's because you were drunk, babe," Cody laughs. "Don't go overboard tonight. I don't want to hear him complain about blue balls when he can't fuck you because you're not thinking straight."

"He has permission to fuck me even when I black out."

"Not happening," Colt growls. "You're welcome to find someone who will."

"Maybe I will," she teases, watching his jaw seize. "What will you do about that?"

"Absolutely nothing."

I can't shake how odd this is. I understand the notion of no strings attached, but I've never seen two people so open about it. So uncaring that they're only about sex.

They sit at the same table, but it doesn't stop Colt scanning the bar occasionally, his eyes eating up other girls, and Anastasia doesn't mind.

It seems counterproductive.

TOO STRONG

Considering what Conor said about Colt being territorial, I doubt he shares, so they're obviously exclusive, yet they're perfectly content with it being purely physical.

In my mind, territoriality is closely interwoven with jealousy. Jealousy means feelings, so I'm curious how this thing between them works.

"If you want my dick, say the words," he clips. "I'm not in the mood for games."

Anastasia shrugs, moving away. "Maybe later. Right now, I need to pee, and I need another drink." She hooks elbows with Kelly-Ann, then zeroes in on me. "You coming, Vee?"

Since the devil's not so black as he's painted, I get up and follow, feeling more myself in this new setting.

"Sooo," Anastasia drawls when I close myself in the cubicle. "What's the deal with you and Conor, girl? Don't say *nothing* because he sure doesn't look at you like it's *nothing*."

I stay silent for a moment, wondering how the hell I'm supposed to answer. We're not a couple. Then again, we've spent the day kissing, holding hands, and I want more no matter how much he gives me.

"I'm not sure," I finally say. It's not a secret and it is the truth. "We've been out on a few dates."

One of them lets out a long *ooooh*.

"Dates?" Anastasia squeals. "He must be serious about you. How did you even meet? You're not in our college, are you?"

"Duh!" Jasmine clips. "Didn't you hear? Her sister takes piano lessons from Nico's girl."

It doesn't slip my attention that they say *Nico's girl* instead of *Mia*, like being his somehow defines her... On the other hand, there's a sudden commotion of butterflies flying all directions in my belly, when I think about myself as *Conor's girl*.

A small yelp slips past my lips, the thought undeniable.
'I want more than dates.'
"You okay there?"

I mumble what I hope sounds like *yes, I'm fine* while inwardly panicking. This is my biggest flaw, one I hoped to control better around Conor—I get involved quickly and then drown in my own tears.

I've done it before, latching onto my ex and the girl I thought would be my bestie forever. I do it to this day, giving my all to everyone way too fast. Abby knows it's an issue, and she's one of the few people who don't abuse the knowledge.

I've always been like this. Whether the lack of a mother and an ever-absent father who worked hard all his life to provide for his family is the reason, I don't know.

I'll likely never know, but I guess the theory is valid. I was only one and a half when my mother died. Without pictures, I wouldn't know what she looked like.

I can't say my relationship with Dad was or is bad. We've always been close, but then he's always been absent, working twelve or fourteen-hour days and missing school events. Never home to help me with homework.

While Rebecca offered me some attention, Rose was her focus. I was just three when she was born. I don't remember much from those times. Every now and then, the topic of our childhood comes up, and Dad boasts about how independent I was. I could tie my shoes, get dressed, and make my bed when I was only four.

Maybe I was a clever kid... or maybe I had no choice but to take care of myself while Rebecca had her hands full with Rose. She was a difficult child. Becca couldn't leave her alone for one minute without Rose finding a way to hurt herself or flip the trailer upside down.

It took years before I realized my problem. I get attached too quickly. For years I've been trying to get a hold of the unquenchable need to be there for everyone, wearing my heart on my sleeve so people would stay with me. So my friends wouldn't move on, leaving me behind.

Not that taming that part of my character works much. I know my issues, so I try and correct myself whenever I go overboard, but with Conor... I failed to keep myself in check.

And now I'm attached. Far too invested for the little time we had together.

We need distance.

I need distance. A few days to get a grip on these silly thoughts. I'm not his.

'*Rich.*'

The word springs to my head unwanted, reminding me I'm not up to his speed and we'll most likely end before we truly begin.

I won't be the silly girl falling in love with a man out of my reach.

I need to be more like Anastasia. '*Enjoy this while it lasts.*' Open up to new things, seize handfuls of Conor's kisses, and how good he makes me feel, but remember it won't last.

We're having fun, but this is temporary.

I'm territorial about you because this is in no way temporary.

His words barrel into my mind, navigating the fuzzy traffic like that ambulance he described. And with that thought sprinting across, flashing its lights, I realize I'm surrendering to overthinking, letting doubt and fear take control.

Not this time.

With a deep, calming breath, I exit the cubicle to wash my

hands. Wherever the road at Conor's side leads... I'm taking it. Consequences be damned.

FOURTEEN

"Stop here." Vee points at a gas station.

Without question, I flick the indicator, certain she needs something from the shop. That thought dies a quick death. The place is shut, and Vee unbuckles her seatbelt, turning to face me.

"Thank you. I had a lot of fun tonight."

My eyebrows knot in the middle. There's no trailer in sight. "This isn't where you live. Vee, I—"

"It's not far from here," she cuts in. "Less than five minutes. I'll be fine."

"You're not walking. It's late. It's dark. What the fuck will your dad think if you come home from a date at this time, and I'm not the one who took you home?" I flip the lock so she can't get out, my blood frothing. "Why are you so embarrassed about where you live? I don't fucking care, Vee. How many times do I have to tell you?"

"I know, but—"

"No buts," I cut in, growing tired of this. "Give me *one* good reason you don't want me to know where you live."

She bites her bottom lip, eyes unfocused.

Fucking tease...

I lean across the middle console, pulling her lip free. "That's my job." Curling my fingers around her neck, I pull her in for a kiss, desire searing through me.

"My dad can't see you," she admits with a heavy, defeated sigh as she pulls back a little.

"What? Why?"

Toying with her fingers, she mutters something incomprehensible. Not audible enough to make out this time. I catch a few out-of-context words that make no fucking sense, but my brain whirs, connecting the dots, looking for meaning.

It's a lesson in deciphering code.

"Vee," I urge, sweeping my knuckles down the side of her face to grab her attention. "Why can't your dad see me?"

"He doesn't like you."

"What?" I fall back against my seat. "He doesn't know me."

"No, he doesn't, but you're—" She swallows hard, eyes rigidly ahead. "You're a Hayes. My dad doesn't like your dad. Doesn't like your whole family. We lied to him about Rose's piano lessons because he went ballistic when he found out Rose wanted Mia to teach her. I've never seen him so angry. Now he thinks some old guy's teaching her."

Okay, *that* I didn't expect.

My father's been part of the Newport scene all his life, a mayor for years now, his second term running out in a few months. All I've heard over the years from people is how much good he's done. How fucking great he is and how much people love having him as mayor.

I. A. DICE

Vee's dad is the first person I know about who *doesn't* like him. It's just plain bizarre because as tough as my father is sometimes, he's a golden retriever inside. Always helpful. Always available.

My mother's done amazing things for people over the years, supporting soup kitchens and women's shelters, donating to the hospital, and funding a brand-new maternity ward...

"I don't know what your dad's problem is with my dad," I admit, poison infecting my voice.

It's fucking offensive he doesn't like my dad. The guy who slaves to make this town a better place, who cares about everyone regardless where they're from or how much they own.

"Me neither," Vee says warily. "He says your dad only looks after the elite. Everyone knows that's not true, so my only explanation is an old-time grudge. Maybe they fell out at school or something. I think it's more personal than Dad lets on, but... I know he won't like seeing you."

I want to say I don't give a fuck, but while that's true, there's also one problem. I won't be the one listening to him rant.

"Whatever the reason, I'm not my father, Little Bee. Sooner or later, your dad will have to accept that. You can't hide me forever. While I'd like to meet him tonight, I'm sure you'd rather prepare him for the news."

She nods, a glint of appreciation in her eyes.

"But I'm still not letting you walk." I start the engine. "Lead the way. Get me as close as possible without risking your dad spotting my car."

She bites her lip, making me groan. I stretch across, replacing her teeth with mine. "Every time you bite, I bite," I say, glancing at the dashboard. "We still have fifteen minutes."

I drag her onto my lap, pulling her sneakers off in the

TOO STRONG

process. She straddles me, her knees dig into the upholstery on either side of my thighs. It's a tight fit, but it works.

A bit too well, actually.

Her hot pussy settles over my rigid cock, just three thin layers separating our skin. Her panties, my jeans, and my boxers.

Not much, and my cock fucking feels it, jutting against her, summoned by the inferno pulsing between her thighs.

Sweet torture amplified tenfold when her body trembles as I grip her hips, fisting her dress.

She takes charge.

Or tries, at least, but I'm in control as our lips touch.

I take her mouth like I want to take her. The kiss deep, hard, bordering on feral. She's so fucking eager, her tongue dancing with mine. For a second, I think she'll push me away as she raises her hands, but instead, she traces the ripple of muscles down my abdomen and keeps exploring, gently gripping my pecs and biceps before weaving fingers in my hair.

She drags me closer to her. Hungry for more. The sweet, musky scent of her arousal perfumes the compact space. Tampers with my sense of right and wrong.

I want her.

I want everything she'll give me. Sounds, touches, pure ecstasy shining from those silver eyes.

Her chest rises faster the deeper I kiss. I move my lips to her neck, biting, teasing, sucking the soft flesh, and her body fucking *sings*.

Pleads with the first circle of her hips against me.

Begs with the second.

Demands with the third.

"Ambulance thought," she pants, arching back and giving me better access to her throat. "No more dates."

Fucking finally. "Say the words, Little Bee."

She tugs my hair, drawing me in as my lips smudge a line from her shoulder to her ear. "We're dating."

"Different words."

"I'm yours."

"You've been mine since I met you. Different words, Vee." I take her mouth again, stoking the fire, working her up until she moans, her body running on instinct as she grinds into me harder. "I know what you want, baby, but I want a *yes*."

She stops moving. Her eyes pop open, sheer surprise shining through like she hasn't fully been here or can't believe I want audible consent.

I do. Since she told me how her mind works, I've paid extra attention to her quiet mutterings. I started coaxing clear answers to all my questions.

Her cheeks are warm, pink, lips swollen from our kisses, pupils blown, and I've never seen a woman so effortlessly *hot*.

"No traffic jams," I tut against the soft spot below her ear. "Don't get out of the moment, baby. Don't overthink." Moving my hands to her waist, I thrust my hips once, checking her reaction.

A little tremor passes through her. Eyes hood over.

"I love the look on you right now. I'll give you everything you'll ask for." I thrust upward again. "I'm pretty damn sure you want me to make you feel good, but *pretty damn sure* isn't enough. I just need a *yes*." More kisses: lower, along her jaw and down her chin. "I need you to be sure because once I see you coming undone, I'll want more. So much more."

Her fingers gouge into my nape when I shift my hips next. A soft moan slips out, and she gives into the need crushing her like an avalanche. It's fucking palpable.

"Yes," she breathes, resting her forehead against mine. "Please."

"If I slide my hand up your skirt, will I find your pussy dripping wet for me?"

Another shudder shakes her gently. "Yes."

I grip her knee and her neck, closing her lips with a kiss while my other hand travels higher. My pulse triphammers in my ears.

The windows start misting over, giving us privacy. Not that I'd care if anyone driving by guessed what we're doing. My focus is solely on Vivienne.

My needy, horny Bee working herself over my cock. I gently brush the smooth, damp fabric of her panties, and she whimpers at the touch, her cheek against mine, lips parting by my ear.

"So needy," I say, my tone dripping with delight. "So fucking perfect." I keep touching the damp fabric, drifting my fingers up and down, loving how her hips arch into my touch. "Good. Always show me how much you need me."

The electric shudder thrashing through Vee hits me head-on when I feel how warm and wet she is, aching for release.

I close my fingers around her throat, gently for now. We'll get to the kinkier stuff later. I press a button on my seat, sliding it back as far as it'll go, increasing the pressure on Vee's neck until her shoulder blades hit the steering wheel. Her legs are bent, feet either sides of my thighs, hands braced against the door and middle console.

'Wrong. So wrong. This won't work.'

FIFTEEN

Conor's eyes snap to me, an airless unease mounting around him. "Wrong? What's *wrong*? What won't work?"

My breath falters. Goddamn. He heard.

I'm turned on to an abstract, incomprehensible point, tumbling through vertigo with nothing but the all-consuming need to come. I quiver softly, my body like an exposed nerve.

The heat of his palm cuffing my neck only intensifies the pleasure coursing through me, but I know he won't tip me over the edge.

No one managed that.

I have to take charge and find a rhythm that does the job, or I'll be left frustrated.

My chest heaves, my nipples so hard they sting. I want him to touch me. Kiss me, and let me take what I need, but he's not budging, eyes on mine as he waits for an explanation.

"You won't make me come this way."

He raises a questioning, ignorant brow. "And why not?"

"Because..." I stammer, the heat of his gaze flaying my skin. "I... I need to set the pace, or it won't happen."

He clamps his fingers over my neck. "Is this okay?"

Okay? It's beyond okay. It's hot even though he's not squeezing hard, barely holding me in place. "That's nice."

"I'm not good at giving up control, Vee, but if I can't make you come the way I want, I'll let you lead." He flicks his fingers over my panties, teasing, building the anticipation. "You think you can let me try?"

My body pulls taut. Dread sinks into my bones.

He'll be left disappointed when I can't reach orgasm. He'll think I'm broken or that he's not good enough. It'll bruise his ego, and *'he'll move on.'*

"Not now, not ever," he says immediately, yanking my panties aside and exposing me to him. "Give me five minutes."

It's unnerving how he stares. Like he's checking whether I meet his expectations. It's in my head; I know this. Ridiculous, self-conscious thoughts. Did I shave well enough? Am I dripping onto his jeans? Is my pussy too dark? Too light? Ugly?

My knees are pressed together, but it doesn't cover me up this way. If anything, it exposes me in a filthier way.

He glides one finger between my lips, sliding up and down slowly. "Such a pretty pussy," he groans, eyes focused between my legs. "Let me try, baby."

I nod, fling my head back, close my eyes, and melt into the steering wheel.

Even if he doesn't make me come, I want him to touch me because when he does, he sends a shock of endorphins roaring through my blood. I want him to tighten the hold around my throat and—

He dips two fingers inside me.

Curls them immediately, and just like that, he finds my G spot. The magical button no man I've been with thus far ever looked for.

"Wrap your arm around your knees," he instructs.

I obey, holding my knees together as a needy moan escapes me without permission. The sensation of being touched by a man who knows what he's doing blurs my vision with pure pleasure.

"Good. Just like that," Conor coos quietly, slowly working those fingers in me. "I'll worship the ground beneath your feet every day, baby. I'll spoil you with cuddles, kisses, dinners... I'll give you the world. And at the same time..." He increases the pressure on my neck, enough for a hot flush to heat my face, "...in bed... I'll own every inch of your body."

God, this man knows what he's doing. Every low, husky word encourages my orgasm, beckons it closer to the surface, the unrushed tempo of his fingers sliding in and out nothing short of amazing. Add the sheer possessiveness filling his tone, and I'm a goner.

"Such a needy girl," he fusses, desire lurking in his eyes when my hips start winding. "Don't stop."

He's got me so close. So *fast*, but... it's not enough. *'I need more.'* Just a little more. A little faster.

"You think I don't know what I'm doing?" he asks, his voice full of lustful amusement. Letting go of my throat, he moves his hand between my legs, and his thumb is there... pressing against my clit, rubbing tight circles. "Wrong, Little Bee. Look at me."

It takes effort to peel my eyes open, but I do, meeting his heated gaze. He rests against the seat, casually sprawled, not a care in the world.

TOO STRONG

Seeing him like this, no one would guess both his hands were between my legs, eliciting expert pleasure.

"You're right where I want you. Almost coming. Almost getting what you need. Ready to be tipped over." He ups the tempo, filling me faster and proving a point when my body purrs toward orgasm.

But it doesn't hit.

He stops before the elation stacks up high enough, making me whimper in protest.

"No, no, *no*, don't stop, it's—"

"You'll come when I'm good and ready to let you and not a moment sooner." His fingers manipulate my G spot, causing faint shudders as I clench around them, rocking my hips to get off.

A lazy smile curls his lips.

His head hits the backrest.

I want to smack his stupid, handsome face, tear his hands away and finish what he started, but...

I love what he's doing.

I love that he knows how to touch me. That he *can* drive me this feverish, this illogical with need.

"Whose are you, Vee?"

I half pant, half moan, the words a jumbled drowned-out mishmash because he tortures my clit again, hard and fast, reducing my bones to liquid.

But when I'm right there, he eases away, lazily pumping two fingers in and out, keeping me balanced on edge. He offers enough to keep me there but not enough to push me over.

"You need to know it with every one of your cells," he continues. "Whose are you?"

He pinches my clit—gently—but I'm so ready to come my

whole body spasms wildly. Another moan tears from my chest. My mind fires up time and time again, but it's not an orgasm. It's a prelude, tiny vibrations, barely a suggestion of what the real thing will feel like.

"Please," I gasp, a hot ball of frustration surging behind my ribs. I'm ready to cry, kick, *beg*. "Please, Conor... I can't take this!"

"*Whose* are you? I need words."

I bite my bottom lip, whimpering when he toys with my clit again, bringing me so close. "Yours," I pant, digging my nails into my knees so hard I leave marks. "I'm yours."

"That's right. Mine." He smiles, exhaling a content breath as his gaze zeroes between my thighs. "Mine to take care of and mine to drive crazy." He increases the pace, crooking his fingers inside me while his thumb rubs my clit, and that's all it takes.

The orgasm rips through me, powerful, mythical, so intense I think I'll black out. So intense I'm deaf. Blind. Utterly useless.

I never came so hard. Never felt so boneless or delusional. The sensation eases off and then comes again like waves crashing against the shore.

And Conor doesn't stop. He still strokes my G spot, still puts his thumb to good use, and the release lasts so long. *So fucking long I think I have an out-of-body experience.*

He finger-fucks me right through it, easing back until he brings me down completely. And only when I tune back into reality Conor gently removes his fingers, licks them dry, then gathers me up like a ragdoll.

In three moves, he's got me flush against his chest, our lips moving in a slow, thorough, attentive kiss. I'm still lightheaded, limp, mellow, my pussy pulsing with little aftershocks.

"From now on," he whispers, tucking my head under his chin as he strokes my back, "you don't touch yourself. Don't get off unless I'm watching, understood? Your orgasms are mine."

"Okay," I sigh, nuzzling my face in his neck.

"I hate to say this, but it's almost midnight. We should get going."

"Okay."

He chuckles, kissing my head. "Orgasms make you very agreeable, baby. I'll keep that in mind." He swipes his thumbs under my eyes, then pulls my scrunchie out.

"What are you doing?"

"You look like you've been thoroughly fucked. Unless that's the look you're going for, I suggest you fix your hair and dress."

I straighten more, spotting the bulge in his pants. "I'm sorry, I... I didn't think."

He grabs my wrist before I get anywhere near his zipper. "This isn't an exchange, Vee."

"But you're—"

"About ready to lock you in my room for a week and fuck you until we're both too exhausted to move? Yeah, but I don't mind waiting." He pats my hip, urging me to get off him. "I'm trying to get into your dad's good books, and making you late won't do me any favors. Lead the way."

SIXTEEN

My phone pings when I get into my car outside college. Cody and Colt left a moment ago, but I'm still digging through my jam-packed trunk, looking for my jacket.

It's too chilly today. December's barely started, and already no longer t-shirt-only weather.

I finally find it, rolled into a ball under a case of beer at the very back of the trunk. It looks like something a dog chewed up and spat out, creased in every direction.

It's too cold to care.

I slam the trunk, not wanting to stare at the mess there any longer. I should probably clean it out one day before rats start nesting in the bags of Halloween decorations. Well, not decorations, mostly trash—cobwebs, paper bats, lanterns... even a few destroyed cardboard tombstones.

I jump behind the wheel and open the Hayes brothers' group chat, surprised I'm the first to see Theo's message. Everyone else must be either working or driving.

Theo: Water broke. Pick up Ares. Talk later.

His messages are usually the longest, but given the circumstances, I'm not surprised he kept the word count to a minimum. I bet he's having a coronary, fussing around Thalia, and panicking they won't reach the hospital on time.

Me: Deep breaths, bro. You've got this. Keep us posted. I'm on my way to grab Ares.

Another message arrives as I'm about to lock the screen.

Logan: Breathe with her. DON'T FAINT, and remember she's the one in pain, so don't be a fucking pussy.

Nico: Call me if you need a punching bag, errand boy, or anything else.

Theo's not reading this, probably halfway to the hospital by now, talking Thalia through her contractions. I tuck my phone away, ignoring the new messages, and dial Vee's number as I pull out of the parking space.

"Hey," she whispers, "I'm still at work. Can I call you back?"

"I'll make it quick. I'm picking you up after your shift, and we're going to the beach. You got a jacket with you, or should I grab you a hoodie? It's cold today."

"Yes, I have a jacket."

"Good. I'll see you in half an hour."

She whispers "*Bye,*" then cuts the call at the same time I hear an overdoor bell sound in the background.

Ten minutes later, Ares almost tackles me to the ground as I enter Theo and Thalia's house. He's whining, jumping, trying to lick my face off, clearly confused about what's happening.

The house looks mostly intact, but it's lucky I came. Soup simmers on a low heat, the air tinged with the mouth-watering smell of manestra: a tomato and orzo soup. Probably my favorite Greek dish from everything Thalia makes.

Looks like she was making dinner when labor started.

A puddle on the kitchen floor proves me correct. *She spilled water or tea*, I tell myself, mopping it up. I turn the hob off, put ingredients for what looks like a roast back in the fridge, and load the dishwasher. Once nothing seems out of place, I open the cabinet where they store Ares's food.

"Wow, your mommy was ultra-prepared for this, wasn't she?" I pat Ares on the head, rummaging through an overnight bag she prepared with essentials.

After triple-checking the house is locked, I let Ares take the back seat in my car, and forty minutes later, he's lying beside Vee on the beach, ears perked, clever eyes watching the waves frothing at the shore.

The sun hid behind a thick, gray blanket of clouds while I waited for the barista to finish our coffee order, and the temperature dropped another few degrees.

"I think it'll rain," Vee says, enfolding herself tightly in her jacket when I sit down, handing her a steaming cup of caramel latte. "We should get going."

"Afraid of a little rain?" I ask, watching the waves loom higher and stronger. "I've not kissed you in the rain yet."

She hides her smile behind the takeout cup. "So romantic."

"I watched *The Notebook*."

It was fucking dreadful.

TOO STRONG

Mainly because I watched it with my brothers. Their commentary could rival the best stand-up comedians. Sounds fun, right? It usually is, but when their pokes and prods are aimed at me, they get annoying after an hour or so.

I'm not a movie person by default. I prefer spending my time with people or getting shit done, but Vee mentioned it's her favorite movie, so I sat through two hours of wet Ryan Gosling.

"Well, it's officially raining," she says, holding her hand out to catch the spaced-out drops falling from the unbroken, steely clouds. "Kiss me and let's go."

I set my coffee aside, drilling the bottom of the cup into the sand, then lean over Vee, covering her small frame with mine. Shielding her eyes from the rain that starts falling heavier, she beams, perfectly relaxed.

Crawling a little higher to stop the rain hitting her face, I watch those gorgeous pale gray eyes look up at me with so much trust... so much wonder. She's finally beginning to feel everything I feel.

And I feel unhealthy, sick, red-flag things. It wasn't as prominent before, but my obsession grows tenfold every day. Each tiny detail I discover about her adds a layer of possessiveness to my territorial mind.

The cupid bow of her full lips is my favorite part of her body. Or maybe those silver eyes. Or the tiny freckles dotting her nose. Smooth, soap-scented skin...

"Why are you looking at me like that?" she asks, her voice barely audible and almost swallowed by the downpour soaking my jeans right through.

"I can't get enough," I say, sealing her lips.

A rush of endorphins ignites my mind right on cue. Slowly, I lick along the seam of her mouth, loving how it parts for me, her hot tongue tangling with mine.

And that little whimpering, moaning sound escaping her… the best in the world.

I move one hand to her jaw, steering her face to sink deeper and draw another sweet little mewl.

She pushes her hands under my clothes, scraping long nails along my ribs and shoulder blades, putting enough pressure to let me know she wants me closer.

Wet sand mats her hair, dancing around us under the attack of heavy raindrops. We should get going. The downpour won't ease off anytime soon, and I don't want Vivienne to catch a cold.

Maybe a small one. A slight fever, stuffed nose, and scratchy throat. Enough that she'll stay in my bed, curling into my chest for a few days.

"We should go," I whisper, nudging her nose with mine. As tempting as having her body warming me all night sounds, she wouldn't stay. "C'mon, baby, you're cold."

Her hands slide under my clothes to my shoulders, dragging me back down. "Just one more." She lifts her head off the sand high enough to reach my lips.

I lose it on the fucking spot. Knowing she wants me as much as I want her has my cock almost splitting my zipper and my heart squeezing like a sponge.

Have I mentioned I'm fucking obsessed with this girl? Falling hard, fast… I don't want to stop.

I want everything she can give me. Everything my brothers have with their girls, and so much more. Her hand in mine, her body tight against mine at night. Morning kisses and cuddles on the couch. I want the light. The love…

And all the depraved things infecting my mind.

I want her tied to my bed, begging for my touch. I want her

TOO STRONG

panting my name while blood rushes to her face from my fingers around her delicate throat, driving her pleasure sky high as they constrict her breath. I want her ass in my lap, my hand streaking down over again until she's so wet she's dripping onto the floor.

I want to fucking own her.

In and out.

Day and night.

And I want her to own me.

She already does, but she has no idea how much power she holds. How quickly she could ruin me.

I kiss her forehead first, letting my warm lips dawdle on her cool skin, every ounce of emotion compressed into that innocent kiss.

Then, I slide my jacket off and pull it over my head, creating a small tent as I weasel between her legs, pressing into her hard. I'm rewarded with a strained moan. Her hips arch against me, eyes fall shut, and she throws her head back, exposing her neck in silent invitation.

I accept. I kiss, bite, and suck a spot above her pulse the way she loves until she whimpers.

Her body's a pool of knowledge.

She might whisper her thoughts, but her pleasure, likes, and dislikes *scream* through her gestures. I kiss a special button in the crook of her neck and rise on my elbows, watching the magic happen.

Her nipples harden, peeking through the fabric of her bralette and t-shirt. When I first found this special button, I thought she didn't wear a bra. She does, just not a standard one. More like a short, tiny top that keeps those beautiful boobs in place.

It does nothing to hide her arousal, though. Nothing in the way of her nipples rising in two candy-hard points.

"So fucking beautiful," I say, watching her lips fall apart as I press my hips forward.

Not to let her feel how much I want her. That's a given. I do it because her body cries for it. It's in her every touch, every moan, every pirouette of her hips.

She's in the moment, not overthinking, guided by need, and that's how I want her always.

"Someone could see," she says, eyes blinking up at me. "We're in public."

Someone could see, but her tiny smile playing tells me she likes that thrill. We're cloaked under my jacket, the makeshift tent giving us a false sense of privacy because *we* can't see anything but each other.

We're shielded, as if in bed under the comforter, getting hot and bothered like we're sixteen, experimenting for the first time.

Instead, we're on the beach. Exposed. In clear view from the pier and the coffee shop nearby. Anyone paying attention, anyone wandering past, would immediately know we're basically fucking with our clothes on.

"Then push me off you." I lower myself back on her, chest to chest.

I skitter my lips to her ear, my warm breath raising goosebumps in its wake. We're moving. Slowly building the moment, getting lost in each other, heating up from the inside out even though our clothes are soaked.

"Do you want me to stop, baby?"

"No, no, don't stop."

I grip her knee, moving her leg high enough that she hooks it over my ass. "Dirty little thing." I lick her earlobe. "You want me to make you come right here for everyone to see, don't you?"

And I will.

Fuck, I *will*.

The sky cracks above us. An almighty roar of thunder explodes with the force of an H-bomb, sounding like a fighter jet crashed into the pier.

The wind howls in our ears as the storm ferments over Newport Beach, gaining strength by the second, air thick with saltwater and ozone. We're in for a fucking hurricane, I can already tell.

Time to go.

Ares yelps, his big claws digging into my jeans, not far off ripping the fabric as he paws my thigh.

I can't see the lightning bolt tearing through the clouds, but a bright-white strobe breaches the makeshift tent like a camera flash, and in an instant, Vee's frozen in place.

Motionless.

Pale.

Silently hysterical.

Her lips part like she's screaming, but no sounds escape. Gorgeous, wide eyes brim with tears, a helpless look contorting her features. Long nails pierce the skin of my back, and her body trembles beneath me...

SEVENTEEN

Conor

"Shit... fuck!" I snap, my blood running cold, when a panic attack throws Vivienne into a frenzied abyss.

Her heart beats against her ribs like a hummingbird's wings, her fear almost tangible.

I cradle her to me, my lips plastered to her forehead, fingers framing her face. "Easy, baby. Look at me. Hey, hey..." I angle her face so she can't see anything besides our tiny jacket tent shielding us from the rain. "We're okay. You're okay. I'll get you out of here."

She bites her lip hard enough to draw blood, nodding once.

"Close your eyes." I whip away my jacket.

Rain immediately saturates my hair. I rise to my knees, pulling Vee with me, then haul her into my arms, grabbing the jacket and Ares's leash along the way.

She quivers. Clings to me like a second skin, face buried in my neck as she swallows big, irregular gulps of air.

TOO STRONG

"Shh, shh... I've got you. You're okay." I wrap my jacket around her shoulders, high enough to cover her head and make a run for the car. "Hold on tight."

She does. Her legs clamp my waist in a vice grip, arms lock around my neck so tight I can't breathe. The rain comes down in sheets now. So hard it jabs my skin like microscopic needles.

I can't see more than a few feet ahead, squinting as the wind tears at my clothes, whipping my wet hair into my face.

Ares tugs on his leash, almost dragging me behind as he barks, bulldozing forward.

Vee's muffled sobs echo against my neck, her heart racing in frantic rhythm.

The palm trees sway, their leaves whipping back and forth, and debris flies in every direction, carried by the gusts.

Another bolt of lightning sizzles into a nearby palm tree that falls onto the road. The world turns blinding white for a split second, illuminating the chaos. Vee's hysterical, screaming and wailing in the thunder that follows. It's so loud it seems to shake the very foundation of the earth.

Fuck, this is bad.

With trees falling already, it'll be category two, maybe even three within the hour. Newport doesn't get hurricanes often, but I remember a couple that stripped the cladding of my parents' mansion when the fallen trees took days to clear, paralyzing the town.

This right now... it feels the same. An aura of impending doom hangs in the air, the scene unfolding like a sequence from a high-budget disaster movie.

The wind whistles around us, thankfully blowing from the sea and helping me along the way instead of blowing in my face to slow me down. The keyless entry in my car is a blessing, no matter how crazy it drives me on a normal day.

The lock clicks the second we're by the door. Yanking it open, I let Ares take the back seat first.

"Baby, look at me," I say, peeling Vivienne off me as I maneuver her inside. "Deep breaths. We'll be home soon. I need you to breathe."

She nods rapidly, still swallowing her sobs, shaking as she leans back, tucking her feet inside. I buckle her up before I round the hood, hopping behind the wheel.

"Head between your knees," I tell her, starting the engine. "Deep breaths for me, baby. Close your eyes."

I wind the audio system as loud as it'll go without blowing the speakers. "Royalty" by Egzod pumps out. The mix of classical music and strong beat muffles the hurricane, so Vee can't hear the rain battering the car from all sides or the thunder roaring more frequently now.

Stamping my foot down, I shoot out of the parking space. Tires skid the back of the car almost fucking level with the front on the wet asphalt. We slide onto the empty main road, half drifting across the intersection. My heart pumps blood faster. My pulse hammers in my ears.

"Fuck!" I slap the steering wheel, spinning it all the way left. A fallen tree blocks the road ahead, forcing me to take a longer route.

Left, right, left again.

We're fucking flying down the streets as I mentally map the roads least likely to be blocked.

Vee reaches her hand to the audio system when the song changes to something less intricate. She pats the controls blindly, her head still between her knees.

I press a button on the steering wheel, restarting "Royalty," my foot stomping the pedal all the way down as I reach across, stroking Vee's back for a moment.

She's still shuddering, her fingers drumming the melody blasting from the speakers like it keeps her grounded.

Trash flies around the streets, bins roll down the sidewalks, leaves whirl in the gusting wind, and a few smaller trees litter the sides, but nothing significant blocks our way.

Halfway across town, my phone connects with the car, and *Cody* flashes on the screen.

The rain falls so heavy my wipers can't keep up, and the deafening sound of his ringtone swamps us in 5.1 surround once the music's cut. If I don't answer, he'll jump in his car and come looking for us.

Fuck. I jam my thumb into the button.

"Where are you?" he asks, a nervous undertone layering his voice. "Tell me you're not still on the fucking beach!"

"On our way home. Five minutes. I need a parking space in the garage, a big towel, and music on full volume."

"Wha—?" Cody starts, but Colt's *on it!* booming in the background cuts him off.

Thank fuck he's bright and doesn't need me to spell this out. I cut the call, music back on, the song the whole ten-minute ride to Nico's.

I don't slow down until we're right in front of the garage. Colt's inside, two towels in hand, and the door rolls down once my wheels come to a full stop.

I kill the engine, shooting out like I'm on springs. Snatching one towel from Colt's outstretched hand, I round the hood, yanking the passenger door open. Ares gets out, barking and shaking off water before he bolts upstairs, leaving a trail of wet sand.

"She good?" Colt asks.

A headshake is my only answer as I unbuckle Vee's seatbelt. "We're home. C'mon, baby, you're safe now."

Slowly, she lifts her head, shuddering softly, her eyes bright, rimmed pink, and teeming with tears. It takes a great deal of maneuvering to haul her out and into my arms. Colt helps me wrap her in a towel, though it won't do much other than keep her warm. Most of the water has pooled on the seat.

She's so fucking stiff as I carry her upstairs. Her muscles bunch so tight she'll get cramps if I can't calm her a little bit.

Music seeps through the house, calm, classical.

Mozart, I think.

I half expect Mia at the piano, but besides Cody, who's toweling Ares dry, the house is empty. I sit on the couch, clutching Vee to my chest, her nose pressed against the crook of my neck, holding me so hard her fingernails turn white.

"Shh," I tut against her hair, pulling a warm blanket to her chin. "We're home. You're okay."

She nods, parting her lips to force a long exhale, and slowly, very *slowly*, her tremors subside.

"Where's Nico and Mia?" I ask Cody as he sets four beers on the coffee table.

Pointless question. The main door opens, then closes quickly with a bang, making Vee jump in my arms.

"God, you're such a brute!" Mia's wail reaches our ears first. A second later, Nico enters, carrying her over his shoulder like a sack of potatoes. "I can walk, you know?"

"Yeah, I know," he grumbles, running his hand down his face. "Is she okay?" he asks me, eyeing Vivienne.

"Scared of thunder," I explain, tracing a line up and down her spine. "We were on the beach when it started."

"Who's scared?" Mia tries to peek from behind Nico, but can't and whacks him hard. "Um, could you put me down now? *Please.* It's bad out there. I won't run. Promise."

"You ran again?" Colt smirks, dropping onto the piano stool with a bottle of Corona. "You sure make his life entertaining, Bug."

Vee stirs, a little less tense, and peeks from under the blanket. "Hey," she says quietly. "I'm sorry, I—"

"Don't apologize," Nico cuts in, dismissing her with a flick of his wrist. "You have no idea what I'd give for this little diva to be scared of thunder." He slides Mia down his front until she stands barefoot. "Fucking reckless," he snaps, his angry voice a stark contrast to the soft, tender kiss he stamps on her head. "We stopped for takeout," he continues, ignoring her folding her arms and the three of us chuckling.

It helps Vee relax, too. She pulls the blanket lower, no longer stiff in my arms, no longer shaking as much.

"Five minutes," Nico says, taking a towel from Cody to turn Mia into a pink ghost so he can dry her hair. "I was gone *five* fucking minutes. I come out, and it's raining, the car's open, her shoes on the dashboard, and she's gone."

"Lifeguard station again?" Colt chuckles, looking at the rainwater pooling at their feet.

A small smile curves Vee's lips when Nico wraps Mia in the towel like a straitjacket, then sets her on the couch beside us.

"I like the rain!" she says, failing to escape the cotton constraints. "Ugh! Let me go! I want wine."

"I spent fifteen minutes chasing her down the beach."

Mia smiles, blowing a strand of wet hair off her face. "You like chasing me."

"Not in the middle of a fucking hurricane, Mia. What did

I say when I went to get the food?"

Her cheeks flush pink. "You told me to be good."

"And were you?"

"No..."

Vee chuckles, moving her hand under the blanket to weave our fingers together.

"Not funny," Nico tells her, but his tone isn't laced with the same aggression he rarely keeps in check. He's watching how he speaks so she won't feel uncomfortable. Something he learned during the last few months. "I'd be much happier if she was scared. At least she'd behave."

Another laugh, much louder, falls from Cody's lips. He passes one glass of wine to Mia, and another to Vee, taking a seat in the corner of the couch. "You'd be bored if she was any more obedient."

"I'd be calm," Nico retorts, looking out the floor-to-ceiling windows where rain cascades down the glass in sheets. "We better find something to keep us entertained because the town may as well be on lockdown with how bad the roads are. You should call your parents, Vivienne. No way we'll get you home tonight. Probably not tomorrow, either."

Wish granted... she'll sleep in my bed.

"Have you checked in with anyone?" Nico asks, pulling his phone out.

"Everyone save Theo called already. They're fine."

Within a minute, Nico's holding his phone at a distance, angling it so we all see the screen.

Shawn's the first one to answer, still in his police uniform, water dripping from his hair. "I was about to call you. How's everything with you guys?"

"All here. You heard from Mom and Dad?"

"Yeah, they're good. They're at Grandma's, so not stuck at home alone," he says, towel-drying his head. "Where's Conor?"

"Here." Nico angles the phone further until we're visible. Vee tenses like she's unsure whether to dive under the blanket. "You heard from Theo?"

"Yeah, River's here now." He pauses until our cheers die down. "Born half an hour ago. I've not seen him yet, but the nurse said he's healthy and a screamer."

"Something to look forward to when we're babysitting," Nico says, hugging Mia closer. "How's Thalia doing?"

"As you'd expect. Good. Absolutely no issues... Can't say the same about Theo, though." He pinches a smile behind his lips. "We've got our first fainter, boys."

"Argh, damn it," I huff, reaching for my wallet to retrieve a hundred-dollar bill.

Nico's already holding one out, and within seconds, Cody's three hundred dollars richer.

"Told you," he grins at Shawn, gripping the back of the couch. "We'll split it when the storm passes."

"Yeah, you still need to collect from Logan. He called ten minutes ago, Nico. They're fine. He was about to put Noah down for a nap, so give him half an hour before you call."

Nico nods and disconnects the call, dialing Mom's number next. He won't stop until he knows first-hand that the whole family is safe.

EIGHTEEN

Vee

With the phone pressed to my ear, I sit in Conor's room, dwarfed by his t-shirt. I keep pulling the strings of his sweatpants tighter, but they barely cling to my hips, bunching at my ankles.

The dial tone rings for the second time as I run my fingers through damp hair, my skin stinging from the steaming shower that relaxed my muscles a bit more than Conor's cuddles.

My heart still threatens to snap my ribs, but it's no longer the roaring thunder or my memories' fault. Nico's mansion has an interconnected speaker system installed. Soothing classical music plays in every room, drowning out whatever sound could seep inside through the triple-glazed windows.

The line rings three more times. I'm about to lie my ass off *again*, and my stomach wrenches at the thought. I should tell Dad about Conor.

I can't keep him a secret forever.

The only reason he's not blowing up my phone is Abby.

TOO STRONG

She called a few times while my phone was still in my purse, locked in Conor's car. Failing to get through, she sent a text saying she told my dad I was with her.

Best friend ever.

"Hey, Daddy," I say, gripping the phone tightly when he answers. "How's it going over there? Is the trailer holding up?"

He chuckles, genuinely amused. "Of course. It's bolted to the ground well enough to withstand a category three hurricane, Angel. We're safe. You know we're prepared for these storms."

Dad's a survivalist, even if he doesn't like to admit it. The small pantry at the back of the trailer is stocked with canned food, batteries, thermal blankets, a first-aid kit, a water filtration system... everything you'd need in an apocalypse. He started collecting supplies after the last hurricane ten years ago.

That's when I grew afraid of thunder. Our trailer wasn't ready for a hurricane back then. Windows gave in, shattering under the strength of the wind, half the roof flew away, and the inside flooded within an hour.

I was only eleven, hiding under the bed, crying as I held Rose close. The roads to the trailer park were blocked for five days. We ran out of food as quickly as the nearest gas station.

My dad hates relying on others, but that time he had no choice. As soon as he could, he started setting things aside, buying a few items each month in case we were ever in a similar situation. Last year, he bought a generator after a town-wide blackout during one of his team's games, so even losing electricity isn't an issue.

It isn't here, either. Nico's home is self-sufficient. Otherwise, we'd be sitting in the dark by now. Most of Newport lost power about an hour ago.

"How's it down at Abby's," Dad asks, emphasizing too

much. "You girls keeping safe? Did your *date* drop you off there?"

A chill slips down my spine.

Shit. He knows...

Not that Conor Hayes is the guy I'm seeing, but he knows I'm not spending the night with Abby.

My pulse quickens, whooshing in my ears.

Should I dig my grave deeper or come clean now? It's been a month since my date with Brian. I've not told Dad who I'm dating, but I assume he thinks it's the same guy.

'I'm twenty-one, for crying out loud.' I clear my throat, finding courage. "Okay, you got me," I sigh, my voice trembling, giving away my nerves. "We were on the beach when the storm started. I panicked, Dad. Like really badly, so he took me back to his place, and now the roads are closed, and—"

"Vee, calm down. You're twenty-one, for God's sake," he chuckles softly, making me aware I said that aloud. "This isn't the first time you're having..." He pauses, voice tense because he accidentally veered into murky waters. He swallows so hard I hear it. "A *sleepover* with a guy, is it?"

"No, it's not, but I've not had a chance to bring him home yet... I know how much you worry."

"I do. I always will, Angel. You're my baby girl. It's only natural that I worry. You're smart, Vee. I know you wouldn't be there if you didn't trust him."

I flop back onto the pillows that smell like Conor's cologne, and my eyes roll back in my head. "I do. He's amazing. I promise I'll tell you everything soon."

"Yeah, okay. I'll let you get back to him." He exhales down the line, so I know he's not done. "Angel?"

Uh-oh.

God, *'please don't let it be about protection'* please, please, please.

"Yes?" I ask, my voice wary.

"It's not about that, but since you've mentioned it—"

"Dad, don't," I squeak, my cheeks scalding. "Please don't. You said I'm smart so let's leave it at that, okay?"

"I might be old, but I'm not senile, Vivienne." He lets out a long breath. "You have a great friend in Abby, you know that? I knew you were staying with your boyfriend, but she was very convincing. She had a whole story stitched about how she was taking a bath, and you were in the kitchen with her mom and couldn't hear her calling."

I chuckle, imagining Abby frantically put on the spot like that. "She's the best. I'll be home once the roads are clear."

"I know. Night, Angel."

"Night, night." I cut the call, roll onto my stomach, and bury my face in the pillow. Shower gel. Cologne. The faint scent of washing powder.

Conor must've changed the sheets a few days ago.

I yank myself upright at the sound of the door handle moving. Conor walks in, freshly showered, hair damp. He left me here, free to use his en suite while he used the guest bathroom. Now the air moves with him, the citrusy, minty notes of his shower gel dazing my senses.

His chest is bare. Obscenely sexy gray sweatpants hang low on his hips, and heat builds between my legs as I examine the hint of muscles rippling down his abdomen.

"Don't look at me like that, baby," he says, crossing the room to crouch before me. "I promised my brothers we'll come down, and if you keep staring like you want me inside you, we won't leave this room until tomorrow."

"Sorry, you're just... ripped." I feather my fingers along his six-pack. *That's so hot.*

"Vivienne," he warns, encasing my hips with big hands, caressing me softly. "You're staying the night. We have time, but right now, we're going back downstairs. Colt's cooking, and Nico's setting up the home cinema."

"Okay," I whisper, my throat parched, desire coursing through my veins. I steal a kiss. A quick, gentle peck.

It doesn't end there.

Conor groans, biting my lip...

He doesn't let me sit up. Grabbing my waist, he scoots me further up the bed, bearing me down until I lay flat.

"We should go," I whisper, not an ounce of conviction in my tone. It comes out like I'm arguing the opposite. "Your brothers are waiting."

"Which is why you'll come hard and fast." He climbs on the bed and pins my wrists far above my head. "You're wet, aren't you?" He spreads his fingers over the middle of my stomach. "So fucking *needy*."

Harsh words spoken with raw, primal delight that sends pulsing need across my nerve endings. I love how he says that, like I'm being bad, and he absolutely craves it.

"Hard and fast," I echo, loving the idea, my brain skipping ahead, drowning in what I know will come... edging, denying, fierce desire. "Please."

He yanks my sweatpants down, palm running the underside of my thigh as he pulls my legs up, knees under my chin.

"Look at you," he whispers, eyeing my pussy, his pupils blown. "All mine."

He's teasing, sliding one finger up and down my folds, up and down... He doesn't give me enough to scratch the itch, let alone make me come. It's frustrating. Blissfully addictive.

I think it might be the greatest weapon in his arsenal. Little touches nowhere near where I want and need him most. The anticipation he builds, how my craving escalating the longer he touches without getting me off... The orgasm he promises and makes me wait. *'Torture.'*

He smiles darkly, pushing my knees to the side as he dips his head to the peak of my nipple. Timing his teeth grazing me through the fabric, he slips two fingers inside me.

"You've seen nothing yet," he whispers, his mouth gliding along my skin until we're eye level, the kiss a breath away. "I haven't even started."

Taking my mouth in a deep, hard kiss, he shows me the truth of his words, pistoning his fingers in and out, teasing my G spot with measured precision.

I moan, gasp, whimper, and he swallows it all, beckoning my orgasm to the surface so fucking fast I forget to breathe.

Minutes.

Three, maybe four. Maybe not even that, and I'm hanging over the precipice, balancing a tightrope, ready to come.

I try to wiggle my hands free. I need something. Sheets, his back, my thighs, anything to sink my nails into. "Let go, please. I need... I need..."

"Will you keep your hands where they are if I let go?"

"No. *God*, no."

He smiles, sealing my lips with featherlight biting kisses. "Then I'm not letting go." His hold tightens, and I'm at his mercy, drowning in pleasure so intense it borders on pain.

The world's shattering at the edges. I don't know how he does it, but the orgasm he's building feels like ten in one and gains momentum every time he brings me oh so close, then eases off.

"Yes, just like that," he encourages, even though *he's* doing all the work.

I can't do much other than take what he offers and dissolve into the mattress, my body in his possession, humming, buzzing like a bee in a watering can.

"Next time, I'll tie you to the headboard. I need that hand." He squeezes the fingers cuffing my wrists. "But you won't keep them here if I let go."

"No," I pant, straining against his hold. I don't want him to let go. Something about being under his command—helpless—adds wood to the fire running rampant beneath my skin. "No, I won't keep them there. God I'm close. So, so close."

"I know, baby." He lets out an amused, breathless chuckle that tickles my nose for a second before he kisses my forehead. "You're clamping around my fingers so hard, but we have a few more minutes. You can wait a little longer."

I open my eyes, staring him down. If looks could kill, he'd be deader than dead. Words clump on my tongue. Instead of telling him off, I'm begging. "Enough. Please, enough. I need... I need, *oh God*—"

The rest is swallowed by my disjointed moans because *now* is when he sends me over the edge.

"Give it to me," he rasps, showering my jaw, cheeks, and eyes with soft kisses.

He crushes his body against me, tethering me in the here and now, and somehow the weight of him magnifies the orgasm. He's not easing off, still working my G spot, teasing out faint tremors, the sensation so intense I'm sure tears stream down my cheeks.

I'm delusional. Overstimulated. Exhausted in the best way. His t-shirt sticks to my damp skin. My moans fill the room, drowning out the music, but I don't care who hears.

"So pretty when you come..." Conor mutters against my forehead. "Shh, baby, I've got you. I'm right here," he adds like he knows I'm losing touch with reality.

Slowly he eases off, gathers me to him, and flips us so I'm on his chest. His hands tangle my hair, lips soothing my temple in slow kisses.

That was by far the most intense orgasm of my twenty-one years. I'm wrung out to the point my bones bend.

"Again?" Conor asks, amusement lacing his voice. "I think you can go again."

"Not for the foreseeable future," I mumble, endorphins roaring through my head as I burrow into his solid chest. "You can't do this to me. Not like this. It's too much, Conor. All I want is to sleep until morning."

"This is nothing, baby. I told you I haven't even started yet. Wait till you come on my cock." He pushes me flat on my back, his eyes glimmering with satisfaction even though he hasn't come. "It doesn't take much to make you look like you've been thoroughly fucked."

"I feel like I've been thoroughly fucked six ways back to Sunday." I run my hands down my face, tucking back a few unruly locks.

Conor huffs quietly, a silent *no, you haven't* hidden in that sound. "Did you call your dad? How are they doing?"

"They're fine. Dad's got enough supplies to last a month."

He leans over me, pressing his lips to mine, and quickly, the sweet peck becomes a full-on, dominant make-out session. As always, he doesn't pass the opportunity to bite my lower lip.

"That'll swell up real nice in a minute."

One more peck, and he rises to his full, over six-foot height. He pulls a black t-shirt from the closet, yanking it over his head.

My breath falters when his back muscles stretch and bulge before the fabric covers the view.

Dozens of different-sized question marks are tattooed over his spine, a long scar running down his right side. I've touched him there but couldn't feel it under my fingertips; it's pale, smooth, and blends almost seamlessly with his skin.

I sit up slowly, certain I'll get a headrush if I'm not careful. Dragging my feet across the carpet, I lock myself in the en suite, wiping between my legs not to make a mess of Conor's sweatpants.

I'm not used to parading around without underwear.

A moment later, we head downstairs. It's not until we're there that I realize the music has changed. Still classical but no longer flowing from the speakers. Now it comes from the piano where Mia sits in crisp white denim overalls, a glass of wine perched on a small, tall table beside her.

Her delicate fingers tickle the keys as she plays "War of Hearts" by Ruelle. Each note reverberates through the acoustic space, electrifying the air and sending goosebumps up my arms.

No wonder Rose wanted to learn from her. She's amazing.

Nico sits on the couch holding a tumbler of whiskey and a remote. A huge screen slowly slides from the ceiling, and a projector hangs on the opposite wall.

"Be a doll, and grab a case of beer from the garage," Cody says, stopping by us with popcorn and eyeing Conor with a smirk. He turns to me after Conor playfully smacks his head while he turns to go downstairs. "What do you want to watch? Action, horror, comedy? Don't say rom-com. Those are banned in this house."

"I don't mind. I've not watched anything in ages, so whatever you choose is good."

TOO STRONG

The microwave dings in the kitchen. The aroma of pizza sauce fills the house, making my stomach remind me I've not eaten anything since breakfast.

"Can I help with anything?" I ask, finding Colt expertly juggling dough.

"Sure. Only the sauce is ready. Grab whatever you like from the fridge and start the toppings." He motions at the island, where three perfectly round, stretched pizza doughs await dressing.

"Anyone here a picky eater?" I ask, checking out the fridge.

"Mia likes cheese and sweetcorn, so make one half just with that. Conor's allergic to asparagus, so none of that. And as long as you don't put pineapple anywhere, it'll be good."

While Colt stretches the dough, I pile up ingredients, wash the vegetables, and slice the cheese before I start layering the toppings.

"First one's ready." I hand the baking stone to Colt, watching him slide it into the pizza oven.

Conor comes back, dropping a case of Coronas by the fridge, then immediately wraps an arm around my middle. A kiss follows. Quick, sweet, and only a touch inappropriate as he sucks my neck, undoubtedly leaving a raw mark.

"You need help?" he asks, snatching a handful of olives.

"Say *no*."

"No, but I wouldn't mind a glass of water."

"Coming up," Cody says, setting a glass of wine beside me. "Grape water."

"That'll do, thanks."

As soon as the pizzas are done, we move to the living room, where Mia's under a thick blanket tucked against Nico. An odd yet soothing visual. I would've never expected a big, scary man like him to act so soft with his girl.

Nico's the kind of man I'd imagine ending up in handcuffs

on domestic abuse charges, but seeing how he handles Mia, it's clear he'd rather break his own hands than hurt her or let anyone else do that. His moves border on extreme protectiveness wherever she's concerned, and I notice that in Conor.

Earlier at the beach, him hanging over me, my mind alight with pleasure... the look in his eyes was nearly as fierce as Nico's whenever he seeks Mia out for a kiss.

I take a deep breath, fanning away the memory of Conor pinning me to the ground. Despite the recent orgasm, I'm ready for more. Ready for him to make good on his promise and *get started*.

Cody picks a movie, pressing play as we all dig in. The takeout Nico mentioned earlier sits in the bin, wet and soggy after he left it on the roof of his car to chase Mia.

She's a great plot twist. Timid and tiny outside, cheeky and brave inside.

"Full?" Conor asks quietly when I fall back after finishing three big slices.

I nod, not wanting to interrupt anyone. He pulls me into his chest, gently manhandling my arms and legs until I'm cuddling his side. Within seconds, his fingers slowly stroke my hair. It's nice. So nice my eyelids grow heavy.

I drink more wine, blinking sleep away, but the next time I blink, the room is dark. I jolt upright, confused for a moment before I adjust and the haziness gives way.

"You fell asleep downstairs," Conor whispers.

I turn to look at him, nothing more than his silhouette visible in the darkness. "I'm sorry. Why didn't you wake me? How did you get me up here?"

Snaking his arm around my middle, he pulls me back down and flips me onto my side, little spoon to his big. "I carried you.

TOO STRONG

Sleep, baby. You're exhausted."

I must be if being hauled up a flight of stairs didn't wake me. "Night, night." I reach under the duvet, take his hand, and wiggle my butt against his warm body.

NINETEEN

By morning, the rain has stopped. The sky cleared, but the mayhem outside hints how bad the storm was. Nico's garden is a mess. Leaves and broken tree branches litter the lawn, and half his furniture drowns in the pool.

Out front, Colt's or Cody's Mustang is damaged, a metal trash can denting the hood.

It's only six am. My biological clock's set to bright and early and won't let me sleep in on a Monday. I should be opening the newsagents right now, but the owner texted last night saying he needs to assess the damage first, so I'm staying put.

I stand in the kitchen, tightening the strings of Conor's sweatpants and wondering if using the coffee maker is overstepping. Conor's brothers are more than welcoming. Even Nico stopped being so scary last night, doting on his fiancée like a good boy, but still...

I've not asked permission so this feels like snooping.

Maybe someone will be up soon.

Sitting by the breakfast bar, I check my phone. There's only one text from Rose—a link to Newport's social page.

The more pictures I scroll, the more my heart sinks. It's a nightmare out there. Debris blocks most roads, and cars lining the curbs are either damaged or trapped under fallen trees. There are pictures of houses throughout Newport with portions of roofs missing, shattered windows, and doors hanging off their hinges. The shops on the main street took a hit too.

Me: How are things at home?

I don't expect a return text until at least eight, but the dots start dancing on the screen a moment later.

Rose: Okay. No lasting damage here or any neighbors as far as I can see, but the big oak tree at the entrance gate lost some huge branches, so we're trapped. Firefighters probably won't get here until they clear the main roads, so you have another night with your boyfriend. How is it at Nico's?

Me: The garden is ruined, and either Colt's or Cody's car got smacked around, but we're all good. Everyone's still asleep.

Rose: I'm surprised you're up. I thought you'd be too exhausted after all the sex to crawl out of bed this morning.

I roll my eyes. She's always been straight to the point, never sugar-coating or tiptoeing around any topics. She blabbed for three hours straight when she lost her V card to her high-school crush a few months ago, then wished the plague on him a couple of weeks later when they broke up.

Me: No sex. I fell asleep watching a movie.

Rose: Jeez, sis! You're so boring. Dad's been asking about Conor.

My heart thumps faster, working pretty well as a caffeine replacement. I put my fingers to work, typing a reply, but another message comes through before I press send.

Rose: Well, not Conor, per se. Just asked if I knew that boyfriend of yours. When will you tell him you're dating a Hayes?

Preferably never. I'm sure his reaction won't be good. While he can't forbid me seeing him, he can make doing so much harder. It would be easiest to move out so he'd no longer have any say in my love life or otherwise, but that takes money. Abby and I are working toward renting a flat together, but we're not there yet financially.

Me: I don't have much choice. I'll talk to him soon.

Rose: Good. He's getting suspicious. Butter him up first. Make Conor sound like a fucking godsend, and maybe it'll go down better.

I don't think she believes that.

Me: You think it'll be rude if I make myself a coffee? No one's up yet.

Rose: God, you're so dumb sometimes! What do you think is gonna happen? They'll publicly hang you or something? Get a fucking coffee.

Easier said than done. You'd think it'd just be a click-of-a-button kind of thing. Unfortunately not. The coffee machine built into the kitchen design is a glorious work of art and high-spec engineering.

There's a touch screen, but the language is set to Italian, so I'm translating the words back and forth on my phone, not daring to blindly click things I don't understand.

After a bit of fumbling, I find the right menu, the right coffee, and even, after searching the cupboards, a cup. But once the machine starts whirring it only pours enough for two, maybe three sips into said cup.

It's not the latte I wanted. This is an espresso.

Something flashes in the corner of the screen, and thanks to Google Translate, I work out it's *milk*. The machine grinds, heaves, and makes me step back from a steam-hissing nozzle.

After two more tries and my frustration mounting high, I give up, settling back into my seat.

The bitter smell wafts in the air, assaulting my senses. While it wakes me to an extent, it's not hot coffee on my tongue.

"Morning," Cody says ten minutes later, making me jump out of my skin when he appears so stealthily I didn't hear him coming until he was right here. "Early bird?" he asks, rubbing sleep from his eyes.

"I normally start work at six. I'm programmed to get up early and don't sleep well in new places."

"You slept just fine on the couch," he chuckles. "Drooled all over Conor's t-shirt."

I scrunch my nose. "At least tell me I wasn't snoring."

"Not that I heard. You had a coffee yet?" He pokes the touchscreen with ease.

"I tried. I couldn't make the machine work. It kept giving me espresso. I clicked *milk*, but it just hissed at me."

Cody opens the fridge, pulling out a small milk jug. "It's a coffee-shop-grade machine. No milk container anywhere, so you need to froth it yourself. C'mon." He waves me over. "I'll show you."

"Why is it set to Italian?"

"It's imported. No English language in the software." He flicks to the main menu, tapping the correct words. "I don't speak Italian like Colt, so I memorized the sequence when we moved here."

"I used Google Translate."

"Now pop the nozzle in the jug," he says once the machine spits another tiny amount of coffee into a tall glass. "Then hold the *milk* button for twenty seconds."

With the grace of an actual barista, he tops up the cup and passes it over, watching me take a sip.

"That's nice, thank you."

"Best coffee you'll ever have, *Little Bee*."

"Keep giving her shit and this..." Conor says, entering the kitchen, finger aimed at Cody's coffee, "will be your last meal."

Cody smirks, winking at me out of Conor's view. "I'm being nice, bro. I like that nickname. Chill. You're starting to sound like Logan."

"Morning." Conor leans in, kissing my neck, then snatches Cody's cup out of his hand. "Thanks, bro."

"Morning. Did I wake you two trying to get this thing working?"

They both shake their heads.

Within the hour, Colt's up, but Nico and Mia don't come down until nine. Since I'm the unexpected, trespassing guest, I offer to make breakfast.

TWENTY

After breakfast, the guys organize another Hayes-wide conference call, checking on everyone. Shawn and Mr. Hayes are the only two at work. Theo's still at the hospital, and Logan's home, or rather in his garden, clearing debris.

We all go out, too. There's not much damage around Nico's neighborhood, but a few smaller trees toppled over, and almost every bin is someplace it shouldn't be. We spend the afternoon clearing the mess with a few other neighbors.

Once again, I'm struck by how considerate the Hayes are. And how overprotective.

Nico growls whenever Mia lifts something he considers too heavy, and when she accidentally slices her hand on broken glass, he's about ready to kill.

"He's very—" I cut myself off, not sure how to finish that sentence as I watch him enter his driveway with Mia in his arms.

"Pick whatever word to finish that sentence, and it'll fit,"

TOO STRONG

Cody supplies with a chuckle, though the way he's watching them disappear behind the bend shows he's equally worried. "It's mostly unwarranted, but he has every right to freak out this time. Mia's got a clotting deficiency. The cut is deep, so if he can't stop the bleeding within half an hour, she needs to go to the hospital, and it won't be easy with the roads closed."

"She'll be fine," Colt says, wiping sweat off his forehead with the back of his muddy hand. "If it doesn't slow down in twenty minutes, I'll stitch her up."

"Shouldn't we check on them?" I ask, hauling a garbage can and picking off trash from the hedges around Nico's property. "Maybe they need help?"

"He won't let us touch her until it's necessary, so there's no point in hovering," Colt explains. "You'll get used to their dynamic," he adds, seeing my questioning eyebrow.

She cuddled into his shoulder yesterday when Nico went upstairs to grab a shower and she sat in Cody's lap this morning, sharing a tub of ice cream with Conor, so the *no touching* makes little sense.

I stop asking questions, busying myself with helping clear up for another twenty minutes before we head inside, calling it a day. Mia's not bleeding anymore, her hand wrapped in gauze.

"C'mon," Conor says. "We could both use a shower."

True. We're filthy, covered in mud, and there's something I really, *really* want that I'd rather be clean for.

***

Conor sits on the bed when I exit the en suite wearing a towel, my skin tingling from the hot shower and anticipation.

I've wanted his hands back on me since yesterday.

I thought he'd jump me the second I woke up last night, but he just tucked me in, even though I could feel his hard cock snuggling against my ass.

I was too sleepy for sex, but when I woke up this morning and Conor still didn't start anything, I realized that despite his deep, passionate kisses, and my two world-changing orgasms, he hadn't once groped me like my previous boyfriends.

I initiated both times, first by grinding into him in his car, then yesterday, too, and even when I pulled him back down at the beach. I think the reins are in my hands. I dictate the pace.

Unless I make the first move, clearly showing him I want him, he won't take until we get carried away again.

I stop between his knees, weaving my fingers through his messy dark hair. I love how the thick curly tangles feel. How he always smells like peppermint, leather, and pomegranates. How he looks at me like there's nothing and no one he wants more.

"You're trembling," he says, his fingertips gently stroking the back of my knee. "Are you cold?" He peers up in time to catch me shaking my head. "Scared?"

"A little."

His other arm immediately loops around the back of my thighs, pulling me the last step forward. "Why?"

"I'm scared you'll say no."

His eyebrows draw together, then relax when I hook my finger in the towel and let it slide down my legs. It lands half-draped over his knee, half-piled on the floor.

"I will never say *no* to you."

Lips first. Warm, soft, full lips kiss my abdomen.

Then his hands glide up my legs until he holds me in the most affectionate yet sensually arousing way imaginable. One arm under my butt, the other lined with my spine, fingers caressing my nape.

He noses a line up my tummy, trailing open-mouthed kisses and leaving goosebumps behind. "Remember our first date?" he whispers, his breath heating my skin.

"Yes, why?"

"Remember what I told you when you stood there with your eyes closed?" He takes my thighs, moving me until I straddle his lap, my pussy pressing against the hard-on beneath his sweatpants. "What did I say?"

"That you already knew it wouldn't be our last date."

"No. Tell me exactly what I said."

I rest my hands on his shoulders, sketching small circles with my thumbs. "You said *I already know, Little Bee.*"

"That's right. I couldn't tell you then. You'd run away screaming, but I wanted you to remember that moment, so when I finally could tell you, you'd know when I knew."

"Knew what?"

"That I love you." Sincerity and fathomless affection shine from his deep, brown eyes.

"We've not had sex yet. How can you love me?"

A small smile twitches his lips as he says, "I can't love you until I impale you on my dick?"

"I didn't say that. I just... I've had a few... *partners*. I know how this goes. Don't tell me you love me just because you think that's what I want to hear."

"I've been in love with you since I first kissed you." He floats his lips along my collarbone, big hands roaming up and down my back. "I'll love feeling you come when I finally get inside you, but I don't need that to know you fit me so fucking right. Otherwise, I would've loved every girl that hit my sheets since I was fifteen."

"But you didn't…"

He smiles, gripping the base of my neck and pulling me down, our kiss a breath away. "Not one. You've been with other guys. You know sex and feelings don't always go together."

"They rarely do," I admit, thinking about the men in my past. It's nothing like that with Conor. He's more. We're more than I could ever anticipate. "I can't tell you I love you. Not yet."

"Good. I don't want you to say it back. I want you to say it when you feel it."

I close the last inch parting our lips, teasing his tongue for a second before he seizes control, dominating the moment the way he always does. Tasting, sucking, nipping, devouring me like this is our first kiss.

"You sure you're ready for me, Little Bee?"

"I'm sure," I whisper in his mouth. "I need you more than you need me."

"Not possible." He gouges his fingers into the flesh of my butt, flipping me over, and crouches on his calves. Dark eyes rove my naked body inch by inch. "God… I want so much from you tonight I don't know where to start."

"Start by taking your t-shirt off."

A tight smirk curves his lips, and he obliges, doing that sexy back-of-the-neck collar tug before his tee hits the floor.

"Now what?"

"Your jeans."

He kicks them off, leaving nothing on but his boxers before he climbs back over me, skimming his hands up my thighs to cup my butt, squeezing lightly.

"I'm on the pill," I blurt out as he drags me lower, pulling me under him, elbows flush with my arms.

"I wouldn't care if you weren't."

My eyes pop wide. "What?"

"You heard me." He nips the conversation as his lips come down on mine.

My entire body ripples.

Waves of pleasant heat hit time and time again, my breaths coming in shallow gasps the more he pushes against me. I'm consumed by him, by the newness of how caring, tender, and passionate he is compared to what I'm used to.

Sex has always been a quick deed. Not much foreplay. No overpowering feelings... it's different with Conor. Every time his fingers touch my skin it jolts me like a mind-blowing, beautiful electric current.

I hook my fingers in the elastic of his boxers, tugging them down in one go and letting him kick them aside. His cock springs out, slapping my thigh. Without peeking, I know he's the biggest I've ever had.

"You think I'll get right into it, don't you?" he humorously hums in my mouth. "Baby... I told you I haven't even started yet. You've no idea what you're getting into with me. I'll make you scream. I'll make you beg for more even while you're coming undone for the fifth time."

He nudges my chin with his nose, hot lips latching onto the delicate skin of my throat, sucking, pecking, *biting* between words. My mind focuses on him, every sense starved for his words and touch.

"I'll bend you to my will."

And I'll bend like a rubber band.

I already do. I can't get enough of him. The way he speaks. The way he looks at me like I'm the most important person in his life, even though we only met a few weeks ago. This thing between us moves at warp speed, and we're both falling hard.

He might have beat me to *I love you*, but I'm not far behind. I'm just trying not to let the thought sink.

It's too soon, isn't it? I shouldn't feel so attached so quick, but I can't help it.

"What do you taste like?" he muses.

The question isn't aimed at me. More like he's voicing his thoughts, twirling his tongue over my pebbled nipple. He toys the other between his fingers, pinching, rolling, and driving me wild.

Satisfied with my hips arching off the mattress, pleading for more, he grips my thighs, pushes my legs back, then rests my ankles over his shoulders. The first tiny kiss to my mound forces the air from my lungs.

"You're trouble," I sigh. "Stop teasing."

"Teasing is the best part, Little Bee."

Spreading me with his thumbs, he licks me slowly, bottom to top, dragging the flat of his tongue up and over my clit. And then he sucks. Hard. The sting lights up my mind. Neurons fire up, and my thighs quiver in time with a surprised gasp.

"You taste like *mine*."

I grasp his hair, forcing him back down, and feel him smile against my pussy.

"Greedy... needy... *dirty* little thing." He punctuates every word with a thorough lick, and then... the show begins.

"Oh my," I mewl, fisting his hair. "*God*. This is so nice."

He doesn't respond with words. Instead, he slides one finger inside, timing the thrusts with the flicks of his tongue.

Just as I expected, just as I *hoped*, he doesn't let me come when the orgasm looms close by. He eases off, kissing and biting my inner thigh as his big hands knead my hips until I cool down.

He does that once.

TOO STRONG

Twice.

And again.

And again...

By the fifth denial, a mist of sweat coats my neck. Whenever he comes up for air, breathing softly on my clit, I spasm, almost crawling out of my skin.

"Show me your eyes," Conor coos. "Show me how much you want to come."

"So much," I pant, looking into his aroused, blown pupils. He holds my gaze, tongue out, licking slowly up to my apex, and the visual of him between my legs, staring at me as he inflicts so much pleasure, is almost enough to tip me over. *Almost.* "So *so* much... I might kill you if you don't let me come."

His eyes light up as he pushes two fingers back in, curling them quickly. "I might spill on the fucking sheets if I don't get inside you soon, so we're cutting this session short."

"Short?!" I gasp, my back bowing off the mattress. "It's been like an hour already."

"Barely ten minutes, baby. We'll get to hours soon, I promise." His head drops down, torturing my clit with his tongue.

I'm so ready for the orgasm it's mere seconds before it hits. I'm vaguely aware I've clamped my thighs around his head, holding him hostage as he licks me through the release.

I'm even less aware of how loud I am because blood inundates my head, briefly muting the world.

I'm here is the first thing I register.

"I've got you, baby."

He's suddenly closer, higher, his arms flush to my sides. He doesn't wait until my boneless ass catches a breath or tunes back into the here and now before he moves between my legs.

One long, slow thrust almost has me coming again. He

drives himself home, letting out a low growl that forces my body into high alert.

"Fuck," he breathes, pressing his lips to my forehead. "So wet. So tight... so fucking *mine*. Are you back, baby? Look at me."

My lips twist into a smile. "I didn't go anywhere."

"Nowhere but higher than the clouds," he admits, buried inside me, unmoving. "Eyes, Vee."

I obey, looking into the abyss of his black pupils as white spots blur my vision. "I'm a little lightheaded... dizzy."

"You're breathing too shallow and too fast when you come, that's why. Take a deep breath for me." He pecks my nose. "Good, another one. Better?"

I nod, wrapping my limp hands around his neck when his hips shift back before he bottoms out inside me. I'm almost bracing for a wild ride, but it doesn't come.

After everything he said, I expected relentless, almost brutal sex. I expected the bed hammering the wall. I thought he'd move my body into ten different positions. I thought he'd make this fast and hard enough my pussy will hurt for days, but his moves are so damn cautious.

Caring. Tender. Slow.

But somehow, the force of his moves quadruples in seconds. Still slow but so thorough I feel every inch sliding in and out like I'm too tight to take him.

His grip on my waist is nothing short of possessive. His thrusts calculated to drive me crazy. Every look of his dark eyes is loaded with emotion. Even though the pace is nowhere near frantic, it's the most stimulating experience in my life.

He's not mindlessly ramming into me as fast as his body allows. No, he's building the moment, and I quickly realize that *this*... this might be the sweetest form of torture.

TOO STRONG

He's got me in a pot, flames licking the bottom. The water's getting warmer. Every nibbling, biting kiss, every time he sinks into me, every push meticulous... the temperature soars.

I miss the moment it gets too hot, and I'm boiling, coming hard. So hard my eyes water. Thighs cramp. I try to swallow the sounds I can't control, biting the back of my hand, but it's useless.

"Eyes, Vee," he rasps, bracing his hand against my throat. "I'll teach you how to breathe evenly when you can't catch enough air." He waits until I look at him before his fingers tighten bit by bit. "Tell me when it gets too much. Breathe in time with my fingers. When I clench, breathe in. When I don't, breathe out. Got it?"

I nod, still delusional, still drifting in pure ecstasy land.

I don't think he wants me to recover. He pistons into me, not changing the pace one iota as he drives himself home over again. The weight of his big body pinning me to the mattress magnifies how erotic this feels. How close we are.

The precise, measured, long strokes, how his cock massages me from the inside, hitting the sweet spot, amplifies pleasure.

My body's weak, my legs quiver, and the little oxygen I'm pulling down multiplies the sensations tenfold. He guides my breathing, and even though I barely feed my lungs any oxygen, I don't feel like I'll faint any second.

I part my mouth, pulling in short, measured breaths, and Conor dips his head, licking my bottom lip, then sucks and bites, never once breaking the torturous tempo of his hips.

"Good, easy, baby. You're doing great. I'll cut you off completely for fifteen seconds. When I let go, take a deep, steady breath. Don't panic, okay? I'll *never* hurt you."

A single nod is the only answer I can give while the pleasure inside me stacks up, growing faster the harder he squeezes my neck. As soon as he completely cuts off my air supply, a shudder ripples my body, and my eyes close in pure bliss.

My ears ring. The pressure mounts so high it feels like I'll burst, and when the orgasm hits, it compresses me from all sides, stripping my mind of a firewall I didn't even know was there in the first place.

"That's it," Conor breathes into my mouth, loosening the hold on my neck. "Steady breath, baby." He smiles against me when I comply. "*That's* how you should come every time. So hard you don't know where's up and where's down. So hard you feel like you're drowning in that high."

White spots dance before my eyes again, dissolving slowly, and his voice sounds distant.

"Yes, please," I mutter, only now realizing he came, too. "But maybe not so hard that I don't notice when you come."

He kisses a line in the valley between my breasts, then sucks my nipple, gently scuffing it with his teeth. "Harder," he says before he gets up, and my breath catches in my throat.

He's still hard and... how he managed to fit *that* inside me with such ease will forever remain a mystery. It's not about the length. I've been with a guy with an abnormally long dick, and Conor's right up there, too. It's the girth that has me stupefied.

None of my exes came anywhere near his size.

Must be why I felt every single thrust.

"You look like you want to lick me, Vee," he muses, pulling a tee from the closet and throwing it for me to catch. "I won't say no to that idea."

"Good luck fitting your cock in my mouth."

"It fits in your pussy." He rests both fists on the bed and leans over me. "It'll fit in your mouth and your ass just fine,

TOO STRONG

too. You were made for me, baby." He bends to kiss my forehead. "Wait here. I'll grab a washcloth."

I swallow hard, watching the door of the en suite close behind him. I'm no stranger to getting guys off with my mouth, but my ass... nope.

That's off-limits.

TWENTY-ONE

Conor

I glance in the mirror, catching sight of long, red lines incised down my shoulders and back.

Vee's beautiful face, all pink from oxygen deprivation, will always be my favorite view.

I planned this session longer. I wanted to make her come on my lips and fingers at least once more, but her last orgasm stripped *my* fucking sanity.

I didn't have to move. In fact, I wasn't moving. I was still, balls-deep inside Vee's pussy, watching her come, listening to the breathless, titillating gasps, and that's all it took.

You'd think I'm sixteen again. No control.

I clean myself off, grab a washcloth, run it under the faucet, and go back to bed. Vee's flat on the bed, my t-shirt draped over her beautiful body.

"Oh, thank you," she says, reaching for the washcloth only to have her hand swatted away. "I'll do it myself, Conor. I—"

"I fill you, and I clean you. That's how it'll work with us, so make peace with it fast." I grip her hips, pulling her closer to the edge of the bed, and nudging her knees. "Open up."

She shakes her head, sinking those white teeth into her bottom lip. A gesture that instantly makes me feral.

"I don't want you to do this. I can clean myself up."

"Either you open your legs and let me wipe my cum off your sweet pussy, or I'll push your knees back to your chest and finger-fuck you until you're dripping... and I'll still get my way."

Her eyes widen, telling me which option she prefers. I toss the washcloth onto the bedside table, drawing Vee even closer. Close enough that her ass hangs over the edge of the bed, leaving her no choice but to pull her knees back far enough to keep her balance.

"Perfect," I say, looking her over. "Next time I have you like this, I want you in knee-high socks and a bralette."

She holds my gaze as I touch the underside of her knee and slide along the back of her thigh, making her squirm.

"You're making a bigger mess," she half-says, half-moans when I dip two fingers in her pussy.

"I don't give a fuck about the mess," I whisper when her head falls back as she grinds into my hand. "I'll have so much fun testing your limits, baby. Something tells me you're tough to satiate."

Case in point. She just came three times, so hard she wasn't far from blacking out, but here she is, soaking wet and a little sticky as I stroke her G spot, dipping my head to her lips.

"That's it. You're loving this, aren't you? You want me to own you, Little Bee? I took it easy on you before. You think you can handle me when my brakes give out?"

I kiss the column of her throat, fastening her wrists to the mattress above her head with my free hand, doubling my efforts the more her walls spasm around my fingers.

Every soft moan flying past her lips adds more blood to my cock. I press it against her hip, letting her feel how much I fucking want her even though I just had her.

"You think you'll love it when I've got you helpless, tied, unable to move, my hand on your throat, controlling how much air you pull down?"

An incoherent whisper is the only answer I get.

Fuck. I thought I could do this, but my cock wants to join the action too much to ignore.

"No, no, please... I'm so close," she whines when I pull my fingers out, flip her onto her stomach, and spread her wider, one knee bending to her chest, the other leg arrow straight. "Oh God..." she gasps when I enter her, falling forward as I brace on my elbows to stop me burying her in the mattress.

"We'll be fucking like bunnies for weeks before we go back to dinners, walks, and spending time with other people," I say, pulling out and pushing back in. "I'd grab the edge of the bed if I were you. And maybe bite the pillow."

The second I plunge back into her, she takes both suggestions to heart and goes one step further, seizing fistfuls of the comforter, her spine denting beautifully.

"Tap out if it's too much, okay?"

"Yes, yes, okay, just don't stop."

I don't. Not when she comes the first time, nor less than a minute later when she comes again, gouging her nails deep enough into my arm to hurt.

My hand lands on her butt, the clap reverberating throughout the room. It probably travels downstairs, too. Her ass pinks up, and she floods my cock with more arousal.

TOO STRONG

"Your pussy tells me you like that," I groan, resting my forehead on the back of her head.

I'll find every single thing that makes this girl tick. I'll make every one of her fantasies come true, even if it fucking kills me.

***

Bunnies might be an understatement. We don't leave the room for the rest of the night. By the time we're ready to take a break, we've gone three more rounds.

We're sweaty and sticky, so I haul Vee into the shower, quickly wash off, and change the bedsheets while she's brushing her teeth.

Mia stopped by—thankfully between sessions two and three—to drop off girly toiletries, so Vee's got the essentials, and I add *shopping for girly shit* to my list.

I want her to have everything she might need here, even if it means buying sanitary pads or pink razor blades.

The next morning I expect Vee to be out of bed already when I wake up, but she's asleep on her back, face burrowed into the pillow. Three minutes later, she's not sleeping. She jerks the covers aside, cheeks bright pink when she finds me between her legs, licking her awake.

"Morning, baby. Don't mind me," I say, pushing a finger inside her. "As you were. Put the covers back."

"You're insane," she muses, her lips forming an *o* when I add a second finger and suck her clit. "Oh shit... I take that back." She covers my head with the comforter. "You're a genius. A very generous, *oh, God...* genius."

I huff a laugh.

Once again, there's no way I can deny myself the pleasure

of feeling her convulsing in climax around my cock.

She's fucking addictive, this girl.

Pretty, soft, wet... mine.

Twenty minutes later, she's too mellow to protest when I fetch a washcloth and clean her up, pressing a few soft kisses on her thigh. I could get used to having her around all the time real fast...

"I should start working out to keep up with you." She stretches on the bed while I pull out fresh clothes. "My legs feel like jelly."

"We'll be back in bed as soon as we eat."

"I'm not hungry, and you... you already ate this morning."

I smirk, tossing her a pair of sweatpants. "C'mon, smartass. How are you planning on keeping up with me if you don't eat? You're a flimsy thing. You'll pass out before noon."

"You want to spend the rest of the day in bed?"

"No. I want to spend the rest of the day in *you*."

She gets up, smiling at me like she did on Halloween before she learned my last name. "That can be arranged."

Everyone's already downstairs when we join them ten minutes later. Cody's brewing everyone coffee while Colt's making breakfast.

The smell of fresh omelets lingers in the air, reminding me how hungry I am. I don't usually go an hour without munching something, but I've not eaten anything other than Vee's pussy since six o'clock last night.

My stomach has wrapped itself around my spine by now.

"Are you going somewhere?" I ask Nico, seeing he's dressed to head out.

"Yeah, the roads to the hospital are fairly clear, so we'll visit Theo and Thalia."

TOO STRONG

"Do you know how the roads are around Bayside Trailer Park?" Vee asks, her cheeks blooming at the word *trailer*. Her eyes flicker to my brothers as if she expects to catch them... I don't know, pulling faces or something?

"Yeah, Shawn said most of the town is clear. You can get over there fine, but the road leading up to the park is still blocked, so cars can't go through."

"It's not a long trek. I should probably get back home." She looks at me, her pretty eyes apologetic. "My boss texted me last night that he's reopening the shop tomorrow, so I guess *The Well* will be back in business, too."

As if her father can hear our conversation, her phone rings, *Dad* flashing on the screen before Vee rushes out, soft footsteps pitter-pattering away until I can't hear a word she's saying.

"You need a soundproof bedroom, bro," Cody heaves, leaning closer to me, so he doesn't have to raise his voice. "Man, what kind of steroids are you on? You were at it for hours!"

"What I need is my own place."

"No," Nico snaps. "You're not even out of college, and you." He points a finger at Cody, his features pinching into his signature expression that makes you want to flee for your very life. "Get some fucking earplugs. I've heard you with different girls more times than I can count, yet I never gave you any shit."

Colt scoffs, leaning against the counter. "He's not giving him shit, bro. He's looking for pointers."

"Find a girl you'll just want to *watch*, and you'll be fine," I chuckle, patting Cody's shoulder before turning to Nico. "We graduate in five months. I'm not sure if you remember, but you're not our father."

He grinds his teeth, temper flaring quicker than a struck match, but just when he's about to go off, Mia's heels click-clack down the stairs and Nico's entire demeanor changes before our eyes. He cracks his neck, inhaling a calming breath. The sheer thought of his girl works wonders on his mental state.

"We'll talk about you moving out when you graduate."

We'll see about that.

TWENTY-TWO

Vee

While the town is still in disarray, the trailer park mostly escaped the hurricane's wrath.

There's more trash littering the ground than on a normal day, but the trailers in sight seem in good shape, ours included. After the hurricane a decade ago, Dad did a great job bolting it to the ground and securing the roof and windows to withstand the worst winds.

The only thing that took a hit is Rebecca's clay-pot vegetable garden, now notably missing. Either it got whisked away by the wind, or the pots shattered, and Dad already cleared the mess. Rebecca never showed much enthusiasm for gardening, so I doubt she's upset.

Dad's not home when I cross the threshold. His car sits in its usual spot, so he must've walked to work this morning. Rebecca's there, though, mixing something on the stove, the trailer stuffy and filled with the scent of burnt potatoes.

TOO STRONG

"You finally made it home," she says, looking over her shoulder. "Your dad was worried."

"He didn't sound worried over the phone," I point out, kicking my shoes off.

"He couldn't tell you to come home with the roads being closed, but he griped for two days that he doesn't even know where to look for you if anything goes wrong." She flips a strand of hair over her shoulder, assuming the same pose she uses when interrogating Rose: shoulders back, chin high, one eyebrow raised. "Maybe if you'd introduce your new boyfriend to us, he'd feel better with you staying over there."

"I will. Once I'm sure he's worth it."

I'm already sure, but introducing Conor to Dad won't go well, so I'm buying all the time I can. With Christmas approaching, I should wait until after the holidays.

"You're awfully secretive about him. Is he much older?"

"No, he's my age."

"A criminal?"

"Of course not. He's in college."

"Ah…" she drawls with a smirk as she turns back to stir whatever she's cooking. "So a rich boy."

Rose enters the living room, arms crossed over her chest, her fringe long enough to partially cover her eyes. "I'm in college, Mom. Doesn't make me a rich girl, does it?"

"No, I don't suppose it does, but you wouldn't be in college without Vivienne." She turns back to me, eyes narrowed. "I just don't understand why your boyfriend's such a secret? He never once dropped you off here, and you've not brought him around. We don't even know his name. If you can't tell us about him, there must be something wrong with him."

"Maybe if you'd stop treating us like kids, you'd know

what's happening in our lives, and we wouldn't keep secrets!"

"Watch your attitude, Rose. We're not treating you like kids. We're worried. You'll understand when you have kids."

Looks like this argument is about more than just my reluctance to bring Conor around.

Something must've happened while I was gone.

"Your fringe needs trimming, Rose," I say, eager to find out what bent Rebecca so out of shape. "Another week, and you won't see anything."

She nods, turns on her heel, and retreats to our room. That's my cue, but Rebecca blocks my way before I can follow.

"You're an adult, Vee, but you still live here, which means you'll respect our rules. Until you bring your boyfriend over, you're not spending another night with him."

My blood boils. "I've been nothing but supportive my whole goddamn life, Becca. I missed out on college so I could help you and Dad. I'm paying for Rose's tuition so I can't save enough to move out but make no mistake: if you force my hand, I *will* start thinking about myself, and you'll either have to find another job or tell your daughter she has to drop out of college. You'll meet my boyfriend when I'm ready to bring him over here."

With that, I follow Rose into our room and slam the door, my chest rigid. "What the hell is her problem?" I ask.

"No idea. She's been bitchy the whole time you were gone."

"Did they fight?"

"Not that I heard. Dad didn't mind you being gone, just so you know. He did ask me if I knew your boyfriend, so I said I don't because he'd start digging, and I wasn't sure how much you told him. It's Mom who kept telling him to find out where you are. She's probably worried you'll move out and stop bringing money in."

"I'll have to move out someday."

"I think she hopes you'll stay until I finish college."

I comb her hair forward, detangling it before I start cutting. "You've just started. I'm not staying here another three years."

"Where will you live?" she asks, her tone cheeky, implying I'll move in with Conor.

"I almost saved up enough to rent a flat. If not for my car breaking down, I could move out with Abby in three months."

"It's going to suck here when you move out."

"At least you'll have the room to yourself. You can invite boys for *sleepovers*."

She chuckles, shaking her head and messing up the parting I made to cut her hair straight. "Yeah, imagine Dad when I bring a guy here to stay the night. He'll whip out the shotgun in no time. Besides..." She looks at me in the mirror, her brow furrowed, a pained expression distorting her pretty face. "Liam and I broke up again. He's such an asshole."

I tilt her chin, urging her not to move as I redo the parting. "What did he do this time?"

"I caught him feeling up some blonde skank at that frat party last weekend. He can't keep it in his pants to save his life, I swear. I mean, it's not like I don't give him any, so I don't know why he's looking for more."

I take half an inch off her fringe before layering and blending. "He's a guy, sis. He's eighteen so his testosterone is raging. It doesn't excuse him, of course, but it's something you should know. Dump his ass once and for all. He doesn't deserve you."

We chat about college, Conor, and whatever comes to mind for over two hours. It's been a while since we had a good heart-to-heart. We've been so busy lately we forgot to make time for each other.

    I've missed this.

TWENTY-THREE

Conor

Bliss. Pure fucking *bliss* for three weeks straight. Dinners, sex, quick strolls on the beach, sex, kisses, cuddles, and more sex.

Sex that's off the fucking charts. Vee's adventurous, fearless, and keen to try every depraved thing that springs to my mind.

I tied her hands to the headboard, edging her for an hour straight last week. She sucked my dick as I navigated Newport, driving from *The Well* back to Nico's so we could fuck before she had to head home at midnight. I had my fingers in her pussy while she sat between my legs on the beach, her back to my chest. My jacket covered the indecency but did nothing to muffle her climactic gasps and moans as we watched the waves foam at the shore.

Pure. Fucking. *Bliss.*

Right until it bursts like a soap bubble.

"No, that's... I can't take this," Vee mutters, holding her Christmas gift at arm's length like a bomb about to explode.

TOO STRONG

It's Boxing Day. I planned to give her the gift before Christmas, but it'd raise questions if she opened it at home, so I held off. Her dad still doesn't know about me, and the secrecy eats away at me bit by fucking bit.

"Take it back," she says louder, shoving the box into my chest. "I can't accept it."

I knew *Gucci* glaring from the box would be enough to start a fucking fight. "Why not? You haven't even opened it yet," I grind out, my temper detonating. She's so stubborn it sets my teeth on edge. "It's a gift, Vee. It's Christmas."

"A very expensive gift."

"So?"

"*So?*" she clips, shoving the box into my chest. "So I can't take it. It's too much, okay? I... I—"

"It's just money."

"Yeah... *just* money because *you* have it."

"I do, and I choose how I spend it. Today, I want to spend it on *you*. Where's the harm in that?" I step back, leaving the gift in her hand.

"It's not fair!" she snaps, throwing the box on the bed, her cheeks glowing. "I don't have anything to give back."

"You do. You just don't want to give it."

Her eyebrows bunch, confusion dappling her pretty face. "What? I don't have anything, Conor."

"You, baby. I want *you*."

"What do you mean? You have me. I'm yours."

"I have you when we're at the beach. I have you when we're at *Ruby's* or *The Well*, but I lose you as soon as there's any representation of money around me. You're shutting me out, Vee. Consciously or not, you don't fucking see *me*. You just see the money and how different it makes us."

I sit on the bed, feeling defeated. Just when I think we're past this issue that only resides inside her head, she proves me wrong.

"You think we won't work," I continue, my insides wriggling into knots. "I don't know how to show you that money doesn't matter. That I'm the same person whether we're eating hotdogs at the pier or lobster at Nico's restaurant, and so are you. You're killing me whenever you pull away."

Silence falls upon us. Deafening. Charged.

Vee's not talking. Not moving either, silent and still while I sit on the bed, my face hidden in my hands, heart ricocheting against my ribs.

But then she makes a sound...

A choked-back whimper penetrates my ears, and my stomach bottoms out. I'm up faster than I can form a coherent thought.

She still stands in the same spot, eyes filled with tears, some already crawling down her nose, lips parted, but no words escape, only a pained wail.

"Jesus," I hiss, feeling like I've been hit in the gut by a bulldozer. I grip her thighs, hauling her into my arms. "Shh, don't cry. It's okay. I'm sorry."

"No." She clings to me, her tears dampening my shoulder. "You're right, I'm shutting you out, but I'm—I'm just..." she stutters, scrunching the t-shirt on my back. "I'm—"

"Scared," I finish for her, taking her to bed, my back against the headboard, her warm, trembling body curving into me. "Don't cry," I whisper, skimming my lips against her temple. "Please, baby, calm down. I can't fucking breathe when you cry."

She inhales deeply, swallowing hard before she speaks. "I'm not doing it to hurt you. I'm just... I'm protecting myself, and I get so angry sometimes because—" Another whimper tears out of her, and I swear, it rips my heart right out of my chest. "I like this," she murmurs, nuzzling her face in my neck. "I like those restaurants you take me to. I like your family, your car, this big house, and the gift, and I hate that I like it. It feels like I'm betraying where I came from. I feel so guilty having lobster with you while my family's eating mac and cheese."

My arms cocoon her, my lips almost glued to her head. "There's nothing wrong with liking nice things. Everyone wants a better life, Vee. It's okay to have it, you know? Your dad would be happy to know you're happy..."

She chuckles into my neck, but the tears keep flowing. "I'm sorry. I know I'm messed up."

"You're not messed up. You're careful. I get it, but you need to trust me. I don't care where you're from or how much you have. You need to do the same."

She nods a few times, then inches away, pouting her lips. For a moment, she's composed, but the dam shatters again, and more tears spill. "I'm sorry."

"Don't apologize." I wipe her cheeks with my thumbs, pulling her in for a kiss. "Don't cry. Please don't cry, and don't think I'll let you forget the gift. I want you to wear it, Little Bee."

She chuckles, kissing my forehead before she leans out to snatch the box. She pulls out a gold watch, smiling as she scrutinizes the bee motif on the face before clasping it around her wrist. "It's beautiful, but—" She bites her tongue, shaking her head to dismiss the thought. "Thank you."

"That's my girl. See? Not that hard, right?"

Vee slips her hand down my stomach, making camp by the zipper. "You're right. Not that hard."

I groan through a laugh. Her cheeks still glisten with left-behind tears, but she's smiling as she tugs the zipper, then crams her hand into my boxers.

She's so fucking bizarre sometimes.

Her small hand winds around my shaft, jerking awkwardly in the tight space. It's not enough.

I flip Vee over until she's flat on the bed, then stand, ripping my hoodie off. She's there in a heartbeat, her big eyes looking up as she yanks my pants over my ass enough to allow my cock more breathing room.

Without a moment's hesitation, she takes me into her mouth.

"Fuck," I groan. The heat of her lips induces a tremor of pleasure intense enough to buckle my knees.

Her long nails bite into my hips, and she slides her lips further, breathing through her nose to hold off the gag reflex from settling in too early. She sucks me as far down as she can, then pulls back, twirling her hot tongue around the tip before repeating the entire thing again.

And again.

And again, taking me deeper every time, driving me to the brink within minutes.

"Do it," she encourages. "I can feel how much you're fighting not to take over. Do it."

She's so fucking perfect.

I grip her in place by the hair as I take over, sliding in and out of her mouth, hitting her throat with every deep thrust. She dances her teeth along the underside of my shaft, barely scratching, but it works wonders, elevating the orgasm that hits when she hollows her cheeks.

I pull out, painting her neck with cum while she holds her hands under her chin so I don't accidentally spill on her face.

***

TOO STRONG

"Should we join your brothers?" Vivienne asks an hour later, even though she looks about ready to fall asleep scribbling small shapes all over my chest. "Technically, it's still Christmas."

Technically it is. Just for a few more hours, but I guess we shouldn't lock ourselves in the bedroom for the rest of the night while they watch *The Grinch* downstairs.

"Probably. But first..." I push her onto her back, resting on my elbow. "I want you to come with me tomorrow."

"Where?"

"My parents' house. Everyone will be there. It's Grandma's birthday, so Mom's throwing a party. I want you to meet the rest of the family."

She takes a while to reply, lost in thought, weighing her options. Before she makes her mind up, her medication reminder alarm goes off.

"I'll grab your purse and a glass of water." I sweep my thumb across the screen, then jog downstairs, snatching Vee's purse from the console table in the hallway.

"Will you join us this evening?" Colt asks with a grin when I enter the kitchen. "Theo's on his way over with River."

"Is that supposed to convince me?" I chuckle, pulling a glass from the cabinet. "Thalia's not coming?"

"No. Theo's giving her a few hours to catch up on sleep."

I doubt she had much of it since River was born. That kid is a screamer. According to Mom, he takes after his daddy. We heard stories last night about how whiny Theo was in the first year of his life.

"We'll be down in a bit," I say, fishing an orange prescription bottle from Vee's purse. "Ten minutes."

He waves me off, and a moment later, I'm back upstairs, watching Vee swallow the pill and dry the glass.

"Okay, I'll come with you tomorrow, but... what do I wear? A dress? Long? Short? Formal?"

I crawl in beside her. "Whatever you feel like."

"I don't want to stand out."

"You won't, I promise. It's not a formal party, baby. No dress code." I pull her in closer. I catch myself doing it often... I'm so fucking clingy it makes me cringe sometimes. "Theo's on his way over, so we should head downstairs, but before that, what about *your* family? When do I get to meet them? When will you start spending the night?"

I want her falling asleep beside me every night and eating breakfast together each morning. It's odd she's keeping me a secret, and it bugs me more as the weeks go by.

It's also odd that her father has so much control over her. She's an adult, more than capable of making her own decisions. He shouldn't have a say in who Vee dates.

And maybe he doesn't.

Maybe she's making this out to be bigger than it is. Vee's got that sense of higher purpose about her. She feels responsible for her family—especially Rose—to the point she could rival Nico's protectiveness, and I think it's *Rose* she's looking out for most when she takes on the obedient daughter role.

Vee shifts position, remaining silent, voicelessly answering the question. It stings, I won't lie, but I don't let it get to me. I try not to overthink and wonder whether she's ashamed she's falling in love with me.

She's not.

Just scared of her dad's reaction and disappointment.

"Should I go with you? Introduce myself? Maybe he won't make it a big deal if he meets me?"

She shakes her head, kissing my jawline. "I'll talk to him

tonight, okay?"

"Whenever you're ready."

Theo's already here when we join everyone downstairs. He shimmies out of his jacket, draping it over the banister, and crouches by River's car seat, pulling his little blue hat off.

"How's the whiny baby doing?" Nico asks, emerging from the living room.

"Watch how you talk about my son," Theo snaps, then makes a weird face at River.

"I was talking about you, bro."

"Yeah, what's with the middle-of-the-night chat group messages?" Cody asks, elbowing Theo aside to lift River out of the car seat. "You woke me up twice last night." He cradles the little boy, softly pinching his nose. "Your daddy's such a wuss. So you don't sleep well; it's not your fault you've got colic, right?"

"I've not slept longer than two hours in one go since he was born," Theo says on a long exhale. "Give him back, Cody."

"No way. Get your own."

"He *is* my own. Give him back."

Cody flips him off, marching into the living room with River in his arms.

"Why don't you crash in the guest bedroom, and we'll watch River for a few hours?" Mia suggests when we follow Cody.

He's one-handedly constructing a blanket nest in the corner of the couch. "Yeah, go get some sleep. Maybe you'll quit whining."

"Asshole," Theo mutters. "Wait till you have a kid."

They bicker for a few minutes, and after more encouragement, Theo takes up our offer, disappearing upstairs to catch up on sleep, just like his wife is at home.

The first half an hour goes without a hiccup, but then River starts pulling horseshoe faces, and before we know it, he's crying. We all take turns trying to calm him, but nothing's working.

"I think we'll have to get Theo," I say, moments away from grabbing Vee and dragging her upstairs to escape the noise. "Maybe he's hungry?"

"Hold him over your shoulder," Vivienne tells Mia, who rocks River back and forth in her arms.

"You're welcome to try," Mia says, and my entire body tightens, my heart cranking up when Vee cradles River to her chest.

"You look good, baby," I say, watching as she moves his head to rest on her shoulder. "You want one?"

She beams at me, taking it as a joke.

It's not, though.

I wasn't kidding when I told her I'd be okay if she weren't on the pill. I wouldn't mind getting her pregnant.

"One day, sure," she admits, gently rocking River, smoothing his back with her hand. "In a few years."

"How about a few months? Nine is a nice number."

"Stop messing around," she laughs softly. "Have you been drinking when I wasn't looking?"

Behind the smile, a glimmer of panic fills her eyes, and I know it's way too soon for this, so I smile right back, shrugging it off. But when River falls asleep on her shoulder minutes later, I know we'll revisit the subject pretty fucking soon.

TWENTY-FOUR

Vee

This shouldn't be so nerve-racking. I'm an adult. Telling my father I'm falling in love with an amazing man shouldn't be scary.

I've never dated anyone as long as I've been dating Conor, and the guys I did spend time with weren't worth mentioning to my dad. They were never serious. Stupid flings. Mostly physical.

Things are different with Conor.

Scarily different, considering we've only known each other two months, and I'm already so attached. The thought of losing him has every cell in my body on high-alert mode.

"Can we talk?" I ask, settling onto the couch.

Dad looks away from the TV, his eyes briefly scanning my face before he grabs the remote. I guess he senses this will be serious, or he wouldn't switch off the game.

He sets his beer aside and straightens in the armchair, giving me his full attention.

"I think it's time you met my boyfriend."

TOO STRONG

A small nod is all the encouragement I get, but before I say more, Rebecca enters with Rose trailing close behind.

"Should we go for a walk?" Dad asks, subtly glancing at his wife like he's asking if I mind her listening.

"No, we can stay."

"What's going on?" Rebecca comes closer, draping her jacket over the back of the couch. "Is everything okay? You look pale, Vivienne."

"Everything's fine. Can you sit?"

Her eyebrows bunch in the middle, but she plops down on the armrest, and Rose settles in beside me.

"So? Do we get to finally find out who this guy is?"

"Yes. I'd like you to meet him, but..." I force out a loud breath. "I'm afraid you'll make him feel unwelcome, and I can't have that. His family's been nothing but kind to me since the start, and it's not fair that he won't get the same treatment from you."

Dad sits higher in his chair. "Why would we make him feel unwelcome, Vivienne?"

I bite my cheek, squirming like a child outside the principal's office. "Because you don't like his father."

A deafening silence falls around us, and the tension's building so high my insides start knotting, and I think I understand why Mia pukes when she's nervous. If *this* is how intense her nerves feel, I'm surprised she doesn't puke more often because I'm not far off bolting to the toilet right now.

"I'm dating Conor Hayes," I add quietly, making sure we're on the same page.

A small, horrified sound escapes Rebecca's lips. Her face whitening, marble eyes expressionless for a second before something I would've never expected takes over and my dad's complexion blanches.

Okay, not the reaction I imagined. They look... *scared*.

"Hayes?" Dad echoes, the word like something rotten stuck to his tongue. "You're dating a *Hayes*?!"

"Dad, I don't know why you hate their father so much, but Conor's *not* his dad. He's great. He's caring and kind, and... I'm in love with him."

Dad jumps to his feet, pacing, almost tearing his hair out of his scalp. This isn't how I thought this conversation would go.

I knew he'd be mad, sure, but not like this. I thought he'd yell or tell me the lies he's fed himself for years, but this... He almost looks in pain. Like I stabbed him in the stomach and twisted the knife.

"You can't date him," he spits out, grinding his teeth. "You have to break up."

"What? Dad, you're overreacting. You know nothing—"

"Now!" he booms, balling his hands into fists. "Take your phone and tell him you're done." He shoves the phone in my hand. "Break it off."

"I'm not doing that." I jump to my feet, my head reeling.

I knew he wouldn't be pleased, but this goes beyond any reaction I imagined. My heart rams against my ribs. The mere idea of losing Conor grips my throat. Not in the pleasant, arousing way he does. This feels like cold, wet, dead hands forcing the air from my lungs.

"I'm an adult, Dad. You won't choose who I date! Why do you hate them so much? What did Robert do to you?"

He opens his mouth, but Rebecca shoots out of her seat, shaking her head, eyes brimming with tears, lips pinched together. She's fighting her tears, but a distressed wail like a wounded animal breaks free, chilling me to the bone.

TOO STRONG

"Don't," she pleads, grabbing Dad's hand. "Remember what you said. Remember what you promised. Please... we can't."

Now I'm even more confused.

"Fuck!" Dad snaps, grappling his hair with both hands, eyes fixed on the ceiling. "This isn't fucking happening..."

I trade a loaded, confused look with Rose. I can't think of a single reason Dad hates the Hayes so much. Whatever his problem with Robert, it shouldn't bleed onto the rest of them. He never even met Conor. I doubt he met any of the brothers.

"I..." I start, taking a hasty step back. "I'll let you calm down."

"You're *not* going back to him," Dad snaps, stomping closer. The pained anger in his eyes takes me aback. "You have to break up. You *can't* date him, Vivienne."

I can't remember the last time he used my full name. I've been *Vee* or his *Angel* for years. *Vivienne* sliding off his tongue sounds like an insult.

"While you live under my roof—"

I tune him out, my stomach lurching with the oncoming tears. That's the last straw. A slap to the cheek.

Big fat *fuck you* for everything I've done and how good I've been all these years.

Dad never had any problems with me. No partying, getting drunk, or experimenting with drugs. No sneaking out in the middle of the night. No arguments or teenage rebellion.

I've been good. I helped, kept my head down, handed over most of my hard-earned money, and took care of Rose for years. I cooked, cleaned, and helped as much as possible since I was *four*.

I don't blame Dad for never having much time for us, I'm not sad about my childhood, and I don't consider it traumatic, but fuck...

This is what I get for being so fucking good? For putting Rose first? For bailing on my education?

No questions, no explanation, just *break it off*?

No.

Dad took it too far this time. Telling me not to stay out late or bring boys over is one thing, but saying I can't date the man I love is entirely different.

He doesn't have that kind of power over me.

No one does.

"Okay," I whisper, my voice cracking, tears escaping my eyes as I back away. "Okay, I'll move out."

"No you won't! You'll stay right here." Dad leaps forward to grab me, but I jump away, signaling with my hand I don't want him any closer. "Vee..." he sighs, his shoulders sag, eyes pleading. "You can't be with Conor, Angel. I'm sorry, I really am. You've been so happy the past few weeks, but... it's wrong, baby girl. So wrong."

"Why? Why is it wrong? I don't care what your problem with Robert is. I don't care what he did to you. Conor isn't him. You can't punish us for whatever happened years ago!"

"I'm not the one punishing you two," Dad says, glancing at Rebecca.

I don't know if he's looking for support or checking something, but whatever he needs, he doesn't get. She silently shakes her head, the gesture almost desperate.

"She has to know, Becca," Dad says. "She has the right to know! It's gone too fucking far, don't you think?! They've been together for weeks!"

"Whose fault is that?!" she snaps, storming into him and poking his chest with her finger. "What kind of father doesn't know who his daughter is dating?! You know *nothing* about her or Rose. You're always working or watching TV!"

"Enough!" Rose yells, her voice sounding alien, high pitched, desperate, close to tears. She never could handle their arguments. "Why can't she date him? You can't break them up because you don't like his father. Conor's great! They all are."

Rebecca turns ghostly white, her chin quivering, pure horror veiling her face as she turns to look at Rose. "You know them? You spent time with them?!"

"Ah, looks like I'm not the only one who doesn't know what our daughters are getting up to," Dad mocks, folding his arms. "None of this would've happened if they knew the truth, Becca."

"No! You'll regret it, Derek. Don't tell them!"

"What else do you want me to do?! Cuff Vivienne to the fucking trailer? She'll pack her bags, and she'll go to Conor! It's time, Becca. You knew it would come out one day. That day is today, whether you like it or not!"

"No... please, don't tell them," she begs. "If you love me—"

"Don't tell us *what?*" Rose cuts in, a little ball of rage. "What the hell are you hiding? Tell us what's happening! Whatever your problem with the Hayes is, it's *your* problem, Dad."

"This is so much bigger than you can imagine," Rebecca says, her voice hitching as she looks at me, eyes beseeching. "Conor's not the boy for you, Vivienne. I'm sorry. I really am, but you need to break up with him."

I shake my head, my mind made. "I love you both, but this is my life. *My* choices. I won't break up with him." I spin on my heel, marching toward my room to pack a bag and stay with Abby until I figure out my next move, but Dad stops me.

"You can't be with him," he says, his voice defeated. He sounds like he's about to cry, too, and I freeze in my tracks, never before having heard that desperate note in his voice.

"Why not, Dad? Give me *one* good reason."

My heart cleaves in two when I see the defeat clouding his face, and then it turns to ash when he opens his mouth.

"He's your family," he whispers.

He's not lying. I can tell it costs him everything to speak as he inhales a deep breath, his shoulders collapsing.

"He's your brother, Angel."

"My brother? How's that—No." I shake my head, my eyes popping, legs like goo. "No. No way. That's not possible. He's not my brother. You're lying!"

"You think I'd lie about something like this?"

Shaking all over, my mind disconnects. The intersection gets choked. So many thoughts careering from all sides, slamming into each other, creating miles upon miles of wreckage. And in the heart of it all, *he's your brother* booms like a church bell.

I can't focus on a single thought.

I can't find a link or any rational explanation. Every time I grasp something that makes sense, it eludes me. Erupts in a puff of smoke, leaving more question marks behind.

I—I...

I can't think.

I can't speak.

I can't fucking hear anything other than the cacophony of horns inside my head, but I am moving.

My legs carry me, my surroundings nothing but a blur while my mind's in riot mode, too many neurons firing at once...

TWENTY-FIVE

Conor

"It's odd," Mia says, glancing out the kitchen window. "Rose is never late." She turns, watching me dial Vivienne's number for the tenth time.

It's almost quarter past five. Rose's piano lessons start at five, but they're not here yet. Vee's cell is switched off, the voice mail driving me fucking insane.

"Have you tried calling Rose?" I ask, flinging my phone aside. "I don't have her number."

"Yes. No answer. It's switched off." She looks out the window again like she might summon them if she stares long enough. "They'd call if they knew they were running late."

"You're sure Rose didn't mention taking a break over the holidays?" Nico asks, foraging through the fridge for something to eat.

"I'm sure."

"Vee mentioned telling her dad about me," I say, verbalizing my thoughts. "He's not a fan of the Hayes."

Nico turns to face me, a bottle of water in hand, as he spits out one short, harsh word, "*What?*"

"He doesn't like our dad. Says he only cares about people with money in this town."

"That's fucking bullshit."

"Yeah, tell me about it. Vee thought maybe they fell out back in school or something, which would make more sense." I run my hand down my face. "If she told him last night, maybe he didn't take the news well."

"And did what? Grounded her? She's a grown woman, Conor. You can't ground an adult."

"Well, her dad seems to think that while she lives under his roof, he has the right to dictate her life, so maybe he did. Maybe he took her phone, too."

I grab my cell, trying her again, and when I hear the machine, that's fucking it. "I'm gonna go there." I jump to my feet, pulling my keys from my back pocket. "I need to know she's okay."

Nico nods, gulping down half the bottle before he says, "You're not going alone."

Now it's my turn for that one harsh word. "*What?*"

"If he grounded Vivienne for seeing you, he's not your fan, Conor. You don't know the guy. You don't know what he'll do, so either Cody and Colt go with you, or I do."

"You're overreacting," I say, pushing Cody back down when he starts getting up. "I don't need a warden."

Nico sets the bottle aside, pulling Mia into his side to kiss her head. "Call us if the girls show up."

"Fine," I snap, knowing damn well I won't win this argument. "Fucking *fine*." It takes little effort to piss Nico off, and he looks ready to snap someone's neck, so he's not the one I want trailing behind me. "I'll take Cody and Colt. Better you don't start growling at the guy. Won't win me any points."

"Smart choice," he agrees.

"Okay, let's go," Colt says, fisting his keys. "I'm driving."

"Of course you are," Cody mumbles, pushing past him to get outside and shotgun the passenger seat.

"You know where she lives?" he asks as we exit the house, jogging down the concrete steps.

"Yeah, Bayside Trailer Park."

He slowly runs his hand down his face, demonstrating that he currently thinks I'm dumb. "That much I know. I'm asking if you know *exactly* which trailer." He bangs the door, getting behind the wheel. "You've never dropped her home, have you?"

I shrug, buckling my seatbelt when he kicks the pedal to the floor, almost fucking drifting onto the main road. He's been disappearing late into the night lately, his destination a secret from everyone, including Cody and me.

At first, we thought he was seeing someone and didn't want to share the news, but Cody followed him last weekend when I was busy with Vee. Turns out he's entering illegal street races just outside of town. We've not confronted him about it yet, deciding to wait until after Christmas, but right now, it'll help get my mind off things.

"I'll ask someone," I say. "Now tell me why the fuck you're racing and keeping it a secret."

His foot falters on the pedal before his grip on the steering wheel tightens so hard that his knuckles whiten. "Who told you?"

"I followed you last weekend," Cody admits, pleased with himself. "You thought you could keep things from us?"

"I hoped I could have a life and not share every tiny detail with you two."

"Yeah... no. Won't happen. Go on, spill. What's the deal? If Shawn finds out, he'll rain fire on your ass."

"He won't find out. That circle's been running for three years."

"Why did you join?" I ask.

He shrugs, taking a left turn. "I needed something to unwind. Managing Nico's businesses isn't a walk in the park. It's exhausting. Don't get me wrong, I enjoy the job, but the pressure gets too much, and fucking random girls doesn't take the edge off."

"Maybe you should fuck the *right* girl? Seems to work for Nico. He's doing better since Mia."

"If I ever find the right one, I'll stop racing. Until then, I'll keep at it. Promise not to blab, and I'll take you with me one weekend. We do offroad once a month, so you can ride at the back."

"You offroad in this?" Cody scoffs, glancing around, looking for a concealed safety cage.

"No. I bought something else." He turns left, and a big sign on the roadside tells me we're here.

The car jolts along the dirt road, stirring up a thick cloud of dust. I've seen pictures of this place online, but they must've been taken years ago when the trailer park was first built.

Every time I dropped Vee off, I didn't get near enough to see the trailers. She made me stop on the main road, the park hidden from view by thick bushes and trees. Now, there's nothing obscuring the view.

The trailers loom like rows of decaying teeth, each one in worse shape than the last. Used-to-be white fences around the porches are either missing or rotted. The metal roofs sag under the weight of trash and time. Windows are opaque with grime, and the paint peels away in flakes, exposing brown-speckled metal underneath.

A big Rottweiler barks outside a trailer, and I no longer need to ask where Vee lives. She told me about the dog and how he wakes her up in the dead of night, barking at a cat or gust of wind.

I look over to where my girlfriend lives, where she spent every day since she was a little girl, my imagination picturing her playing with neighbor kids.

Despite the happy images my mind creates, this place gives off a vibe of abandonment. A place where dreams go to die.

"Park here," I tell Colt, pointing ahead. "And wait in the car."

They both nod but unbuckle their seatbelts. The air's thick with a musky scent, a mix of damp earth, rotting leaves, and dirt. The rickety steps up to the door creak under my weight, but I don't get to knock before the door flies open, and I'm staring into the barrel of a hunting rifle.

It takes my brothers a second to exit the car, the door slamming shut, but I don't dare look over my shoulder. There's a gun pointed at my head, so stopping my brothers making this worse is the least of my problems.

I doubt this can get any fucking worse.

"Leave," Vee's father spits. "You're trespassing."

"I'm looking for Vivienne." Surprisingly my voice sounds steady as I look past the barrel, shepherding the twinge of fear resonating through me. "Is she home?"

"Which part of *leave* don't you understand, kid? You have ten seconds to get off my property."

"Dad!" Rose cries in the background. A second later, she comes into view, her horrified eyes swinging between the gun and me. "What's wrong with you?! Put it down!"

"Get back in your room! Now!" He cocks the gun, aiming between my eyes.

The conviction in his gaze could rival Nico's.

I know he won't fucking shoot me, but he sure knows how to make an impression.

Although... who knows, maybe he will shoot me.

Shawn told us plenty more fucked-up stories, so I shouldn't underestimate my future father-in-law.

A hell of a way to meet the guy, that's for sure.

"Stop aiming at him!" Rose yelps, fixing her fear-ridden eyes on me. "Just go, Conor. Please, just go. She's not here. I don't know where—" She's cut off by Derek, who shoves her back, then slams the door in my face.

"He's nuts," Cody says when I turn around and head back toward the car. "Good thing Nico isn't here. He'd fucking break him in half if he saw him pointing a gun at you."

Better he never finds out.

TWENTY-SIX

Vee

"You'll make yourself sick, Vee," Abby scolds, glaring at the untouched toast on the bedside cabinet. "You need to eat."

"I'm not hungry," I say, my voice croaking from the ocean of tears I've cried.

"Thank fuck," she breathes, whipping her hair over her shoulder, relief blazing from her eyes. "You're talking again. You scared the hell out of me, you know? You've barely said three words since last night!"

I cover my face with my hands, expelling the air from my lungs. "I'm sorry, I…"

I don't remember anything but the express train of thoughts polluting my head for what must've been hours judging by the daylight seeping into Abby's bedroom.

I really need to call my doctor. Whatever dose he's got me on now isn't working. I feel like I'm running around in circles, my attention distracted from something more important by a vicious cycle of identical thoughts.

"At least drink something," she pleads, perching beside me on the bed. "C'mon, just a glass of water. You've not eaten or drunk anything since you got here."

I sit up, the comforter slipping lower, revealing a wrinkled t-shirt plastered to my skin. It's the same one I wore yesterday... I should probably shower. Wash off the lack of sleep, tears, and countless hours I spent thinking, remembering every word Dad spoke about the Hayes, analyzing my entire childhood, scrabbling for clues, and coming up with nothing.

I don't remember how I got to Abby's. I don't even remember how I left home. Did Dad chase me? Did Rebecca? Did Rose say anything when I was leaving?

My mind was in disarray. Utter and complete chaos, the same line bouncing around my head on repeat.

He's your brother.

I've got glimpses, little flashbacks, nothing solid until about midnight when I'd calmed down enough to realize I was at Abby's. Before that, there's mostly emptiness interwoven with a sense of impending doom.

I drove here.

At least, I think I did... I shouldn't have gotten behind the wheel, but I don't remember doing it, consumed by shock.

That's the best way to describe it. A deep state of shock.

Denial, too.

So much denial.

It wasn't until the early morning hours that I started piecing together a story. Answering questions I should've asked my father last night. Maybe I did, but I *don't* remember.

Slowly but surely, I've realized that if Conor's my brother then Monica Hayes must be my mother. I look too much like my father for us not to be related.

While this part makes sense, nothing else does. Things I'm confident about one second topple over the next whenever I try to piece together a convincing timeline of events.

So my father had an affair. Okay, that's plausible. Less so that a blue-collar man like him could snatch a woman like Monica Hayes, but then again... look at Conor and me.

It's the same, just reversed.

Plausible, I decided sometime around five in the morning.

My father had an affair with Newport's most powerful woman. And she's my mother.

Again, *plausible* when I think about how similar we look. Gray eyes, similar hair color...

But what about the pregnancy? How in the world would Monica walk around pregnant with no one noticing? Did she leave for nine months? Hid somewhere to avoid scandal, then returned once she gave me up?

Why did she give me up? Did she not love my father? Was it just a one-night thing? What are the odds of getting pregnant after one night? Pretty low, I bet, and that's why the foundations of this plausible idea seem built under a sinking city.

Then again, maybe she really disappeared for a while.

She could've been hiding the pregnancy until it was impossible, and that's like... what? Five or six months? Then left for three or four, gave birth, and came back. The elite have a way of making things like this happen on the down-low. Rehab, charity work in Uganda, long vacation because she was stressed.

Plausible with seven sons.

The Hayes always had money, so sending Monica away for a few months wouldn't be an issue.

But why would she give me up? She has seven sons. She

adores kids, and Conor said she always wanted a daughter.

The foundations crack again.

But... maybe Robert threatened divorce if she kept me. Or perhaps she didn't want me and palmed me off on Dad as soon as I was born?

Why would she cheat on Robert in the first place?

Every next question breeds more questions.

Do the older brothers know about this? Are they keeping this secret as close to their hearts as my father?

Doubtful.

From what I've learned, they're family oriented. Very close to each other. If they knew I was their sister, they'd stop Conor dating me, wouldn't they?

I feel sick the second he slips into my head, demanding attention. He's worried by now. I'm sure he is, he always worries, and it's already almost six o'clock in the afternoon. My phone's been off all day. Rose should've started her piano lesson at five...

Rose.

God, I've left her there alone to deal with whatever Dad and Becca throw her way. They've probably locked her in our bedroom and taken her phone.

"Vee, you're scaring me, babe. It's been almost eighteen hours, and you've said three sentences. Your dad's calling every hour checking on you."

"He knows I'm here?"

Abby frowns. "Of course he knows. He dropped you off."

My eyes narrow. I could've sworn I drove myself. "I don't remember that."

"Yeah, I know. You were in la-la land when he hauled you over here."

"What did he say?"

"He said you needed some time away from home to think. What the hell happened?"

I shake my head, fresh tears springing to my eyes.

He's my *brother*...

Half-brother, but that doesn't change much. We have the same mother. We...

God, we kissed. So many times. The best kisses of my life. All of them. The short pecks, the long make-out sessions on the beach, those meant to soothe and show emotion, and those designed to start a fire.

We fucked.

Jesus Christ... we *fucked*. Not once. Not twice. A lot.

And every time, I wanted more. Needed more of him, his closeness, his touches, those reality-altering orgasms.

We fell in love. Deep and fast. Strong, *too strong*, irresistible, real... sick, depraved love.

I slept with my brother.

I'm in *love* with my brother...

"Conor and I are over," I say, the words flooding out in a wail.

I know I have to break up with him. I know we can't keep going, that even the idea of us together is unequivocally fucking wrong, but... my heart knows different. It feels different. It's not rational and refuses to let him go.

"What?" Abby clips, confusion distorting her face. "Why? What happened? Did he hurt you? Cheat on you? I'll fucking kill the bastard!"

"He didn't cheat. He didn't hurt me—"

"Then why are you breaking up with him? Shit, Vee, if you tell me this is about money again, I'll flip the fuck out."

I take the glass from her, another tumult starting in my mind.

Do I tell him what I learned? Do I annihilate his world the

same way my father shattered mine?

The Hayes are a movie-worthy family. Close, tight, always there for each other, loving and caring.

Do I have the guts to destroy that? Because telling Conor I'm his sister will unravel a chain of events that will change them forever... and it won't help *us* in the slightest.

Nothing will. Not one answer to the questions plaguing my mind will alter the facts. The truth won't set us free. It won't make loving Conor acceptable. Not the way I want to love him.

Nothing will change the fact we're related.

Monica obviously didn't want me. She must've had her reasons, and despite how unwanted that makes me feel, my pain isn't enough to drop a bomb in Conor's life.

Just because I don't belong with him and I'm not wanted as a part of his family doesn't mean I should pulverize it. I love him too much to intentionally cause so much hurt.

And that's why I need a lie.

Powerful enough to make him walk away.

TWENTY-SEVEN

Conor

After four hours, countless phone calls, and pointless driving around town, I finally get the address I've been desperate for since Colt drove away from the trailer park.

Abby St Clair, Vee's best friend.

While Cody and Colt got all our friends on high alert, asking everyone to track Abby down, I've left no fucking stone unturned. We've been to *The Well*, the newsagent she works at, the beach, the arcades, and every other place she ever mentioned.

But she was nowhere to be found.

My chest feels so tight it might fucking choke me. I know something's terribly wrong. Whether her father's hatred of me drove Vee away or something else entirely, she's alone while she should be with me. She's dealing with whatever happened without my arms around her, and that won't fucking cut it. Ever.

My foot jitters nervously as Conor pulls up outside Abby's apartment complex. I know this street. I was here when all the

TOO STRONG

Hayes brothers moved Cassidy's things out of her flat two years ago.

Abby lives further down the street, but the building is almost identical. Outside and inside, too. The same dark-red, cheap carpet in the hallway, the same numbered doors on either side and even the same ceiling lights emit an ugly yellow glow, highlighting dirty walls that haven't been painted in decades.

Despite the *wait in the car* order I barked, my brothers follow suit, keeping a safe, three-step distance when I stop at the door where a number eight is glued with too much glue.

Shaking the tension off my limbs, I push my contradictory emotions aside for now. There's a shift in the air. An intense impression of danger prickles my skin kicking the rhythm of my heart into high gear.

I just want to see her.

Check that she's okay, that *we're* okay. I want to lock her in my room and hold her all night, but the nerves strangling my stomach hint it might not happen.

The door opens after three knocks and a girl roughly my age appears, arms folded over her chest, blond hair swishing around her shoulders.

"Conor Hayes," she drawls, looking me over. "My, my... to what do I owe the pleasure?"

"I'm looking for Vee. Is she here?"

She cocks an eyebrow, clearly taken aback. "No, why? What happened? Did you guys fight?"

"Nothing happened. We're fine, but I can't find her. She's not home, and her phone's off. Any idea where she might be?"

An unworried shrug betrays her, even though her words sound genuine. "If she's not at home, work, or here, she's with you, so I have no idea where she might be."

Too casual.

She's acting way too fucking casual about this. If my best friend had gone AWOL, I'd be more concerned. I'd dig deeper, ask more questions, but Abby stands there like she believes her answer should satisfy my curiosity.

"I need to talk to her," I say, stepping forward.

So does she, trying to barricade the doorway. "Well, I don't know what to tell you," she seethes, emphasizing every next word, "...but she's not here."

"You can keep saying that, or you can save us both time and let me in."

Her stance hardens as she shields the entrance with her body, bracing both hands against the doorframe. "She doesn't want to talk to you, okay? She's fine, but she needs space."

"Abby, we've not had a chance to meet, so I'll give you a quick rundown. I'm not usually an asshole, but I'm losing my fucking head here, so I'm sorry about this." I grip her waist and push her back hard enough that her elbows bend, forcing her to let go of the frame. Not hard enough to hurt her, though. "You won't win with me," I say when she shoves me back. "Stop fidgeting. I'm not leaving until I talk to her."

"I'll take it from here." Colt steps inside and takes Abby by her arm. "We'll wait outside while they talk, sweetheart. You can tell me all about yourself."

"What is it with you and girls whose names start with A?" Cody muses when Colt drags Abby out to the corridor.

"Stop manhandling me!" she whines, then looks over her shoulder. "I'm sorry, babe!" she yells, loud enough for the whole building to hear. "I couldn't stop them!"

She's not struggling against Colt, her eyes sparkling, lips falling apart in a soft gasp when he wraps an arm around her, holding her close to his side.

"We'll wait here," Cody says, reaching to close the door when I step further into the small space.

It's tiny. I forgot just how fucking tiny these places are, nothing more than a kitchen slash living space and two doors either side. A bedroom and a bathroom.

According to Colt's friend who got us the address, Abby lives with her parents. How they manage is beyond me. My bedroom is bigger than this entire flat.

In Cassidy's apartment, the bathroom was on the right, bedroom on the left. I take a step to where I think I'll find Vee and stop when she emerges first.

My stomach drops faster than a lead weight in a pool. She's been crying. A lot, judging by the web of tiny red veins in her eyes. Traces of mascara smear down her cheeks, and her hair is a mess of tangles and loose locks.

"Fuck," I breathe, the capacity of my lungs decreasing. "What happened, baby?" I can't stand her tears. The thought she's been so vulnerable, *alone*, has the fine hairs on my neck standing to attention. "Why were you crying? Why didn't you call me to come get you?"

She sniffles pathetically, pulling her lower lip between her teeth as she holds her hand out, silently keeping me at a distance. "You should leave."

"What? I'm not going anywhere." I take another step closer, reaching out to grab her, but she staggers back, shaking her head.

"Please, Conor. You need to go."

No way in hell I'm leaving. I take another step, and she reacts exactly the same.

She's moving away from me... fuck.

She could slap me, and it wouldn't hurt as much as her refusing to let me touch her. "Stop," I plead, my hands growing cold, my back arrow straight. "Fuck, baby... *stop*. If you take one more step away from me, I'll lose my fucking mind. Just *stop*, okay? Talk to me. Tell me what's wrong."

She wipes her nose with her sleeve, almost choking on her tears as she looks up, meeting my eyes. "We're over."

My ears fill with high-pitched ringing. "What? What the hell do you mean? We're *not* over."

"We're done," she says louder, quivering like a lost pup. Fresh tears twinkle in her eyes, the sight turning my stomach. "I can't be with you."

"We're not over, Vee. No way. Whatever happened, whatever the fuck your dad said, I don't care. We're not done. You're mine, and you don't get to throw this away without telling me what's wrong, without trying to fix it."

"It can't be fixed," she whispers. "Please... go, okay? I don't want you here. I don't want to be with you."

"Don't say that," I snap. "Don't fucking lie to me. Tell me what happened!" She doesn't mean it, I know she doesn't, but it still hurts that she's so determined to shove me away. "You love me. You're happy with me."

"I never told you I love you. I don't."

"Bullshit."

"It's not bullshit!" she snaps, swiping her tears away. "I told you we'd never work! I told you we're too different, Conor."

"Jesus, this about money again? You're unbelievable, Vee. What the hell do you want me to do? Donate it to charity? Burn it? Will that make you feel better? Will you be happier then?"

Tiny rivers spill free, trailing down her pale cheeks when she looks up, so much distress in her eyes I can fucking taste it.

"I cheated. I told my dad about us. He wasn't happy. He said we won't last, and I went out for a drink to calm down," she mutters, words falling from her lips at the speed of light, each breaking a little more than the previous. "A guy was there, and... he made me feel... *normal*. Like I belonged. I didn't worry about my car or where I come from, and..." She pushes a sharp gust of air past her lips. "He fucked me in the restroom."

The whole time she's ranting, I watch her chapped lips move and wonder how much she's cried since last night. How many times did she chew her lips to leave them this sore?

I hear the words she speaks loud and clear.

Every single fucked-up word.

She met someone. Likes him because he's broke. Fucked him for the same reason.

"Who do you have me for?" I ask when she falls silent.

Closing the distance between us, I wait for her to back away, but she doesn't this time. Of course not. She thinks she won. She thinks I'll lash out, scream, and storm away.

"Goes to show how much you know me," I add, taking her face in my hands. "I don't believe anything that just came out of your mouth, Little Bee. Not one word. You're pushing me away. I don't know why, but that's what you're doing." I pull her in, engulfing her in my arms as I kiss the top of her head. "You didn't cheat."

She doesn't hug me back. She's motionless, maintaining her composure, trying to trick her body into showing me she meant what she said, but she's failing.

Her body stabs her in the back when she sags into me. Barely, just a little, but she does.

Gestures speak louder than words.

"I don't know what happened, baby. I don't know why

you're upset or why you're lying, but I know you need space." I push her away, every instinct rebelling against what I have to say next. I don't want to, but it's either that or making her talk when she's clearly not ready. "I'll give you time to think. I'll be waiting when you're ready to tell me the truth." I kiss her forehead, curling my fingers under her chin. "I love you. There's nothing you can say that'll change that."

More tears escape, but she doesn't stop me from crossing the room toward the front door. Doesn't say a word when I leave.

I hope to fucking God I didn't just make the biggest mistake.

TWENTY-EIGHT

Conor

A day goes by. I don't get much sleep, but I get up in the morning all the same.

I wash up, get dressed, and eat breakfast, fighting not to blow the shit happening between Vee and me out of proportion.

She just needs time. I can give her that. I don't know how long I'll cope without seeing, touching, or kissing her, but I can give her time because that's what she needs right now.

Cody and Colt steer clear, either acting considerate and giving me space or scared I'll lash out if they say one wrong word. The first person who starts a conversation is Mia. She joins me at the breakfast bar while I'm on my third cup of coffee.

"Cody told me what happened. What's your plan?"

She places her small hand on my shoulder, the gesture designed to soothe or reassure me. Too bad it does the exact opposite. The weight of her tiny palm and the concern in her eyes remind me of what Vivienne said.

TOO STRONG

I grip my cup with both hands, shepherding the Molotov cocktail of emotions Mia's question reels to the surface. I've been wrestling myself all morning, forcing my ass to stay planted on this stool, or else I'd storm out, drive over to Abby's, and fucking *beg* Vivienne to talk to me.

The option is valid. I've not ruled it out, but as much as I want to see her, I know that...

"She needs a few days to work through some things." Knowing this and letting her take those few days away from me are two different things, though. "Her mind's not a standard one. It gets so overwhelmed sometimes she can't pull a single rational thought out of the chaos. I'm sure you've noticed she talks to herself. She just needs time to settle."

Mia nods, squishing my shoulder a little tighter. "Rose told me she's got ADHD. Do you know why she needs time? Did she tell you what's wrong?"

"She tried lying," I scoff, recalling the shit she spewed about the guy she met at a bar.

He's not real. He doesn't exist, but the need to skin him alive wreaking havoc inside me is very fucking real.

"Her dad doesn't like our family, and..." I groan, hiding my face in my hands. "I kept asking Vee to tell him about us. It fucking sucks being a secret, but if I knew her dad would find a way to make her question whether she loves me, I would've kept my mouth shut."

She squeezes my shoulder once more like she wants to show she listened, then, without a word, she lets go, crossing the kitchen to brew a pot of coffee.

"No advice?" I ask, the ground falling away beneath my feet. Mia always knows how to comfort people, but right now, she's at a loss for words. "What would you have done if your dad didn't approve of Nico?"

I'm surprised Jimmy had zero issues with his daughter dating my brother. There's a whole list of things the guy could've found wrong with their relationship, starting with the ten-year age gap and ending with the fact that Nico and Jimmy were friends long before Nico met Mia.

She pauses with her hand on the fridge handle, silent while she thinks. "I don't think my answer will help you."

"Try me."

"I'd pack my bags and move here," she admits, a tiny smile playing across her lips. "It's my life, Conor. As much as I love my dad, I'd never let him dictate what I can or can't do."

Yeah, she's right. Her answer doesn't help me one bit. If anything, it makes me feel worse. It proves I'm not as important to Vee as she is to me.

Despite what Vivienne says and the progress she's made since we met, there are still moments I think she'll dump my ass because of how different she claims we are.

Loud thudding on the staircase is our only warning before Nico enters the kitchen. He goes straight for her, stamping a kiss on her head even though she's only been gone five fucking minutes. It's already ten in the morning, so they must've started the day with sex, but he can't walk in a room and *not* kiss Mia to save his fucking life.

"You good?" he asks me, adjusting his gray t-shirt as he sits opposite me at the breakfast bar. "How are you holding up?"

My temper flares more.

"So I guess everyone knows Vee tried to leave me..." I blink my eyes closed, massaging my temples. "Did Cody and Colt hold a Hayes-wide conference to brag?"

It's not fair. I know it's not, but the turmoil of my emotions means *fair* doesn't fucking matter.

"They're worried about you," Nico clips. "We all are. Cody and Colt don't know what the fuck it feels like to find the right girl, but I do. So do Theo, Logan, and Shawn, so we're your best bet if you need help. Though I have to tell you... I'm fucking proud of how you're handling this."

My eyes snap to him, unsure whether I heard right. Nico's not the guy to voice such opinions. He's more the show-don't-tell type, more prone to showing us he's proud than driving the actual words out.

"Proud," I echo, shaking my head. "What are you proud of? Vivienne's going through shit, and I just fucking left her to it."

"Everyone needs time to think, Conor. Considering she told you she cheated, I'll go out on a whim and say she really does need space."

"She *didn't* cheat."

A hint of a smile that hardly lives up to the name curves his lips. "Glad to hear you're so certain."

"She made that up to push me away."

"Which means whatever she's going through isn't easy. She was desperate enough to hurt you so you'd give her space, Conor. You did the right thing stepping back."

"Would you sit on your ass and wait if this was you and Mia?"

His jaw clamps tight. Any support he had in his eyes flashes away. I struck the right nerve.

No way in hell Nico would just sit and wait for Mia to work through her shit. None of my brothers would. Maybe Shawn, though I imagine Jack's the one running around like a headless chicken, trying to apologize whenever they argue. Shawn's too stubborn.

Theo, Logan, Nico... they wouldn't hang about. Theo would

get us all together and numb himself with eight or ten drinks. He'd whine and vent all night, but come morning, he'd glue himself to Thalia until she'd have no choice but to work shit out with him.

Logan hardly lets Cassidy get away from him as it is, always close, no fucking space or distance. It only works so well because Cassidy's the same. She loves the small codependent ecosystem they've built. If they ever argue—and that's a big *if* since Logan never mentioned a single argument—it can't be serious. I can imagine, though, if he was in my shoes, he'd be circling Vee's apartment, looking for a window or balcony to climb through.

And Nico... Nico would come with metaphorical guns blazing. He'd break the fucking door down if Mia was one iota sad or uncomfortable. He's not exactly rational when it comes to her.

Maybe their behavior isn't healthy. Maybe that's not the way to go about issues, but it makes me feel weak to just sit here waiting for a fucking miracle.

"I wouldn't," he admits. "And that's probably why it'd take me longer to work shit out with Mia than it'll take you with Vivienne. There's nothing wrong with space, Conor, and with her mind working different than mine or yours, giving her space to think and align her thoughts is the best thing you can do right now." He slides a cup of fresh coffee across the breakfast counter. "She loves you. She'll come back."

"You know about the ADHD too, huh?"

He nods, tightening his fists. "Was it a secret, or are you just trying to start a fucking fight? You need to let some steam off? Go downstairs and work out."

Better that than pissing off Nico. I'm in good shape, but

one right hook, and I'd be unconscious.

***

Three hours later, my muscles burn, my head spins, and my t-shirt's drenched in sweat. I'm exhausted, my system ready to crash, but my mind won't stop.

I might be too wrung out to drag my feet up the porcelain stairs, but my mind is in high-alert mode. Millions of thoughts fight for attention, urging me to hop in my car and drive over to Abby's.

Instead, I grab a quick shower, then fall on the bed, earphones in my ears and Nirvana as loud as the setting allows. I don't know how long I'm there, staring into the distance, before Cody pops his head in, a frown marking his forehead.

"What?" I snap, losing the earphones. "What do you want, Cody?"

"We're leaving in fifteen minutes. I know you'd rather stay in bed feeling sorry for yourself all day, but you're coming with us."

"Where are we going?"

He huffs an exasperated puff of air down his nose. "Grandma's birthday party ring a bell?"

Fuck. I completely forgot.

My stomach twists into a double knot because I was supposed to bring Vee with me today. Get her to meet my parents, grandparents, Shawn, Jack...

Guess that's not fucking happening anymore.

"Can't you just tell them I'm sick?"

"You're not sick, Conor. And we both know Mom will be here in under an hour with chicken soup if you don't show." He

I. A. DICE

opens the door further, leaning against the frame. "You know... If there's beef between Vee's dad and ours, he probably knows about it, right? You could ask him a few questions, find out what happened. Maybe if you know, you'll know how to fix it?"

Now that's an idea I can't turn down.

It's good to have brothers. They annoy the shit out of me on a regular basis, but when the situation demands it, they step up.

With a deep groan, I drag my legs over the edge of the bed and stand. "You're not completely useless after all."

He whacks my shoulder as I pass him. "Remember that. I expect the same support, bro. I have a feeling I'll be in your shoes sooner rather than later."

"What?" I halt halfway down the corridor. "What do you mean? You met someone? Who?"

Colt exits his bedroom at this exact moment. "I heard that, and I sign my name under every one of Conor's questions, Cody."

"I've not met anyone, relax. It's just that seeing you with Vee makes me realize we won't all be past twenty-five by the time we get snatched up like the others. I thought we had more time, but..." He smacks his hand on my head, messing up my hair. Not that it's styled in a particular way, but it still grinds my gears. "Look at you. Twenty-one and ready to pop down on one knee."

"And you think you're gonna have the same thing soon?"

"I don't know when, but I'm not stupid enough to think I'm some kind of exception to the rule and I'll live out my years as a bachelor." He looks over his shoulder at Colt. "But I think you're gonna go down first. You have a thing for Anastasia, don't you? It's not just sex."

His eyebrows draw a deep eleven in the middle of his forehead. "It is just sex. She's good."

"Good enough to keep your attention for two months."

He ups his tempo, passing Cody on the stairs before he turns with an incredulous look. "I know you two prefer a different girl every weekend, but I like knowing I'm the only guy fucking her. I don't want to change them like socks, especially when it works. That doesn't mean I'm after a relationship. And definitely not with Anastasia. She's annoying, to put it mildly, but God, that girl sucks dick like a vacuum."

"So classy," Mia's voice calls as we walk into the living room. She's on the couch, phone in hand, purse beside her. "One day, you'll regret talking about women like this."

"Oh, please," Cody huffs, strolling over to her. "Don't act so innocent. You think we don't know what girls talk about? You think we don't know *how* women talk about us? Why saying a girl sucks dick like a champ is a bad thing, but saying a guy eats pussy like he's starving is a good thing?"

"Because you make it sound so derogatory. When women say it, it's meant as a compliment. When you say it, it's bragging."

Cody leans over, kissing her head. "You're cute. It's the age of equality, Bug. We're not bragging, and we're not derogatory. It's a compliment, Mia. It sure is meant as one, but women take compliments differently than men. Eating pussy and sucking dick is on par, but you'd rather be told you're pretty than that your mouth turns a guy incoherent."

"He's right," Colt adds, leaning against the doorframe. "There's more honesty in *you suck dick like a pro* than *you look beautiful*. We tell every girl we're into that she's beautiful, Bug."

She thins her lips, the look on her face betraying she knows it makes sense, and she's in the wrong. She takes a deep breath before rising to her full five-foot-nothing. No dress today. Instead, she's in jeans and a baggy navy sweater. If I didn't know better, I'd say she's trying to hide a pregnancy belly.

But I do know better.

Mia won't be getting pregnant for at least another two years. Nico's adamant about letting her party until she finishes college.

The night Logan told us he got Cassidy pregnant with baby number two, I thought Nico would drag Mia upstairs and put a baby in her there and then. I don't think I've ever seen him so jealous, but he reined it in, and for now, he's happy being an uncle.

"We've veered off topic," I say, looking back at Colt.

"No, we haven't," he insists. "There is no topic."

With that, he grabs the keys to Nico's G Wagon and heads for the garage.

I think Cody's got this all wrong. I've seen Colt with plenty of girls over the years, and he doesn't act any different with Anastasia than with the rest of them. I'm sure he'll change completely when he finds the right one.

***

Another day goes by. Probably the longest day of my fucking life.

And then another one. Even longer.

And one more.

How can four days feel like a whole goddamn month?

Maybe because I'm not sleeping, eating, or leaving my room. Or maybe because I still have no answers.

I asked Dad about Vivienne's father. If I'm to believe him, he has no idea who the guy is. Never heard of Derek before.

That's not much help to me.

TOO STRONG

I'm losing my goddamn mind more with every passing hour. Vivienne hasn't texted or called. I haven't seen her, and now I'm questioning this entire thing.

I was fine at first. Convinced giving her time to think was my best bet, but the longer she's not coming back, the more I regret leaving her with Abby. I tried calling Rose, but her phone's off, and I'm too chicken to try Vee.

I've not left my room in twenty-four hours. My phone's charging at all times, so I don't risk running out of battery and missing a call or text message.

Maybe it would be easier if college was in session to distract me, but I'm stuck at home with nothing but my thoughts keeping me company.

Sure, my brothers are downstairs, ready to lend a listening ear or drink a few beers with me. I would if not for the pitiful looks I can't fucking stand anymore. They're worried. I know they are.

Even Nico.

He knocked on my door this morning for the first time since we moved in, asking me to come down for breakfast. I said no. Ten minutes later, there was another knock. Mia this time, armed with eggs on toast and a steaming cup of coffee.

I drank the coffee, but the eggs waft pungently from my nightstand, untouched and unmoved on their bed of toast. Normally I'd take the plate downstairs, but I don't want to budge.

And so I sit in the same spot, checking the screen of my phone every thirty seconds, wondering what the fuck I'll do if Vee doesn't show up by the end of the week. I don't think I'll survive any longer than that.

TWENTY-NINE

Vee

Dad and Becca stay out of my way since I came home. A blessing, considering I'm not ready to talk. I'm still processing the news, trying to understand what I learned.

Whenever I think I've figured out what happened, new questions pop up, screwing with the timeline of events I've assembled. My mind's reeling. The constant galloping thoughts sap my energy, but I can't sleep no matter how tired I am.

Things took such a quick, sharp turn that I begged my doctor for an emergency appointment.

He prescribed me new meds again.

Well, not exactly new. I took Adderall a few years ago, but now I take a long-term release every morning and a short-term release in the afternoon to boost the morning dose as it wears off.

It's only been a day. The adjustment period usually lasts about a week, so I'm in for a few more days of blindly navigating the emotional labyrinth.

That's if the dosage is correct and won't need adjusting...

In the midst of all the chaos, or maybe despite the chaos, there's not a minute I don't think about Conor.

I shouldn't. I know I shouldn't. It's wrong to remember every time he kissed me. Even worse to recall every time he touched me. How he looked when his big, toned body hovered over me in bed. How he sounded when he said he loves me.

Wrong. All of it.

While my mind knows it, my heart disagrees because my relationship with Conor doesn't *feel* taboo. Kissing him, holding his hand, or coming undone beneath him never felt wrong.

Not once.

I keep thinking about the scene in *Back to the Future* when Lorraine kisses Marty and immediately knows something is off. I've never had that with Conor. The opposite, actually. It felt so fucking *right* to kiss him.

It's not, but I can't seem to let the thought sink.

Rose tried talking to me a few times. At first, she was sympathetic. She held my hand or climbed to my bunk and spent a monotonous hour brushing my hair. When playing nice didn't work, she changed her tactic to plain rude, saying I should call Conor and tell him what Dad told me. That maybe he'd help me piece together what happened twenty-one years ago.

But what's the point?

Telling him we're related won't change anything. We can't make it work, no matter what. I could risk blowing his family wide open if there's a chance his parents don't know I exist, like if Robert Hayes was my father and my mother never told him, but that's not the case.

They know I exist.

They chose to give me up, which means I'm not welcome.

Unleashing that news will devastate Conor's life... it's not worth it. I love him too much to hurt him when there's no chance of a good outcome.

Gripping my phone, I lay in bed late in the evening. Rose is here, watching a movie on her phone, earbuds in.

I scroll through the pictures of Conor and me, then read every single text he ever sent. I've been doing that for the past five long days. I should delete every single one, convince myself we never happened. That we were never happy.

It would be safer for my heart, but whenever my finger hovers over delete, I can't bring myself to click.

Those photos are all I have left of him. I'm not throwing them away.

Another thing I've been doing a lot is googling Monica Hayes to find myriad pictures of her at the many galas and balls she organizes.

We look similar. Not identical, but similar enough that our relationship makes sense. It's not our features that match. I inherited my face shape from Dad, but Monica has my eyes. Or rather, I have hers. When she was younger, her hair was the exact same shade as mine.

I find a picture of Monica in her thirties and climb down the ladder to fetch an old shoebox from my closet. There's not much here, just a few Polaroids of the woman my father claimed was my mother.

I look like her too. Silver eyes, caramel hair, freckles.

I guess if you look closely, you'll discover similarities in everyone, but the sense of familiarity I get from the woman in the picture isn't there when I look at Monica Hayes.

I grab the box, joining my dad in the living room. I can't piece together a convincing story, and he's the one who blew up my entire world, so he'll have to help me out.

He sits in his armchair, eyes glued to the TV. Becca's not here, working the night shift at the Motel by Costa Mesa.

That's good.

I don't need her listening to our conversation.

I don't mind Becca per se. I've never particularly liked her because she's so strict toward Rose and because she doesn't try harder than she has to. She could work overtime to pay at least half Rose's college tuition, but she relies on my dad and me to do the heavy lifting around here.

Dad looks up, eyes dull as he looks me over from head to toe. He's worried. I've not left my room much this week. I skipped work and hardly spoke a full sentence the past five days, but it's time to get some answers.

"Who is she?" I ask, throwing a picture at him, carefully watching his expression. "Who's the woman in those pictures?" I fan more out on the table, but he remains silent, his face stoic. "She's obviously not my mother. My mother's Monica Hayes, so *who* is this woman?"

A long, tense moment passes before he looks up at me, eyes full of pain and remorse. "You really love him, don't you?"

I clamp my teeth, squeezing my eyes shut tight to not let another tear fall. I've cried every day, and I'm exhausted. So fucking weak. Tired of the pain ripping me wide open. Tired of the sinking, sick feeling wrenching my stomach whenever I force myself to eat, and tired of missing Conor.

"It doesn't matter," I whisper, eyes still closed.

I hear him get up, and his arms circle my back as he cradles my head, holding me flush against him. "It does, Angel. It matters a great deal." He kisses my head, pushing me back a little. "Is he everything you ever hoped for?"

I want him to stop, drop the subject and stop reminding me how much I love Conor, but something in his eyes has me bobbing my head, barely holding off tears.

"More than I hoped for. I miss him so much."

A heavy sigh deflates him. "I know. You're so consumed by the pain you didn't even stop to think."

"I've not stopped thinking," I spit out, pulling away. "That's all I've done for days! I wonder why you never told me. Why Monica gave me away, why—"

"Promise me one thing, okay?" he cuts in like he hasn't heard a word I said. "Things are about to take a turn, and we'll need to be here for each other. Promise me you'll be here."

I move away to look at him, his words making less sense by the second. "What do you mean? Dad, please, I'm tired. I just want the whole story. I want to forget. Tell me who the woman in the pictures is."

"She's your mother," he coos, moving to sit in the armchair. "I'm sorry, Angel. Everything happened so fast, and Becca..." He shakes his head, clamping his jaw, holding back words he might regret. "You're young... I didn't think your feelings were valid, that they were enough to risk our family, to trade one daughter for the other, but I've watched you all week, and little by little, it's killed me to see you hurting like that. You reminded me of myself when I lost your mother. It was the darkest time of my life, Vivienne. I don't wish it on anyone, so I want to make this right." He grabs a picture, pinching the corner between his fingers. "Look at the very beginning. When's your birthday?"

My eyebrows bunch together, anger skyrocketing. "You don't know when my birthday is?"

"October twelfth," he replies with a sigh. "And when's Conor's birthday?"

It strikes me like a lightning bolt.

How have I *not* realized this sooner? Monica can't be my mother. She had the triplets two months before I was born. It's physically impossible. I look to Dad, but instead of hope filling me up, my heart threatens to burst.

"So..." I whisper, eyes brimming with tears. "You're not my real dad?"

"I'm very much your dad. Always have been, and always will be." The softest smile brightens his face before he starts talking again, flipping my world on its axis for the second time this week.

***

"No, no, no..." I chant, patting the steering wheel. "*Please*, not now. Just a little longer. We're halfway there. Keep going."

It doesn't. The engine sputters, growls, jerks a few times, and stops. The sudden silence is almost deafening, punctuated only by my shallow breaths.

"Not now!" I snap, my mind still in overdrive, racing as Dad's words linger, replaying like a broken record. "Fine," I huff, reaching for my jacket, aware how ridiculous my words are, how stupid I'd look to a passive observer, scolding my car. "I don't need you. I'll call a taxi."

A quick pat-down proves me wrong. I don't have my phone, so a taxi is out of the question. "Well, I have legs. I'll run."

I'm not surprised the street's deserted. It's Sunday. Almost eleven o'clock at night. No traffic around at this time in Newport Beach on the eve of New Year's Eve. Streetlights cast eerie shadows on the sidewalks, illuminating the shopfronts.

"I wish I scrapped you a long time ago," I snap, beating the steering wheel with my fist, my heart racing, adrenaline pumping through my veins at the sharp burst of pain. "Ouch!"

Yanking the door open, I leave the keys in the ignition. "I hope someone steals you and saves me the trouble of taking you to the scrap yard." And *bang*. The door snaps shut, but the window stays intact despite my unvoiced pleas that it shatters.

The cold, dark night envelops me like a cloak. It can't be more than forty degrees. The coldest day of the year, I'm sure. Undeterred, with Dad's words spurring me on, I take a deep breath, steeling myself for the ride, and take off at a sprint.

The wind whips my hair, the chill of the night air stinging my cheeks as I dodge parked cars and leap over the cracks in the sidewalk. Everything blurs together, a sea of dark buildings. My breathing ticks like a metronome, my footsteps echoing over the silent streets, counting time.

I don't get far before my muscles burn with the effort. Instead of taking a short break to smooth my breath, I push myself harder, ignoring the ache in my legs and lungs.

Just then, as if this couldn't get any worse, the first raindrops strike my head. I make myself stop, my brain hitting the brakes so fast my legs barely have time to react.

"Please don't let it be thunder," I whisper, peering at the dark, starless sky.

Swallowing big gulps of air, my ears perk, listening for any sounds that'd strip my courage in a flash. My heart painfully screams against my ribs.

Rain. It's just rain. Not even heavy. No gusting winds or roaring strikes of lightning. Just a typical California shower.

With a sigh of relief, I recognize the neighborhood. It's not been here long, a few years at most. The houses still look brand new, with lush lawns and gray cladding.

TOO STRONG

Reassured, I cross the street, settling into a walking pace until my pulse slows. I'm still subconsciously waiting for lightning to burn the sky wide open with a bright flash, but after five minutes of gentle rain, I calm down enough to sprint again.

I'd consider myself physically fit, but no more than three streets over my body tells a different story, every muscle rebelling against my brain urging me forward.

"Not far now. Just five more minutes." And after those five minutes... "Almost there, just five more minutes."

The poor attempts to trick my brain work to some extent when—panting and heaving—I stop at the bottom of Nico's driveway twenty minutes later.

The rain's still just a soft, misty drizzle, but it's soaked through my clothes, leaving me chilled to the bone.

Two Mustangs sit to the left of the garage, the house dark save for the soft glow of LED lights embedded in the concrete steps.

On my last legs, I rest my forehead on the door and rap my fist against it, perfectly aware I'll wake more people than I'd like. I don't even know what time it is. It can't be past midnight, so maybe they're not asleep, watching TV in the living room that's not overlooking the driveway.

Point invalidated when my hand starts turning numb from repeated banging. If someone was downstairs, they'd open the door by now.

I keep at it, ignoring the pain increasing with each blow. Conor's bedroom is right above, the balcony shielding me from the rain. Just when I think I'll have to climb up there to wake him, the upstairs light suddenly floods the driveway. Within seconds, the hallway light blinks, and I hear the characteristic sound of the lock being turned.

A touch too late... I'm still slathered to the door and fall forward as soon as it opens, but two strong hands grip my shoulders, steadying me before I face-plant the floor.

"Vivienne, shit, you're all wet," Cody clips, pulling me inside, eyes roving my frame. "Did you run here?"

"Sorry," I mumble, dark spots coruscating in my eyes as I find my feet. "Sorry I woke you, I—" I press my hand to my wet forehead, feeling like I weigh a ton. "I need to talk to Conor."

"Whoa, easy there." He grips my shoulders again. "You're swaying, Vee. Are you feeling okay? C'mon, you need to sit down. I'll go get Conor in a minute."

"What's going on?" Colt's voice sounds on my left when Cody helps me to a breakfast stool in the kitchen. "Is she alright?" he asks his brother, pulling a tee over his head as he approaches. "What the hell happened?"

"I think she ran here. Go get Conor."

Colt turns on his heel, his bare feet slapping against the marble floor.

An unpleasant thought materializes out of the blue.

What if Conor doesn't want me back? What if, during the last week, he took a step back, considered everything I told him at Abby's, and decided it was true?

My mind's screeching so loud I can't understand what Cody's saying as he sets a glass of water in front of me. His lips move, but the words hit an invisible wall between us, dispersing before they reach my ringing ears.

THIRTY

Five days. Five whole days and nothing.

Not one message. Not one phone call.

I'm tossing and turning in bed, my face smothered by the pillow that no longer smells like Vivienne. I'm starting to wonder if maybe I dreamt the whole thing.

Maybe she never really existed.

Maybe I made her up.

Maybe it was all a fucking dream.

I groan, tugging my earphones out. Music helped at first, both to pass the time and refocus my mind, but it's not fucking working anymore. I've been listening to AC/DC for hours but can't recall a single word. I tuned it out, my screaming mind louder than Angus Young at full tilt.

Sitting up, I flick the nightlight on, rubbing my stinging eyes. I'm sleep deprived. Coming up with the most ridiculous ideas.

Vee's not a dream. She's real. Every last, perfect, smooth

inch of her is real, as are the moments we spent together.

I squeeze the back of my neck hard. The clock on the nightstand shows a quarter past midnight. I've been in bed since seven and slept zero minutes.

No wonder I'm losing my fucking mind.

The idea of getting wasted seems tempting. At least when I got drunk the other night, I passed out instead of laying awake, glowering at the ceiling, my mind going a million miles an hour.

Not one explanation I've come up with thus far is plausible. Not one problem I conjure good enough to destroy what Vee and I had.

Have.

She's still mine.

I'm not letting her go.

She's done with you, my mind screams, almost drowning out the *she needs more time*, my heart coos.

How much more time, though?

It's been a week. I can't fucking stand this. I want her here. I want to see her, kiss her, and watch her fall asleep cuddled into me. Watch her smile.

I get up, padding across the room toward the balcony door. The house is silent. No wonder... it's the middle of the night. New Year's Eve already. I've got less than twenty-four hours to win Vee back if I don't want to start next year without her.

Looking out the window, I stare at my car. I could drive to the trailer park. See her in less than twenty minutes.

But it's the middle of the fucking night, and if her dad spots me, he could make good on his threat and put a bullet between my eyes. Doubtful, but can't rule it out.

I grab my phone from the side table, scrolling through my contacts to *Little Bee*.

Fuck space.

This has gone on long enough.

I swipe the screen, watching her name appear in the middle. A jolt of relief and excitement hits me at once. I've missed her so much that the *thought* of hearing her voice lifts my mood in a flash.

"We're sorry, but you have reached a number that has been disconnected or is no longer in service."

Excitement hisses out, replaced quickly by a sense of dread. My heart ups the rhythm, galloping against my ribs as the operator's words sink.

She changed her number.

For days, I was convinced she needed time to arrange her thoughts. That the only reason she started to doubt us again was the argument with her dad. That she'd come to her fucking senses and realize no one can dictate her life.

Now the doubt creeps in.

What if this has nothing to do with her father's disapproval, and something else changed her mind about us?

A knock on my door has me almost jumping out of my skin. It's not soft like you'd expect a knock to be in the middle of the night. No, this is a bang. Loud, urgent.

"Conor! Get up!" Colt yells, apparently not giving a damn that he'll wake Cody.

Nico and Mia are hidden away one floor up, the entire space soundproof, so there's no need to worry about waking them, but Cody's grumpy if you pull him out of bed when he's not ready.

My brows furrow as I cross the room, yanking the door

open just as Colt grabs the handle to do the same.

"Vivienne's here," he says, looking like he was actually pulled out of bed, his hair disheveled, t-shirt creased.

"Vee?" I'm struggling to catch up. I just called her... now she's here? When did she get here? Why is she—

Why does any of that matter?

She's here.

I shoulder past my brother without a word or a backward glance as I race down the stairs, my heart pelting faster than my legs. It's not until I'm halfway there that I hear Cody.

"We need to get you into some dry clothes. You're shaking."

I enter the kitchen, ready to fucking burst when my eyes land on her pretty, teary face. Her lips are a ghastly shade of blue, and she's trembling all over, clothes saturated, skin pallid.

She looks up, either hearing me approach or seeing movement from the corner of her eyes, and the tears spring free.

"I'm sorry," she whispers, twitching to get up. "I'm so sorry."

I don't stop.

I get to her before she gets one foot to the floor. My fingers disappear in her wet hair, and my lips come down on hers, the words unnecessary.

She's here. Mine.

"I love you," she whispers in my mouth, then inches away, cupping my face like she wants to make sure I'm paying attention. "I love you, and I missed you so much." She kisses me again, pouring her all into one desperate kiss.

"I missed you too, baby. I—"

She presses her frozen, quivering finger to my lips. "I'm not done talking. I know I hurt you. Everything I said... wasn't true. I swear, I didn't cheat. I'd never do that to you."

I cuff her wrist, peeling her hand off my face. "I know.

Now stop for a minute. You're soaked through, Vee."

She shakes her head so hard her wet hair whips cool droplets everywhere. "Let me explain. Please, it'll all make sense if you let me explain. I—" She tries to stand, but her legs give in.

"Stop," I say again, slipping my hand around her back to keep her steady. "How did you get here? Where's your car?"

"I think she ran," Cody supplies. "She couldn't catch a breath when I opened the door. You should get her showered and into dry clothes, bro."

"No," Vee stomps her foot, bracing against my chest to push me away. She's so weak I hardly feel her efforts. "Let me speak. It's important."

"You're wet, cold, and pale, baby. I'm not going anywhere, okay? I know you didn't cheat. I told you I didn't believe a word you said. You can tell me once you're in dry clothes."

"We're *family*!" she yells, her newfound strength pushing me away with both hands, her eyes aflame, starkly contrasting her ashen skin. She grips the counter like she doesn't trust her legs to do their job. "Have I got your attention now?"

"I think she's running a fever," Cody mutters. "She's delusional, Conor."

"I *don't* have a fever and I'm *not* delusional!"

"Here," Colt says, stopping beside me holding sweatpants and a hoodie out to Vee. "Put this on, and then you can talk."

Her eyes gape in horror. Lips fall open. "Why aren't you reacting?! I just told you we're related!"

"There's no way in fucking heaven or hell that we're related," Cody clips, his patience wearing off. "That'd mean one of our parents cheated, and that's not an option, Vivienne. You're walking a fine line right now, so you better think through what you're about to say."

"Watch your fucking mouth," I snap, turning to him, my chest heaving as I shove him back a step. "Don't *ever* threaten her again." Snatching the clothes from Colt, I rein in the unexpected torrent of rage that's pushing me to break Cody's nose. "Wait in the living room. Both of you."

They leave us alone, whispering between themselves on their way out, and I turn back to Vee. She's holding onto the counter with one hand, the other grasping the glass of water.

"I'm sorry," she says, her eyes wet again. "I didn't mean to say it like that. I just had to make you listen."

A heavy weight settles in my gut because the fire in her eyes morphed into uncertainty and fear, like she's second-guessing whether telling us what she knows is a good idea.

"C'mon, you need to change," I say, helping her out of the wet clothes, then into the sweatpants and hoodie.

Given the circumstances, the sight of her body dressed in just black panties and a bra shouldn't make my dick stiff, but I'm a red-blooded man. I've got no control around this girl, especially after almost a week of celibacy.

I itch to kiss her, taste her again, touch her... anything. Even a peck on her forehead, but what she said comes back like the kickback of a gun, stopping me before I move in.

We're family.

It doesn't make fucking sense, but Vee never gave me reason to doubt her. A part of me is generating ideas *how* that could be possible, while the other begs for an explanation that doesn't mean I fell in love with a girl I'm related to.

"I promise that this..." She points between us, "...isn't wrong in any way." She takes a step closer, no longer as shaky, no longer swaying on her feet. Even her lips are growing pinker.

"I think it's fair my brothers hear this, too."

She nods, sucking her bottom lip to bite hard. With a deep breath, she follows me into the living room, her steps cautious, a little wobbly.

"Last week, after I went home, I told my dad about us," she starts, once she's sitting in the corner of the sofa picking her nails. "He wasn't happy. He told me I had to break up with you, that we couldn't date. I always knew he didn't like your family, but I never understood why. Rose was there, and her mom, Rebecca. She kept telling my dad not to say anything, that he'd regret it... She almost begged, but I said I won't leave you and—"

The end of the sentence falls off the edge of a cliff, Vee's voice cracking like eggshells. Using the back of her hand, she wipes her eyes, driving me up the wall.

Every muscle in my body tenses painfully. I fucking hate seeing her like this. I hate when she cries. My immediate reaction is to grab her, wrap her in my arms and hold her until she calms down, but the heavy aura stops me moving.

"He said that line... *while you live under my roof*," Vee says, a scoff slipping past her lips. "So I told him I'll move out. I was going to pack my bags, but he flipped everything on its head when he said that..." She peers up, a lone tear suspended from the tip of her nose, "...he said I'm your sister."

I know that's not true, but the words steal my breath anyway. Steal my ability to verbalize my thoughts while my head floods with visions.

Every time we kissed, touched, *fucked*... the thrill that burst in my chest when I watched her come undone. The emotions she awoke and the feelings that were born the day I first saw her.

She can't be my sister. It's... no. Just *no*.

"You're not our sister," Cody seethes, his temper rearing

its ugly head. He's usually good at keeping himself checked, but when life gets too much, he's leaking gas and only needs a spark to fucking flame on. "No way."

"Let her finish," Colt snaps, his jaw ticking, eyes never veering from Vivienne. "Keep going."

She straightens in her seat, wiping her eyes again. "I don't remember much after that. I think I was in shock. I thought I drove myself to Abby's, but she told me the next day my dad took me there. My mind was going so fast, question after question, no answers, just guesses."

"What kind of guesses? How the fuck did you validate that idea?" Cody snaps once more, dangerously close to forcing my hand, so a gentle reminder to zip it is in order.

"Snap at her again, and you'll be explaining the blood stains on her favorite rug to Mia." Brother or not, I will shut him up with my fist if he doesn't stop barking at my girl.

"How can you just sit here like that?" He jumps to his feet, pacing the room. "This is fucking ridiculous, Conor. She's lying."

"I'm not lying," Vee whispers, tearing her cuticles off. "I stayed up all night, thinking, and it made sense after a while. My mother died when I was little. My dad hates your family... I thought maybe he was in love with your mom, maybe they had an affair, and I was an accident she didn't want."

"You thought our mother was *your* mother?" Colt asks, his tone controlled, even a little sympathetic. "Vivienne, you're only two months younger than us."

"I know. I know that *now*, but when it was all happening, I didn't think about that. There were so many other questions and so much chaos in my head... My doctor changed my meds not long ago, but they weren't working. I thought it was taking longer to adjust, but they weren't working at all." She looks up, pinching her lips like she's about to break down. "I saw him a couple of days ago, I've got new meds again. I should be getting back on track soon."

"Meds?" Cody asks, taking a seat at the far end of the sofa, his tone softening. "For ADHD? I didn't know there were meds for that."

"Not to cure, just to manage," she explains, tapping the side of her head. "I've got it mild. It mostly affects my processing speed."

"Why didn't you tell me what your father said when I came to Abby's? I would've told you it's not possible."

"I didn't want to drop a bomb like this on you. We've..." She swallows, making room for words. "We've done things no brother and sister should, Conor. At least if you didn't know why I left, you wouldn't feel as bad as I did."

Both my brothers scoff in sync. "He didn't think he banged his sister, I'll give you that, but there was nothing *good* about how he felt, Vivienne."

She looks at me again. "I'm sorry. I tried not to hurt you. Breaking up is one thing, but finding out your family's bigger than you thought is something else. I thought your mom gave me up. She couldn't have hidden a pregnancy for nine months, so your father had to know, too."

"Wow," Cody huffs. "You really did think it through, didn't you?" He rests his back against the couch, knotting his fingers on his head. "Okay, keep going because this can't be over. You found out our mom's not yours before you came here tonight, right?"

"I'm not your sister," she firmly states. "We're not related by blood in any way, but... you do have a sister."

THIRTY-ONE

Conor

The silence that falls upon the living room could be cut with a knife it's so fucking thick.

It doesn't last long, though.

My heart leaps, the answer to this riddle easy to find after everything Vee has told us.

"What are you—" Cody starts, but Colt shuts him up, jumping in with a question, his face a picture of self-control.

"It's Rose, isn't it?"

"What the fuck, Colt?!" Cody booms, staggering to his feet. "You think Mom had another kid?! That's ridiculous."

"Not Mom. Dad. That's why Vee's not related to us in any way. Because Rose isn't her biological sister. They've got different moms *and* different dads."

"She's still my sister," Vee says defensively. "We might not be blood, but she's been my sister since the day she was born."

"You're insane. It's one thing accusing Dad of having an

affair, but a different thing entirely to say he's abandoned his daughter!"

"He didn't," Vivienne chips in quietly. "Becca never told him about Rose. He doesn't know she exists. I don't know the details. Dad only told me enough to explain why Becca begged him to break Conor and me up. She doesn't want your father finding out. I think she's afraid to lose Rose."

"Shit..." Cody mumbles, more to himself than either one of us. "This... this is above my fucking pay grade. I'm gonna go get Nico. You call the others."

"It's almost one in the morning," I remind him.

"So what? If *this* doesn't warrant a crisis meeting, I don't fucking know what does. Call them."

"He's right," Colt huffs, pulling out his phone. "I'll call them and start the coffee machine. I have a feeling we won't be getting any sleep tonight."

Vee looks at me when Colt leaves. Wet strands of hair plaster her forehead, eyes uncertain. "I said this isn't wrong, and technically, it's not. We're not related, but—"

"There is no *but*, baby," I cut in.

She had so much conviction in her voice when she told me there's nothing wrong about us. She believes it, but she's unsure of something. I love that I read her with such ease. She's unsure because she's scared I'll see a problem with our relationship.

I don't. I really fucking don't. There's no blood connection. We've not grown up together. I didn't know Rose until a couple months ago. She's Vee's sister because they were raised together, and mine because... my dad's an adulterer.

Regardless what anyone thinks about us, I don't give a damn. She's mine. She's so deep under my skin I don't think I'd give her up even if she really were my sister.

I mean, I probably would, but... who the fuck knows?

No one, and thank God I don't have to find out.

"We're not related, Little Bee."

"No, we're not," she agrees, worrying her bottom lip, a tiny, cheeky smile lighting her eyes.

"That's my job," I say, taking over, biting that sweet, swollen lip, then devouring her mouth and savoring every second.

Never breaking the kiss, I pull her onto my lap and wrap my arms around her, turning the sweet kiss into something more profound. Deeper, greedier, Almost fucking brutal.

A ball of lust burns through my ribs. I'm not far from ripping off her sweatpants and impaling her on my cock right *here* to remind her who she belongs to.

As much as I'd love that, heavy footsteps on the stairs stop me before the idea sprouts roots.

I cut off the kiss, stroking my thumbs under Vee's eyes. "I missed you. Never try leaving me again."

She rests her forehead against mine, eyes closed, fingertips ghosting the line of my jaw. "I promise."

"Nice to see you back," Nico says, entering the living room.

He's had the decency to put on sweatpants and a t-shirt, his hair a mess, jaw set tight.

Vivienne slides from my lap, looking him over and cowering a little. "Did Colt tell you?"

"He told me there's something I should hear. Considering he dragged me out of bed at one in the morning, I guess I won't like whatever it is."

She looks at me, question marks swirling in her silver eyes like she's nonverbally asking whether to tell him now or wait for the others to arrive.

"Go ahead," I say, just as Colt comes back with a pot of

coffee and a handful of cups.

Nico pulls the piano stool closer, legs spread wide, elbows on his knees as he runs his fingers through his tangle of hair. "I'm all ears."

"You have a sister," she utters.

I thought she'd start from the top, explain why she'd been gone and what her father said, but no. Straight out with the big guns. Maybe it's better to just rip the Band-Aid.

"Excuse me?" He looks between me and Vivienne, distress crossing his face. "What do you mean, a *sister*? You?"

"No, not me. Although that's why I wasn't around the past few days. I thought it was me, but... it's Rose. Her mom, Rebecca, had an affair with your father."

Nico's jaw tightens, and his hands ball into tight fists. It costs him a lot of effort not to lash out and scream every question streaming through his mind.

The fact no one says anything tells Nico all he needs to know. This isn't a joke. It's real.

He grinds his teeth, eyes on Vivienne, pressuring her to explain. I don't think he trusts himself to say a word yet.

"Start from the top," I tell Vee, tracing a hand down her spine.

Nico's rage isn't for her, but I understand why she might feel it is. It's hard being in the same room with him sometimes, even when he's in a good mood, and right now, he's raging. Though doing a better job of keeping it in than six months ago.

Mia worked magic on his mental state.

Vee explains everything she learned the past few days, keeping nothing back. She tells him how she thought she was our sister and our mother gave her up, and then what she learned from her father earlier this evening.

"He was trying to protect Rose and Becca. Becca more than anything, I think. Maybe himself a little, too. He loves Rose like she's his. Always did, but he loves me, too, and he couldn't stand seeing me hurt any longer. Becca has been lying to Rose her whole life. She thinks my dad is hers. She has no idea she's your sister."

"Whose fucking fault is that?" Nico grinds out the words at no one in particular. "Jesus fucking Christ. I can't believe Dad gave her up just like that. I can't fucking believe he cheated on Mom."

Vee squirms in her seat. Nico's tone sends chills even down my spine. "Your father doesn't know about Rose," she says quietly. "Rebecca never told him. From what I know, it was a brief affair. I don't know the details and don't want to speculate, but I know she never told your father she was pregnant."

I can tell from the look on Nico's face that this information changes a whole fucking lot. He's still incandescent, but he's fuming less. The fact our dad doesn't know doesn't vindicate him, but it explains why we only *now* find out we have a little sister.

Logan, Theo, and Shawn arrive not long later. Vivienne tells the same story again, answering question upon question, sometimes the same ones repeating, for over three hours. Once they stop asking, a plan of action is formed.

We're visiting our parents tomorrow to confront our father. And then... we're telling him he's got a daughter.

It's going to be one hell of a fucking day.

***

Shortly after five in the morning, the door closes behind Logan,

Theo, and Shawn, and I immediately haul Vee into my arms, running for the stairs, deaf to Colt's *hold on a minute.*

I held on for four fucking hours.

Enough is enough.

It's light outside, but sleep is the last thing on my mind when I stand Vee in the bathroom, her eyes heavy.

"Tell me you love me," I say, watching her in the mirror. I've not had time to stop and appreciate her telling me earlier. "Tell me."

"I love you."

All air leaves my lungs, my heart wrung out like a sponge. "I love you more, baby." I wrap my arms around her, clinging to her as I nuzzle the crook of her neck, then whirl her round to face me, our kiss a breath away. "I love you so fucking much. Never leave me."

"I promise." Her lips meet mine, the kiss slow, gentle, until I take control, sinking deeper, tasting her like a starving man.

I am. A week without her is too long.

"You haven't told me why you ran here," I say, trawling the hoodie over her head then yanking the sweatpants to pool at her feet. I land a hard slap on her ass, tearing a needy whimper out of her mouth that has my cock swelling and jerking. "*Why* did you run, Vivienne? Where's your car?"

"It broke down halfway here." The sentence ends with a sweet gasp courtesy of my fingers gliding over the soaked fabric between her thighs.

"You need a new one."

She taps the back of my head. "Don't even think about buying me a car, Conor."

I can't say it hadn't crossed my mind, but I can't. I don't want Vivienne to feel out of place in our relationship. As much as I'd like to provide, I know she's more than capable of doing this alone and needs her independence.

"I didn't say anything. I know you won't let me buy you a car, but you need to compromise." I spin her around so her back is to my chest. Hitching her panties aside, I slip two fingers into her warm, wet pussy, arching them to stroke that sensitive little button. "Let me help you find a replacement, or at least take a look at that death trap."

Her head falls back against my shoulder, and her lips part as she softly replies, "Okay, but promise you won't pay for repairs when I'm not looking."

Peeling her bra cup away, I toy with her nipple and dip my head, kissing her neck. "I promise, baby."

Taking my sweet time, I summon her orgasm, then ease off. "But once we're married, my money is yours. Deal?"

She answers with a whimper, followed by a moan when I up the tempo, edging her again.

"Married? Slow down, and... oh *God* I can't think when you're touching me," she wails, clutching my wrists. "This isn't fair! You can't manipulate me with sex."

"I'd never do that, Vee. You know I wouldn't." I kiss the back of her head before turning her around. I'm *not* slowing down. No fucking way. "We'll talk after you orgasm. There'll be time for teasing later. Right now, I need to feel your walls quaking around my cock."

"Yes, please."

I strip off my clothes, help peel her panties down her smooth legs, and whip off her bra before we both get under the shower. With one arm around her waist, I spread my fingers in the middle of her chest, dotting her neck with open-mouth kisses.

"I want this little heart beating faster, baby," I say. God, I love when she shudders in my arms. The anticipation sends us sky high as I push her against the wall. "Legs apart and arch that spine."

She takes a broader stance, lifting her chin and presenting her perfect ass, the dimples on her lower back begging me to sink my thumbs in and drive myself home.

So I do.

"Fuck," I groan, guiding my cock inside her hot pussy, sinking balls-deep as I brace against the wall with one hand, the other restraining her wrists. "Fucking perfect. Don't move, Little Bee..."

"Feels nice," she breathes, tilting her head far enough to rest against my pec, and tips her chin up further, expecting a spider-man-style kiss.

She gets it as I pull my hips back. Sliding back in, slowly for now, savoring the moment, a low growl leaves my lips. I'm fucking drugged by this intimacy with her warm, familiar body.

"If you ever try to hide anything from me again—"

"I won't," she interrupts, pressing closer to me. "I promise. I... oh *shit*."

"Good?" I question, upping the tempo when her legs quiver.

She bobs her head. "So good."

I'm almost all the way out when I drive back into her. Hot water trails her back, forming a puddle where her spine dents. I whip her hair to the front, dipping my head to kiss her nape. The kiss turns into a nibble, and then I bite her shoulder.

She's on her toes, and my knees are bent, or this position wouldn't be easy for us. She's seven inches shorter, the top of her head fitting under my chin without an issue.

I reach down her stomach, two fingers strumming her clit

while my thrusts quicken every time a needy whimper leaves her lips.

"Let me have it," I say when she's bucking against me. "Come for me. Come with me."

Her knees jolt, her loud breathless moan swallowed by the wet sounds our bodies make as our hips connect. The second she pulsates around me, I come too.

"I love you," I whisper, dark spots dancing on my eyelids. "You're fucking stuck with me now."

She slumps against me, nowhere near as exhausted as I'd like. We took the edge off, but it'll take a while to get my fill.

Although I don't think I ever will.

Once we shower, I tuck her in, curving her into my side, drunk on how good it feels to have her back in my bed. Back in my arms, safe and mine.

"I realized something when you were gone," I say.

She lifts her head, looking into my eyes with a flake of uncertainty. "What's that?"

"I've tiptoed around you too much."

She rises further away, bracing on one elbow. "Tiptoed around me? You started by kissing me without asking permission then proceeded to stalk me, disregarding everything I said about not wanting a date. How's that tiptoeing?"

"I don't mean the start, Vee. I mean everything since. I let your mind steal you away time and time again. I've been so fucking scared to lose you I let you dictate the rules. All of them."

She sits up, her shoulders tense. "How have I been dictating the rules? You got everything you wanted."

"Not even half of what I want, baby. And not fast enough. I let you keep me at a distance because you're strong. Too strong, baby, despite your fragile mind. I won't make that mistake again. No more tiptoeing."

She smooths her loose hair behind her ears. "I wasn't keeping you at a distance. I just... we're still so fresh, Conor. We only met two months ago. What if you get bored? What if, after a while, I'm not enough?"

"There you go with that attitude again." I take her waist, bringing her closer. I move her so she lies flat on the bed and dip my head to her lips to kiss slow, gentle biting pecks full of promises. "I never want to hear you say you're not enough. You're more than I ever hoped for, but you've had one foot out the door since you gave in and admitted we're dating. I'm not letting you go, Vee. You need to understand this thing between us is in no way temporary."

She smiles small, her hand meeting my cheek. "I know."

"I don't think you do." I rise on my elbows. "This is it, baby. You and me. We're leaving your slow-ass pace. I've accommodated it long enough, and it's your turn to compromise."

"I don't know what you mean. You have me. I'm yours. We're together. I just blew a gigantic hole in your family because I couldn't stay away. What else do you want?"

"I want my forever with you."

"Forever?"

"Yeah. Forever. I spent the last week thinking. Trying to imagine my life without you, but I couldn't. Somewhere deep down, I knew you'd come back to me. I knew you wouldn't throw this away."

Her bottom lip quivers like she's about to cry. "Thank you," she whispers, taking a calming breath.

"What are you thanking me for?"

"For *not* believing me at Abby's. For *believing* I love you. For giving me space when I know it was the last thing you wanted to do."

"Don't thank me for that. There's nothing I regret more than not staying with you that day. I'm sorry I wasn't there. I'll never leave you alone with anything ever again."

She pulls me down for a kiss like she's trying to seal that promise. I let her take charge this once.

"Move in with me," I say. "But not here."

When I try to kiss her again, she turns her head to the side like she knows I want to shut her up so she can't say *no*.

"You're moving this along really fast, Conor."

"Not fast enough. Move in with me. I bought a condo."

Her eyebrows draw together. "You bought a condo? When?"

"I spent three days barely moving from my bed when you were gone, and I realized it didn't matter how long it took. I knew you'd come back and when you did I'd want you for myself, so on day four, I called Logan. They're finishing that development uptown, and he got me a good deal. The paperwork will take a while, but we should be okay to move in about two months. It's not huge, but it'll be enough for now."

She's silent for a while. I think her mind needs a moment to settle, so instead of pushing for an answer, I fold her into my chest waiting, stroking her hair. She doesn't protest, which is half the battle won. I think she's just weighing the pros and cons and making her peace with what's happening.

Because it is fucking happening.

I'm yet to tell Nico I'm moving out. I expected Logan to call him the second he hung up with me, but he didn't, so it's all on me. I'll tackle that issue soon.

"Ambulance thought," Vee says, lifting her head to kiss my chin. "I don't know how to navigate this as easily as you, but I'll try not to let fear choke me. I'll follow your lead."

"Is that a yes?"

"Yes. I'll move in with you."

I kiss her head, a sense of calmness washing over me. "Good. While you're so agreeable, stop taking the pill, baby. I want you pregnant."

"I'm not *that* agreeable." She playfully whacks my head, then pushes me off her and sits cross-legged under the comforter. "You're crazy, Conor. We've been dating two months."

"And?"

"What do you mean *and*? That's definitely too soon! Slow down."

I rest against the headboard, looking her over. "Why do you think it's too soon? You have doubts about me?"

"No, that's not what I meant. It's just... people don't do this so fast."

"Are those people living your life, Little Bee? Because you only get one shot, you know? No replays."

She toys with my fingers. "I know that."

"Then stop worrying what people think. Do what *you* want to do. Don't hold back because some hypothetical someone might think it's too soon. They have their own lives to live. This is ours."

She tugs her lip, taking a moment to think before her eyes meet mine. "We're not even engaged. Nowhere near the status, and you're already talking about *kids*. It's crazy!"

"I can put a ring on your finger tomorrow if it'll move things along."

She laughs.

Fucking *laughs in* my face like she thinks I'm joking.

I'm not. I watched Shawn break things off over and over again with Jack because he listened to his friends when they said he should try different things.

Sometimes, when he gets drunk, he rants, eyes tearful, lamenting the years he wasted listening to people who should have no sway over his life choices.

I watched Logan waste three fucking years, pretending he's over Cassidy. He regrets those years more than anything else.

I'd rather be like Theo or Nico. Probably mostly Nico. Grab the girl and never let her go. Theo took too long pretending he wasn't into Thalia, keeping her as a friend because good old fear held him back.

Over the years, I met, fucked, kissed, and even dated my fair share of girls, but I never had such a powerful longing for anyone but Vee. I know she's it for me. It seems to be the case with all Hayes men. Once the cupid hits hard enough, we're done.

Maybe it's in our DNA. Though considering recent events that's up for debate until Dad paints the whole picture. Still, save for him, it seems once the Hayes fully commit, it's for the rest of our lives.

Or maybe we're just fucking stubborn.

Either way, I'm not wasting time. I don't want regrets. I want my forever, and I want it to start now.

"I'll make you a deal, speedy," Vee says, crawling to rest her head in the crook of my neck. "Give us a year without racing ahead like I'm about to run, then we can talk about wedding venues, rings, and kids."

"A year?" My head slams the headboard. "Jesus, woman... Fine. A year is doable, but your ass better not be on the pill next New Year's Eve because we're spending that day in bed making babies."

She jerks away from me, eyes blinking in panic like she just grasped the topic. "*Babies*? Shit... you think we'll have triplets?!

TOO STRONG

What are the chances?"

Now I'm the one laughing. "Pretty low, unfortunately, but I'll do my best."

THIRTY-TWO

D-Day comes only a few minutes after I close my eyes.

Cody knocks on the door at eight o'clock in the morning, pulling me out of a deep, dreamless sleep. If not for Vee cuddling into my chest, I'd have paced the house all night, nervous about facing Mom and Dad.

Having her close works wonders on my head, though. Not even the news about a sister could keep me awake while she mussed my hair and kissed my neck before drifting off.

"Downstairs in thirty minutes." Cody pokes his face inside, a shit-eating grin curving his lips as his eyes sweep across Vee drooling over my t-shirt. "Aren't you two *cute*?" he muses quietly. "C'mon. We're meeting Theo, Shawn, and Logan at Mom and Dad's at nine, so better get moving."

"Yeah, alright. I'll be there in ten. Make me a coffee, will you? Quadruple espresso should do it."

Or maybe two...

TOO STRONG

He jabs his thumbs up, closing the door without any noise, uncharacteristically considerate.

Reluctantly, I wash up, brush my teeth, and shimmy into a pair of jeans and a hoodie. As much as I hate letting Vivienne out of my sight, I know it's better if she doesn't come along to witness... whatever the fuck is about to go down.

Nothing good for sure.

I kiss her head, nose, cheeks, and eyes, rousing her as gently as I can without diving beneath the comforter to lick her awake.

"I need to go, baby," I say when she opens those silver eyes. "I don't know how long I'll be, but feel at home, okay? Don't leave until I'm back."

She nods, sitting up. "Okay, I'll wait here."

"Get some more sleep. Mia's staying, and I'm sure Cassidy, Thalia, and probably even Jack will come over at some point, so you won't be alone when you wake up."

And who knows? Maybe I'll be back before then.

She slumps back, nuzzling her cheek into my pillow. "Just a few more minutes," she whispers. "I'll be up in a few minutes."

I kiss her forehead and pull the comforter up to her chin before leaving, my body tense.

Everyone is already downstairs. Nico looks like he hasn't slept at all. He's gripping his coffee cup just shy of hard enough to break it as he glares at the floor. You'd think it offended him with how intensely he stares at it.

"How's Vivienne doing?" Colt asks, shoving a cup of freshly brewed coffee into my hand.

"She's okay. She hasn't said anything, but I think she worries whether telling us the truth was a good choice."

"It was," Nico grinds out.

Before he says more, there's a knock on the door, and Cody

goes out to let in Theo, Logan, and Shawn.

"I thought we were meeting there," he says, following them into the kitchen and immediately starting the coffee maker.

"I thought it would be better if we all went together. I don't think I could hold off from screaming my fucking head off if I arrived first," Logan says, searching the fridge for an energy drink. Dark circles under his eyes hint he didn't sleep either. "What's the game plan?"

"There is no fucking game plan," Shawn cuts in. "I think it's best I do the talking."

Reserved laughter bubbles from Theo's chest. "We all know Nico won't let us get a fucking word in until he gets everything off his chest."

"Can you blame me? We have a sister we never knew about, Theo. She's *eighteen*," he emphasizes. "She spent eighteen years alone while she should have been a part of this family."

"You need to remember Dad had no idea she exists. I don't think he'd let her fend for herself if he knew."

Nico breathes out, trying to cool his jets, but this time not even Mia's hand gently smoothing the nonexistent creases on his chest can help the situation. He usually calms instantly at her touch, but today there are too many emotions raging inside each of us for anything other than answers to bring us a semblance of peace.

"Keep Vee company for me," I tell Mia before turning to Logan and Theo. "Are Cassidy and Thalia coming over?"

"Maybe later. We'll see how things go," Logan says. "I don't want her worrying. She's had a tough few weeks throwing up every day and not sleeping well. If she comes here, the girls will talk, and she'll worry."

"What about Jack?" I ask Shawn.

"He's waiting for my call. I have a feeling we'll circle back here once we're done with Dad. We still need to figure out how we're gonna tell Rose."

On the one hand, I'm not sure we have the right to tell her; on the other, expecting her mother to administer the truth might not be the best idea. She's been hiding it for eighteen years. Despite it being less then nine hours since we found we have a sister, everyone already considers her family. No way we'll let her live her life not knowing where she belongs.

Five minutes later, the seven of us ride out in two cars. None of us speaks during the trip. The tension grows taut enough to play with a bow.

And it only gets worse when Mom opens the door. Her face clouds at the sight of her sons outside, all tense, silently watching her with a mixture of anger, empathy, and apology.

We've never arrived en masse unannounced like this—a united front—so it's no surprise she immediately senses something is very wrong.

She doesn't say a word as she opens the door further and lets us in, accepting a kiss we stamp on her head or cheek, her nerves creeping with every I *love you, Mom*.

"Should I get your father?" It's the first thing she asks once she's closed the door behind us all with a click.

"Yeah," Logan huffs, keeping his tone as light as he can given the situation. "Go get him, please."

She nods, gesturing toward one of the living rooms, and rushes down the hall.

We try and make ourselves comfortable. Or as comfortable as we can while we're this tightly wound.

This is a real-life nightmare.

This isn't just about Dad's affair.

This isn't just about Rose, either.

It's about Mom, too. She's the one who'll hurt most because she'll have to deal with her husband's betrayal and a lifelong reminder of Dad's infidelity in the shape of a new family member.

The one time he cheated—I hope to fucking God it was just this once—he made a person. A girl. A daughter my mother always wanted.

I can't begin to imagine how much she'll be hurting in a few short minutes, and it already makes me reassess this whole thing. We should've prepared better. Thought this through.

Instead, we're here, still shell-shocked ourselves, and Nico's doing the talking, which doesn't help the situation one fucking bit.

Too late to turn back now.

Shawn parks by the window, his arms crossed. Logan perches on the armrest of the Chesterfield sofa with Theo and Colt while I stand to the side, leaning my shoulder against the wall. Cody's on the piano stool, cracking his knuckles like he's gearing up to knock Dad out the moment he comes in.

Nico takes center stage in the middle of the room, shoulders squared back.

Dad hesitates as he enters the living room, glancing around, his expression dubious and tense.

"Sit down," Nico grinds out, his tone not much above a whisper but imperious enough to chill me to the fucking bone. He points at two armchairs, waiting until Mom and Dad sit. "There's no easy way to say this, but we need answers."

"What answers, son?"

One rude sentence from Nico wrapped in arrogant superiority, and Dad's matching the stakes, shooting words with an equal dose of venom.

Takes one to know one.

Nico got his explosive character from our grandad. While it partially skipped Dad, there are times he can rival Nico's viciousness.

"Honest would be fucking best," Nico rumbles, unfazed by Dad's tone. He knows he's got the upper hand. "Let's start with why you cheated on Mom eighteen years ago."

As expected, Dad's attitude slips. His face blanches in a flash. And so does Mom's, her mouth falling open but no sounds escaping. In fact, the room falls perfectly silent. So fucking silent you can hear the dust settling.

It takes about twenty heartbeats that feel like eternity, before Dad rights his stance, spine straight, chin lifting in gesture of admission.

"I don't know how you found out, but the reason or the details are none of your business," he says, putting stern authority behind his words while his seven sons watch his every move. "Some things are between your mother and me. Not meant for your ears." He grabs Mom's hand, and I almost fucking kneel when she lets him, squaring her shoulder back.

She knew.

She knew all along.

"It's in the past," she avers, eyes pleading as she looks at each and every one of us. "Let's leave it there, okay? We've made our peace with what happened."

"Too late for that now, Mom. This isn't in the past. It's the fucking present, so he'll talk."

You'd think Nico said that. Maybe Logan. Even Colt would fit, but it's *Shawn* who snaps, his hands shaking, eyes shooting daggers Dad's way.

"Let's take a step back, alright?" Theo cuts in, grasping at straws as he adds, "What was her name, Dad?"

He had the hardest time believing Vee last night. He and Dad were always very close, and it doesn't sit well with Theo that we're blaming Dad for something we can't verify. The confession he just heard definitely changed his mind, but he's still not convinced Rose is our sister.

"The woman," he clarifies. "What was her name?"

"What does it matter?" Dad squares up. "This is none of your business, boys."

"Answer the fucking question," Logan snaps, losing his questionable temper.

"Watch your mouth!"

"Rebecca Bloom," Mom says, defeated, her face a picture of sadness as she unwittingly flushes Theo's arguments down the drain.

Maybe she forgave Dad for cheating but unearthing this secret they've kept from us for so many years opens wounds she fought to close. It's clear as day the reminder cuts deep.

Despite holding Dad's hand, she shrinks in on herself, and her eyes lose their glow as if those memories rush straight to the surface. As if she's reliving the fucking nightmare all over again.

"I made a mistake," Dad continues, backing off.

I bet he knows damn well that won't be enough to appease us. That this conversation won't be over until we get the information we came for.

"I didn't deserve forgiveness, but your mother's an extraordinary woman. She gave me a second chance." It's his turn to look us in the eye. "I love her and all of you more than you can imagine. My family has always been my priority."

He means it. I know he does, but his words don't appease

any of us in the face of the news.

Least of all Nico.

His clenched fists are the only warning we get before he lashes out. "Tell that to your daughter," he seethes. "Wait, you can't because you don't know she fucking exists!"

Dad pales. Turns so white he looks like a dead man walking. He's almost see through, eyes wide, hands shivering. Not a word out of his mouth while Mom's distressed *Daughter?* pierces my heart like a knife.

It fucking flays me alive.

I didn't realize how much hurting Mom would hurt me. It might be a necessary evil, but that doesn't make this any less painful.

"I'm sorry this is how you're finding out, Mom," Logan says, his tone soft, jaw working as he fights to keep himself in check. "We didn't mean to put you on the spot like this. We only found out yesterday... we've not wrapped our heads around this yet."

"A daughter?" Dad finally gasps, fear lacing his voice. "What are you talking about?"

"Her name is Rose," Cody supplies.

"She's eighteen, smart, talented," Nico lists, already fiercely protective of our little sister.

He's spent most time with her while she's studied under Mia's wings, and it's clear he likes the girl.

She's snappy, funny, and utterly unafraid of Nico's mood tantrums. I think he found it pretty impressive. Now he knows she's family, she's made the list of people Nico would give up his arm for.

"She should've been a part of this family from the start," he continues. "She should've been under *our* protection, but instead, she's been living in a trailer park her whole fucking life!"

"What makes you so sure she's my daughter?" Dad asks quietly, eyeing nothing in particular before he ramps up the courage to look at Nico, recognition flashing on his face. "Just because the timeline fits—"

"She looks like you," Theo supplies. "She looks like *us*. Well, mostly like Nico, so you'd think she's ultra fucking ugly, but she's really pretty. Black hair, black eyes. Like you say, the timeline fits, and..." He glances at me, checking it's okay to relay Vee's words.

"Rose is my girlfriend's sister," I supply, garnering Mom and Dad's attention. "At least that's what she thought her whole life, but now we know they're not related." I stare Dad in the eye. "Remember I asked you about Derek Atkinson?"

"Yes. I told you I don't know him."

"He's my girlfriend's father. He's married to Rebecca. She's no longer *Bloom*, obviously."

"The point is," Shawn takes over, impatient to get to the bottom of this without veering off topic. "No one involved has any reason to lie. Rebecca kept Rose hidden from you for years. Conor's relationship almost fell apart because she was so desperate to keep it that way. I think your first move should be reaching out to Rebecca. You should talk. And you sure as fuck should meet your daughter. Take a look at her then decide if you need a paternity test. It can be arranged."

THIRTY-THREE

Vee

I fidget in my seat, wiping my sweaty hands up and down my legs. Rose is in the chair beside me, her eyes rimmed pink from crying all night, but a ghost of a smile back on her lips.

She's wearing her best black A-line dress, her hair in a bun, courtesy of me. It took two hours before she was happy with the updo. It would have been quicker had she let me part her fringe in the middle straight away.

She's glancing at the door every five seconds, waiting to meet her biological father and his wife.

After the seven brothers confronted him about his affair yesterday, Robert Hayes arranged to meet my dad and Becca.

He didn't waste any time, visiting the trailer park last night. Today, they're meeting again, with Rose and me present.

Conor dropped me home ten minutes too late last night. Dad and Becca had already told Rose the truth and when I entered the house, all three of them were crying.

TOO STRONG

It took four hours, two packs of tissues, and a lot of cuddles before Rose started coming out of the initial shock. We dropped our mattresses onto the floor, bunching them together, and I held her all night, stroking her hair as she slowly came to terms with what she had learned.

She cried this morning, panicking that Robert and Monica would call off the meeting, then panicking that they'd try to pay for her silence to avoid a scandal.

She cried again when she figured we're not sisters and Dad's not her biological father. Then again when she realized she has seven brothers she knows nothing about.

I cried with her, so right now, we're both pink-eyed, sniffling, snotty messes.

We're waiting for Mr. and Mrs. Hayes in a private function room at the Country Club. We rolled up half an hour early because Rose was pacing a hole in the trailer floor, and Dad decided it would be better if we got her here already.

The door opens ten minutes later. Mr. Hayes walks through, his wife on his arm.

I watch with teary eyes as my younger sister meets her biological father for the first time. I listen to their conversation and Becca's *I'm so sorry*s, interrupted by teary apologies from Robert Hayes. Monica can't hide her welling emotions. She full-on bawls her eyes out when she hugs Rose.

I didn't expect that. I didn't expect her to be here at all. Not only has she shown up, but she's doing her best to make Rose feel welcome and part of the family.

It truly shows the depth of her and Robert's marriage. The strength of her character. She didn't have to be here. Rose is a living symbol of Robert's infidelity, yet she's making an effort. Taking a stand at his side, even though it means sharing the same air as Rebecca.

Monica Hayes just became my idol.

It takes time for the apologies and promises to stop, and we all sit back down, Rose at the head of the table, both sets of parents on either side. I'm next to my dad, swamping my sleeve in my tears.

There's a lot more empty seats, the room intended for larger celebrations: birthdays, christenings, bar mitzvahs etc.

"I hope you don't mind..." Robert says, turning back to Rose after nodding at a waiter who slipped into the room a moment ago. "But I thought you'd like to meet the rest of your family."

The waiter pulls the double door open, and the entire Hayes family pours into the room one by one.

"Hey there, sis," Logan starts, beating everyone to the punch as he pulls Rose out of her seat. "If you tell me I need to introduce myself, I won't like that."

Rose chuckles, cheeks blushing under the weight of everyone's gaze. "Logan," she says, her nerves fading. "No need for introductions."

"Attagirl." He pats her head, then pulls her into a hug.

"Stop monopolizing her," Theo huffs, shoving Logan away.

Rose's smile amplifies until she's beaming at me over Jack's shoulder, happy tears sliding down her cheeks.

I can't help it, my eyes go again, and I grab a napkin, wiping away tears as Conor approaches. I'm not the only one who noticed. My father's eyes look past me, and he rises from his seat, his face bleak.

My heart thumps a little faster as I attach myself to Conor. "Daddy, meet my boyfriend."

"Conor Hayes," Conor offers, holding his hand out for my dad to shake.

TOO STRONG

A loaded, silent moment passes between them before my father's face relaxes, and he takes Conor's hand. "I gotta tell you, I'm glad I didn't shoot you, boy."

"Excuse me?" Nico's head snaps to us. "*Shoot* him?"

"It's a long story," Cody supplies, squeezing Nico's shoulder. "Funny one, too. I'll tell you later, now go growl at the waiters. I'm fucking starving, bro."

"Cody! Language," Monica scolds, narrowing her eyes. "Behave yourself."

The Hayes boys all burst out laughing, and just like that, the tension in the air winks out of existence.

***

Conor summons a waiter as soon as my glass of wine empties. After the main course, the table's cleared of plates, and we're waiting for desserts.

Rose has been relaying her life story for the past hour, goaded by question after question from every Hayes at the table. It's amazing to see how easily she fits in with them all, bantering and joking around.

There's nothing left of last night's teary girl. She's back to her confident, cheeky self, and I'm glad she's so resilient. Put in her shoes, I'd have a harder time accepting the news.

Not Rose. She absolutely loves this. Well, not all of it, she's closemouthed and on guard talking to Robert or Monica, but as soon as one of her brothers draws her attention, her entire demeanor flips.

"I always wanted a brother," Rose admits when Cody asks what she thinks about having older brothers. "And now I get seven. How cool is that?!"

"Pretty cool if you ask me," Logan affirms.

"Yeah, no," Cassidy chuckles, looking over at Rose. "Don't get so excited. They'll drive you insane soon enough."

"Why?"

"You got a boyfriend?" Thalia asks, sipping her Coke.

All seven brothers zero in on Rose, anticipating the answer, the room suddenly silent, save for the kids.

"Well... kind of."

"Kind of?" Theo asks, cocking an eyebrow. "What the hell does *kind of* mean?"

"We've been on and off for a while," she explains, looking to me for help.

"Don't look at me. You know I don't like Liam."

"Liam?" Colt asks, eyes narrowed. "Liam who? Don't tell me you're dating Liam Montgomery."

"Justin's brother?" Mia gasps.

Rose nods, prompting Cody's fork to rattle on his plate as he drops it. "No way you're dating Liam. He's an idiot, Rose."

"Told you," Cassidy sing-songs, wiping chocolate off Noah's face. He's a cute kid, a spitting image of his daddy—dark hair, dark eyes, the cutest little dimples when he grins. "From now on, every guy around you will have the seven of them breathing down his neck."

"You're barely eighteen, Rose," Nico says, slinging his arm over the back of Mia's chair. "You've got time for boys. Focus on school."

"Hypocrite," Mia mutters. "I'm nineteen. Maybe I should just focus on school instead of—"

"You're mine," he cuts in, brooking no argument as he signals a waiter when she sets her empty glass of wine back on the table. "You run, I chase."

A hum of laughter echoes over us. I tune out the conversation for a moment when Noah crawls over to Conor's chair. He hauls him up, bouncing the boy gently in his lap. It doesn't last long. Within ten seconds, Noah's bored, and once Conor puts him back down, he crawls to Cody.

"I'll deal with Liam," Colt muses, grabbing a beer from a passing waiter. "If you can honestly tell me you like the guy, I'll have him working like clockwork by tomorrow."

"He might not be too pretty for a few days, though," Cody chips in, barely tearing his eyes from Noah as he feeds him tiny pieces of chocolate muffin. "Colt explains shit best with his fists."

"Don't scare the girl," Thalia huffs. "Think whatever you want, but neither of you gets to decide who she dates."

"Like hell," Conor breathes so quietly I doubt anyone but me hears.

"You know…" Rose muses, flopping back in her seat, a cunning smile stretching her lips. "I wouldn't mind if you had a good heart-to-heart with him. He's such a whore."

"*Rose!*" Logan snaps, theatrically holding his hand to his chest. "*Language*, sweetheart."

Another wave of laughter travels around the table.

"Welcome to the family, sis," Theo says, raising his glass. "We're all fucking crazy here."

"We sure are," Cassidy admits, bending down to grip Noah underarms now he's finished circling the room, going from hands to hands. "Some more than others, right, baby?" She grins at Logan, who stops her lifting Noah off the floor.

"What did I say about lifting?" he snaps, hauling the kid into her lap.

"You work, Logan. It's not like I don't lift him all damn day."

"All the more reason to let me do it when I'm around." He kisses her head and stamps a kiss on Noah's head, too. "He's not getting any lighter."

"You should've waited until Noah started walking before you got Cass pregnant again," Shawn retorts. "That way, she wouldn't carry him around as much."

"Seeing how he can't tone it down, we're waiting until Eli..." She pats her small bump, "...starts walking before we have another."

I bite my cheek to stop laughing when the look of a child who had his toys taken away crosses Logan's face.

"No, no, no, that's like... what? Two *years*," he whines. "I'll tone it down, okay? We'll have another once Eli's here."

"She's not a gumball machine, bro," Conor chuckles beside me. "Let her rest."

"But... I want a daughter. C'mon, princess, you promised. Just one more, okay?"

"One more kid?" Nico narrows his eyes at him like he doesn't believe that.

"Yeah. One more, and we'll take a short break."

Jesus... how many kids does he want? It seems the Hayes men are baby-making machines because Theo's next to announce they'll be trying for Irish twins.

I love this family. Their relationship, interactions, and banter. I love that they call it as they see it while supporting each other through the best and the worst. And I love that if I throw caution to the wind, I'll be part of it by the end of the year.

EPILOGUE

The Yountville Estate is closed for the duration of the wedding weekend. Logan booked one hundred and twenty-two rooms, twenty-two suites, a spa, a pool, and the entire twenty-acres to accommodate his wife-to-be.

Colt's beside me, his head almost visibly steaming while Abby never fucking stops babbling.

It was Vee's idea for Colt to take Abby as his plus one. When he said last week he still hadn't asked anyone, she said Abby would love to come as his friend.

No expectations.

And since *no expectations* is what Colt's looking for, he agreed. Now he looks ready to tuck and roll out the moving car and sprint back to Newport. Abby hasn't shut up since we picked her up this morning. She's been talking non-stop throughout the flight, too.

"Babe, you're forgetting to breathe," Vee mutters, looking

as sick of it as Colt. "How about you just zip it for a while, hmm? No one's listening anymore."

Abby pouts, folding her arms across her chest. "Well, excuse me, but you know I don't like silence, and no one else has struck up any conversation. I'm excited, okay? I've never been on a plane, I've never been to a fancy hotel or even a wedding. I mean, have you *seen* my dress?! It's fucking beautiful! I look like a movie star!"

"I was there when you bought it," Vee reminds her, sharing a look with me in the rearview mirror. "Music?"

"God, yes," Colt huffs, switching the radio on at full volume.

That seems to do it. Abby's mouth doesn't move until I park outside the hotel, next to Nico's G Wagon. He and Mia got here last night. Refusing to watch his girl panic throughout the flight, he drove five hundred miles.

Talk about whipped.

Rental cars throng the parking lot, though not even a fifth of the guests are here. It's just close family and bridesmaids for the rehearsal dinner tonight. The other two hundred guests are due tomorrow for the ceremony.

We check into our rooms, and two hours later, I'm outside, taking a quick moment to get my fucking act together.

"You ready?" Logan joins me while everyone's flocking toward the venue where we're about to sit for the rehearsal dinner.

My hands shake as I spark my Zippo, inhaling a deep drag. I've not had a cigarette for six months now, but tonight, I need something to take the edge off.

I don't even know why I'm nervous. I'm sure I want to do this tonight, with our whole family watching, but I also remember I promised Vee a year, and it's only been eight months.

"Yeah. What's the worst that can happen, right?"

"She could say *no*," he chuckles, glancing over his shoulder as the door flings open, and Nico exits the building with Theo and Shawn hot on his tail.

All six of my brothers know what's coming. I had to check Logan and Cassidy didn't mind me crashing their rehearsal dinner like this, and news travels fast among the Hayes.

The only Hayes who doesn't know is Rose. Mia wasn't supposed to know either since she and Rose are almost fucking inseparable, but I wanted Mia to play the piano, so pinky-swears and all that.

Rose is terrible at keeping secrets, which is why I made Vivienne's father promise not to breathe a word. I did ask his permission, old fashioned as it may be. It felt right and I didn't want a shotgun pointed at my head. Luckily it didn't end that way.

We've grown closer over the last eight months. Even more so when he, Rose, and Becca moved into a townhouse two streets over from mine and Vee's place.

My father rose to the occasion when he found out he had a daughter, instructing Nico to set Rose up a portfolio and deposit the child support she would've been due had he known about her. Given my parents' hefty monthly income, Rose's total came close to a million dollars for the eighteen years she should've been receiving it.

At first, she fought like a lioness, saying she didn't want the money, but after a lengthy chat with Nico and my father, she caved.

Two months later, she used a third of it to buy a small townhouse. It was a renovation project that Derek, Logan, and Cody gladly took on.

Once they moved out of the trailer, Rose used some more to pay off her college tuition and buy two cars: one for herself, and one for Vivienne—a thank-you gift for all the years she put Rose first. It's not the brand-new convertible Mustang I would've bought, but Vee loves her tiny VW Beetle.

Colt joins us outside, one hand fishing out a packet of cigarettes while the other massages his temple. "Thank God Abby's got a separate room, or I'd strangle her in her sleep," he huffs. "She's still *talking*."

"Is Cody here yet?" I ask.

"No, sorry, bro. He rang ten minutes ago, they only just boarded the plane, so they won't be here for at least two more hours."

"Anyone knows who he's bringing?" Logan asks, letting out a gray cloud of smoke. "All he told me was, *you'll see*."

We all nod in sync because that's the line Cody treated all of us with whenever we asked who he invited. I don't fucking like the secrecy. It's putting me on edge more than popping on one knee.

"Right, let's get inside," Logan says, opening the door. "Mom's been panicking worse than Cass all day. I don't want to set them off over dinner starting a minute too late."

Time stands still while we eat. Well, they eat. I barely touch anything on my plate, my stomach clenched, mind in riot mode. Fuck. I shouldn't have made this so official. It would've been easier without my whole family watching, but it's too late now.

The satin box in the inner pocket of my suit jacket burns a hole in my chest once the waiters clear the tables.

Mia shoots me a reassuring look, rising to her feet. I asked her to play Vee's favorite song as a backdrop. As soon as she's up, I know this is it.

No turning back now.

My nerves evaporate in a flash as if the build-up to this moment was the only reason my heart triphammered in my chest. With a deep breath, I rise, pushing my chair aside.

But then Mia freezes mid-step, her green gaze trained on something behind me. Her cheeks pale a touch, her face a picture of deep shock. The same look settles onto Colt and Nico, and a goddamn massive weight tightens the atmosphere.

I turn, checking what got them this alarmed. My heart pounds again when I spot Cody in the doorway, his bulky frame dressed in a three-piece suit, hair in a bun.

And then my attention shifts to the girl on his arm.

What the fuck were you thinking, Cody?

Thank you

I hope you enjoyed *Too Strong*. Cody is next and I hope you'll love his story. Pairing him with a hated character wasn't an easy decision, but I wouldn't change a thing.

Love,

T. A. Dice